CW01664706

THE HORSE SHIFTER'S MATE

HARMONY RAINES

The Horse Shifter's Mate

The Bond of Brothers

Book Two

* * *

Sign up to the Harmony Raines Newsletter by going to:
http://www.harmonyraines.com/newsletter-sign-up/
Never miss a new release!
You'll also receive the EBOOK '*A Bond to Bear*'
Just to say thank you!

SERIES ORDER

1. The White Wolf of Wishing Moon Bay

2. The Horse Shifter's Mate

3. Her Fae-vorite Bear
4. Fae-ted to the Bear
5. The Snow Leopard's Love
6. The Dragon Shifter's Desire

US LINKS

Website and Newsletter: harmonyraines.com

Facebook: facebook.com/harmonyrainesauthor

Amazon Author Page: amazon.com/Harmony-Raines/e/B0090Q3DWM

Bond of Brothers Series Page

On Amazon: amazon.com/dp/B08T6JF1QZ

On My Website: harmonyraines.com/all-books/bond-of-brothers-series

UK LINKS

Website and Newsletter: harmonyraines.com

Facebook: facebook.com/harmonyrainesauthor

Amazon Author Page: amazon.co.uk/Harmony-Raines/e/B0090Q3DWM

Bond of Brothers Series Page

On Amazon: amazon.co.uk/dp/B08T6JF1QZ

On My Website: harmonyraines.com/all-books/bond-of-brothers-series

THE HORSE SHIFTER'S MATE

THE BOND OF BROTHERS

Book Two

A silverback shifter romance

Horse shifter, Dario, returns to Wishing Moon Bay after learning his brother has met his mate. His return sets in motion a surprising chain of events.

Helena arrives in Wishing Moon Bay. But what exactly is she running from? And whatever it is, can she escape it?

Spooked by an incident in her apartment, Helena takes the fateful decision to join her sister, Penny, in Wishing Moon Bay. If she can find it!

The sudden appearance of a horse in the middle of the road steers her in the right direction. There she meets Dario, a man who soon captures her heart. However, the town also holds the secret to her past. A secret that could be deadly.

Dario has searched for his mate all over the world. But finds her on his return to Wishing Moon Bay.

However, if he expected to settle down with his mate and enjoy a quiet life, he's in for a surprise. There's something lurking in Helena's past. Someone who means her harm.

He might not be a predator like his brothers, but Dario intends to do whatever it takes to keep her safe.

With the help of family, and unlikely friends, can they solve the mystery and find the happy ending they had both almost given up on?

1

HELENA

"A horse?" Penny studied her sister as she ate a delicious pastry in the restaurant at the Wishing Moon Hotel. Outside, the ground was covered in a two-inch layer of snow. If more snow fell today or overnight, Helena might be stranded in the small town of Wishing Moon Bay.

"A horse. Yes. It just appeared like that." She clicked her fingers and Milo, Penny's son, jumped and fixed his attention on his aunt.

"And that's how you found the road leading to town." They had gone over this a couple of times already since Helena had arrived, but Penny kept asking for more details, even though there were none.

"Yes. I told you, I followed the directions you gave me. I drove back and forth along that one stretch of road but couldn't see you or a sign for Wishing Moon Bay. I was just about to give up since you weren't answering your calls or your texts..." Helena's jaw tightened as she fixed her sister with an accusing stare.

"Sorry, we had a long day yesterday and Milo was so tired I didn't want him woken up by my phone. Then I forgot I'd set it to silent." Penny's excuse sounded plausible, but Helena was suspicious she was holding something back.

"Well, I guess it all worked out all right." She took a bite of the croissant she'd carefully cut into pieces. The buttery flakes of pastry melted in her mouth. "These are the best croissants I've ever tasted."

"Ivan baked them. He's the chef here. All his food is incredible." Penny took a bite of her blueberry muffin.

"Is he single?" Helena asked.

"Ivan?" Penny coughed and took a sip of her coffee.

"Yes, I could marry a man who bakes this well and forgive him a lot of faults." She grinned at Penny's shocked face. "I'm joking."

"Sorry." Penny cleared her throat and frowned. "So the horse..."

"He appeared from nowhere, I turned down the road leading to Wishing Moon Bay and when I stopped the car and got out to check if he was all right, he was gone. Not a sign that he was ever there." She rubbed the crumbs off her fingertips. "Maybe he wasn't there at all. Maybe he was a figment of my imagination." Helena rested her chin on her palm and stared out of the window, lost in her own thoughts. Perhaps there was something wrong with her.

"Helena." Penny reached out and clasped her sister's hand. "What's wrong?"

"Nothing." She smiled brightly and picked up another piece of her pastry. "I'm just tired, that's all."

"I know you, that look doesn't say you're just tired." Penny let go of her sister's hand and glanced at Milo. "Perhaps I can ask Logan or Rift to take Milo for a couple of hours and we can go for a walk on the beach."

"The beach!" Milo, whose attention had been firmly fixed on what was on the other side of the restaurant window until now, turned around to look at his mom. “I'd like to come to the beach. Maybe Logan can come, too.”

“I'd like some time alone with Helena,” Penny explained. “We need to talk. You know, catch up on what's been happening in our lives.”

“Oh!” Milo's eyes widened and he looked from his mom to Helena. “Are you going to tell Aunt Helena about Logan?”

“What about Logan?” Helena tilted her head to one side as her sister's cheeks flamed red. “Oh, now I'm interested.”

“Logan is the sweetest, most incredible man I've ever met, that's all.” Her breasts rose and fell as she inhaled deeply. “I think I'm in love with him.” She closed her eyes for a moment. “I know I'm in love with him.”

“Love? Isn't that fast? I mean, I know people say love at first sight is real. But it's also possible to get caught up in a dream, a romantic dream, that won't last long.” She pressed her lips together as she looked at her sister, who had been hurt so badly by Milo's father. “I don't want to shoot down those dreams, but I also have to protect you. You and Milo.”

“We don't need protecting from Logan. I promise.” Penny was so certain. Her sister had loved her first husband, Milo's father. But this was different. Helena longed to have the same certainty about a man even if it was for a fleeting moment. Surely it was better to experience love, heady, giddy love, for a short time and have your heart broken than to never experience it.

Helena had never felt that kind of love. Not ever. The sad truth, that she'd never admitted to anyone, not even Penny, was that she had never been in love. Lust, yes. And sure, she'd convinced herself she was in love a couple of times just so she didn't feel like she was a freak of nature. It wasn't as if she didn't know what love was. She loved her dead mom, she loved Penny and Milo. But real, earth-shattering, I'd-die-without-you love, that had evaded Helena her whole life.

"I'd like to get to know him while I'm in town." Helena finished her muffin and eyed up a buttery pastry.

"How long are you staying?" Penny's eyes darted toward the door leading from the restaurant to the kitchen. The same door Logan had used when he left them alone. Could she sense him out there?

Helena tensed. Was he out there listening to their conversation? What if he wasn't who he said he was? What if this was one big conspiracy? She swallowed hard and grabbed her coffee cup, taking a long drink. When she met Penny's gaze, it was filled with concern.

"Sorry."

"You seem a little jumpy." Penny's eyes narrowed. "Are you sure you're okay? You can go take a nap in our hotel room if you need to."

"No, I'm fine. And in answer to your question, I'm staying as long as it takes." She looked down at her empty plate. Would it be greedy to have another one? Or perhaps she could wrap one in a napkin and slip it into her purse to eat later.

"As long as it takes to what?" Penny's suspicions were raised.

"As long as it takes to make sure that what you have with Logan is real and you are doing the right thing." She leveled her gaze at Penny.

"Helena..." Penny leaned back in her chair and shook her head. "You had me for a moment there."

Helena chuckled. "I thought you might throw the rest of those delicious pastries at me."

"The thought did cross my mind, but that would be an insult to Ivan's baking skills, and I do not want to upset my future brother-in-law." Penny waited for Helena's reaction.

Helena wasn't sure how to react. "You aren't joking, are you?"

Penny shook her head. "He's the one, Helena. The man of my dreams and he'll be there for me no matter what. Unlike a certain other person."

"And Ivan is Logan's brother?" Maybe Helena could seek Ivan out and while congratulating him on his amazing culinary skills, find out about the real Logan. If the man had stolen Penny's heart in a matter of days, then she wanted to find out all his secrets and any skeletons he might be hiding in his closet.

"Yes. Adopted brother. There are six brothers all together. Logan, Ivan, Rift, Caleb, and Aiden. Plus, Dario, who I haven't met yet. Valerie, who owns the hotel, adopted them all when they were young."

"Six boys, she must either be crazy or superwoman." Helena could understand the need to adopt a child, her biological clock wasn't just ticking, it was starting to wind down. If she didn't meet the right man and settle down in the next couple of years, she would never fulfill her dream of being a mother. Penny might have been emotionally scarred by her jerk of a husband but at least they had a child together. Milo was an incredible boy. Who deserved an incredible father.

"She's quite a woman," Penny agreed. "They all love her very much."

"And what about Milo?" Helena switched her attention to her nephew. "Do you like Logan and all the people here?"

"Logan is fun. Not as fun as Rift, but fun."

"Maybe Logan doesn't need to hear that," Penny told Milo quietly.

"He knows, Rift told him." Milo slipped off his seat and ran up and down the window, staring at the snow outside.

"Of course he did," Penny rolled her eyes.

"Do the brothers get along?" Helena asked.

"Yes, they love each other and are there for each other

whatever they need." Penny reached across the table and took Helena's hand. "Like us."

Helena's tight smile didn't reach her eyes. "I'm happy for you, Penny. You and Milo."

"But..." Penny didn't let go of Helena's hand as she studied her closely. "What's wrong?"

"Nothing." Helena slipped her hand toward her, but Penny didn't let go.

"You've been acting weird since you arrived. And I don't think it has anything to do with being tired." She studied her sister closely and Helena's cheeks flushed pink under her scrutiny. "You didn't come here to check up on us, did you?"

Helena's gaze slid sideways, and she watched Milo as he ran in and out of the tables, so carefree. "Do you ever wish we could turn back the clock and go back to being Milo's age?"

"You are skirting around the question. I know that's part of your job, but not when you are talking to me." Penny squeezed Helena's hand tighter. "Tell me what's wrong."

"I think I'm going crazy." Helena kept her eyes fixed on the plate of pastries in front of them.

"Going crazy?" Penny asked. "Why do you think that?"

"Because..." She shook her head. "I don't know, it's stupid."

"No, it's not stupid. Whatever you think is obviously bothering you. So tell me. You know there's nothing you can't tell me." Penny's soft tone of encouragement was the reason Helena had traveled here to Wishing Moon Bay.

"You always were the best listener." A tear rolled down Helena's cheek and she dashed it away.

"You're not so bad yourself. I don't know how I would have coped if you weren't at the end of the phone every time I called and needed a shoulder to cry on or someone to listen to me rant about..." She glanced at Milo and stopped talking.

"That's what sisters are for."

"Then tell me, this is my turn to listen. My turn to repay the favor." She nodded as she squeezed Helena's hand again. "Come on."

"It's probably nothing..."

"You don't think it's nothing."

"I met someone."

Penny rolled her shoulders back, her eyes darting to the door leading to the kitchen once more. "You met someone. Is it serious? Did you come here to tell me you are getting married or something?" She covered her mouth with her hand. "Are you pregnant?"

"No!" Helena shook her head. "None of the above."

"Then what?"

"I met this guy. We bumped into each other outside work. I mean *actually* bumped into each other. I dropped the stack of files I was carrying on the ground and he helped me pick them up. Our eyes met..." She gave a lopsided smile. "No, I didn't think it was love at first sight. That doesn't mean that I wasn't attracted to him. I'm a single middle-aged woman and he was cute, dimples, nice smile."

"That's a healthy response." Penny nodded. "What happened?"

"He called and asked me to dinner the next day." She looked down at her hands. "I thought it was romantic that he went to the trouble of tracking my number down."

"Romantic would be one word to describe it. But I'm guessing that's not how it turned out?"

"At first I'd call it romantic. We dated for a couple of weeks. I liked him a lot."

"You never told me you'd met someone."

"You were in the middle of your divorce. It felt wrong to tell you I was happy when you were in such a dark place." Helena shook her head. "I know what you're going to say. I know that you would have been happy for me, I really do.

But it was a call I made. I figured that if the relationship lasted, I'd tell you about it when things settled down for you, if not then it made no difference."

"What happened?"

"He was a very sweet guy. He treated me nice. With respect. He never pushed himself on me, if you know what I mean." She sighed, recalling their dinner dates, of dancing in his arms, resting her head on his shoulder as he held her close. "I really thought I'd found a good guy. Someone with whom I could make a future. He had a good job in a similar field to me. We were a good fit."

"Okay, so that's the good, what's the bad?" Penny asked.

"He wore this expensive cologne." She inhaled and closed her eyes. "A mixture of exotic spice and musk. Very distinctive."

"What happened?"

"The day you were due to arrive..." She put her hand over her mouth, her face pale. "After you called, I went home..."

"Honey, what did he do?"

"Nothing." She shook her head. "Not to me."

"Tell me."

"I think he'd been in my apartment."

"You *think* he had."

"I could smell him. His cologne." She shook her head. "I'd never invited him back to my place. We never got that intimate."

"Do you think he let himself into your apartment?"

"Or maybe I just imagined it, in the same way I imagined that horse today." She took a shuddering breath. "What if I'm going crazy? What if I'm losing my mind like Mom did?"

"Oh, wait, no. The horse, I'm almost certain you saw." She glanced over her shoulder to check on Milo. "As for the guy, is there anything else about him that makes you think he would go into your apartment like that? Was there anything missing?"

"Not that I know of." She shook her head. "I could have just imagined it. But the smell, it seemed so real."

"Okay, well, you're here now, you're safe here in Wishing Moon Bay." Penny nodded. "And when you go home, I'm coming with you."

"No, you've already said you want to stay here. I don't want to get in the middle of what you have with Logan. A real chance at happiness."

"And that happiness will still be here waiting for me when I get back. Although, I suspect that Logan will want to come with us." Penny got up and came around the table to hug Helena. "You're not in this alone, I promise."

"Thanks, Penny. I don't know who else to turn to. I couldn't call the police, they'd laugh at me if I said I can smell an intruder in my apartment." Helena leaned on her sister. "I'm just scared I'm going crazy like..."

"Like Mom. I understand. But I don't think Mom was crazy. Not really."

"She used to believe in monsters in the closet and all that crap."

"I think she just saw things differently." Penny sighed heavily. "But that doesn't mean what she saw wasn't true."

"Now you believe in monsters and magic?" Helena pulled away from her sister. "Where did that come from?"

"There are things about this town that I need to tell you," Penny said cryptically. "But for now, let's just drink coffee and eat these delicious pastries. The rest can wait."

"I don't think it can, Penny." Helena was just about ready to bundle her sister and nephew in her car and drive out of town. But as Penny poured the coffee, Helena had a feeling she was right where she was supposed to be.

2

DARIO

"The horse lord returns." Logan entered the hotel kitchen where Dario was devouring a plateful of Ivan's food. He'd traveled all over the world but there was nothing like his brother's cooking.

"Logan. I came as soon as I could." Dario placed his plate down on the counter and hugged his brother. "Congratulations."

"Thanks, Dario." Logan patted his brother on the back. "And are congratulations in order for you, too?"

"Have I missed something?" Ivan's sharp inquiry was met with a sheepish grin from Dario. "I have missed something." His dragon shifter brother looked from Logan to Dario and back again. "One of you needs to tell me."

"Dario, this is your news." Logan let his brother go and stepped back.

"I have found my mate."

"You're joking!" Ivan shook his head. "You aren't joking."

"He's not joking." Logan's eyes narrowed as he stared at his brother.

"Ivan tells me there was some trouble with a witch who

kidnapped your mate." Dario scraped the fork across the plate and glanced at Ivan. "Any more?"

"I'd forgotten how much you eat." Ivan fetched a covered plate from the fridge and set it down on the counter. "Help yourself. It's leftovers from last night."

"Oh, leftovers, my favorite." Dario peeled back the aluminum foil from the plate. "Spaghetti." He inhaled deeply. "Smothered in your famous tomato and basil sauce, with just the right amount of garlic."

"Dario," Logan said sharply. "Explain."

"Explain?" Dario heaped the spaghetti onto his plate. "Your tone hasn't lost its sharpness."

"Not when the subject concerns my mate." He drew in a shaky breath. "And this does concern my mate, doesn't it?"

"How does Dario finding his mate affect Penny?" Ivan recovered the plate and stowed it back in the fridge, his tone hostile.

"I'm sorry." Dario set his fork down on his plate. "I am being insensitive."

"Just explain." Logan ran his hand through his hair. "Please."

"Logan..." Dario nodded. "I was coming back here to meet your mate. Ivan called me and told me you had found her, and I dropped everything to come back. It's a big occasion."

"Get to the point," Ivan told him.

"I was outside of Wishing Moon Bay this morning when a car came by and I got this feeling." He rubbed the back of his neck. "It knocked the wind out of me. Then I realized that whoever was in the car was special to me."

"You are the horse Helena saw." Logan rubbed his chin and turned away.

"Helena?" Ivan leaned back against the fridge. "Penny's sister, Helena?"

"She is your mate's sister?" Dario asked.

We had no idea, his horse told him. No wonder Logan is in shock.

But why the hostility? Dario asked.

Maybe he's afraid we won't take this seriously. We spend our days traveling the world. Running wild and free. A mate means settling down. A mate means family.

"Yes, she's my mate's sister." Logan glanced toward the restaurant.

Dario could sense his mate, she was close, she was safe. That's why he was in the kitchen eating, because she wasn't going anywhere. The moment she did, he would follow.

He would follow wherever she went. They were bound together.

"And you are afraid I will...what?" Dario rolled his shoulders. If Logan planned to come between Dario and his mate, he was ready to fight his brother just as they had fought as children.

Grow up, his horse told him.

Logan believes I am not serious about this. He thinks I won't do right by my mate. He's wrong! Dario clenched his fists, then immediately relaxed.

"I'm afraid if we don't handle this well that Penny and Helena might both leave Wishing Moon Bay."

"Handle what well?"

"Penny had no idea that shifters or magic were real. That was a shock, and then Penny was kidnapped by a witch. Not exactly the best new experience of life here in town." Logan went to the back door and pulled it open, sucking in the fresh air.

"That must have been traumatic. And now you are worried that Helena might freak out when she finds out about shifters?" Dario asked.

"I am." Logan turned back around. "We planned not to tell Helena since we figured this was a fleeting visit."

"I am not going to hide who I am and what she is to me," Dario replied hotly.

"That's not what Logan is suggesting." Ivan tried to smooth over the situation. "Listen, this isn't like you. Either of you. You are not enemies. I suspect the nearness of your mates has elevated your testosterone. So just calm things down and let's work this out together. Like brothers."

"Ivan is right."

"As always," the dragon shifter muttered under his breath.

"We are in this together. We both want the same thing, for our mates to be happy and stay in Wishing Moon Bay." Logan held his hand out to Dario. "Or wherever it is that you are living these days."

"I have no fixed home." He pressed his lips together. "I've spent the last few years exploring the world, joining with the few remaining herds that roam wild and free. I lost myself to that freedom. But now it's time to start a new life."

"So, you're agreed. The plan is to make sure that Helena accepts that shifters and magic are real without freaking out." Ivan looked up, at the same time Logan took two long strides toward the door leading from the restaurant.

"Penny's coming." He half-turned to face Dario. "We need to tell Penny about you and Helena."

"No!" Dario shook his head. "When Helena finds out about us being mates, I want it to be from me. I certainly don't want her to think we were plotting and scheming behind her back."

"And I am not going to lie to Penny." Logan's shoulders rose as his muscles bunched. "Trust me, Dario."

"Logan." Penny burst into the kitchen but came to an abrupt stop when she saw Dario. "Hi. Sorry, am I interrupting?"

"This is Dario," Ivan said quickly.

Penny's eyes widened. "The horse shifter?"

Dario inclined his head. "It's good to finally meet you, Penny."

"And you." She pointed at him as she drew closer. "It was you."

"What was me?" Dario got the feeling no one needed to tell Penny about her sister being his mate.

"Helena said a horse suddenly appeared in front of her and steered her toward Wishing Moon Bay. She'd driven up and down the same stretch of road a half dozen times and never saw the turnout and then you..."

"And then me." He inclined his head.

"You're her mate?" The question was direct and one he could not deny.

"I am."

"Oh." She glanced over her shoulder toward where her sister was still seated in the restaurant.

"Oh, what?" Logan placed his hand on his mate's arm. "What's wrong?"

"That's what I came to tell you." Penny eyed Dario, not with suspicion, but with sympathy. "Helena is in trouble. At least I think she's in trouble."

Dario stepped closer to Penny, but Logan inserted himself between them. "It's okay," Dario told his brother. "I just want to hear what Penny knows. If my mate is in danger, then I intend to do whatever it takes to ensure her safety."

"I know and I understand, but give Penny some space." Logan patted his brother's chest. "This is all new to her, remember?"

"I'm sorry, Penny." Dario stepped back, his hands curled into fists. "This is all new for me, too. Having a mate. When I felt the connection to Helena in the car, it was like being hit by a freight train. It's like being a teenager again when my first shift was close and the hormones in my body were out of control."

"I understand." Penny pressed her lips into a thin line as she switched her attention to Logan. "I assume that's how you felt, too, Logan?"

"When I saw you walking down the street, I just knew you were the one. Then panic took hold. And my head filled with all these thoughts, what if you didn't like me, what if you ran away and I never found you again. After so long waiting for my mate, it kind of makes you crazy."

"Okay. Well, you're gonna need to deal with that crazy and fast." Penny's firm tone alerted him to the presence of danger. Not here in the hotel, but somewhere danger threatened his mate. That was the reason for Penny's sympathetic gaze. Her sister's problem was now his problem.

"What's wrong?" Logan asked gently. "Did something happen to Helena other than a wild stallion jumping out in front of her car?"

"I think so. Before she came here, a man...he seems to have inserted himself into her life."

"Inserted himself into her life?" Dario frowned.

"He literally bumped into her on the street. He then called her at work even though she never gave him her phone number. She's a grown woman and had no reason to be suspicious of him. She figured it was a cute gesture. She really liked him..." Penny placed her hand on Dario's arm. "I know this isn't easy for you to hear."

"If you're expecting me to celebrate my mate being in love with another man, then no, this is not what I need to hear." He shook his head and turned from Penny, pacing the kitchen.

"She isn't in love with him if that's what concerns you," Penny told him. "If anything, it's the opposite."

"The opposite." Dario spun around to face her, his feet planted hip-width apart as his anger simmered below the surface. "What happened? Did he hurt her?"

"No, he never touched her." Penny's forehead creased as she shook her head. "And maybe it's nothing but Helena doesn't scare easily."

"She's scared?" Dario headed toward the door leading to the restaurant. "I should be with her." Every part of him wanted to hold his mate in his arms and tell her it was all going to be okay now that he was here to protect her.

"Slow down a second, Dario." Ivan grabbed his brother by the arm and spun him back around to face Penny. "Let's hear the rest of it, shall we?"

"A couple of days ago, Helena went home, and her apartment smelled like this guy's cologne. Expensive cologne." She locked eyes with Dario. "And before you think...*those* kinds of thoughts, the guy had never been back to Helena's apartment. There's no way the place should have smelled of him."

"On her clothes?" Logan asked. "Expensive cologne can linger."

"Since when did you wear expensive cologne?" Dario asked.

"I don't. But we have guests who do, and the scent can linger for days. So what if Helena went on a date with this guy and it rubbed off on her clothes? It might have been on her coat or her purse." Logan spread out his hands in defense as the others looked at him. "Hey, I'm trying to make sure we check out all the alternatives before we unleash a territorial stallion on the world."

"She isn't my territory, she's my mate," Dario told his brother.

"Believe me, when you have a mate, anywhere she is *is* your territory." Logan inclined his head toward Penny. "I try to keep it under control, but when I first found out you were my mate, it was hard not to rip the head off any man who so much as looked at you let alone talked to you."

"I'd say I didn't notice but I'd be lying," Penny answered smoothly.

"So what happened now?" Ivan asked. "We can't just dismiss what Helena believes happens."

"Does she have any idea why he might have gone to her apartment?" Logan asked.

"No, she had never met him before he bumped into her. And while they were dating, he never acted unusual, never questioned her about anything that raised her suspicions."

"Could it have to do with work?" Dario asked.

"She doesn't have any information on anything that would warrant anyone going into her apartment."

"What if it's not about Helena?" Ivan asked. "What if this is purely about the apartment itself? Perhaps there was something hidden there that the guy needed. He might have wanted to gain access by dating Helena."

"She didn't take him back there. That's what she said, and she has no reason to lie. We tell each other everything. If she took a guy home for sex, she would tell me," Penny insisted.

"What if he had access to her keys and got one duplicated?" Logan asked. "That way he could get in and out without arousing her suspicions."

"Stop!" Dario held up his hands. "This is a conversation we need to have with Helena present."

"Dario is right." Penny hugged herself as she turned back toward the restaurant. "You should come and say hello, Dario. And then I suppose we should tell Helena all about shifters and all the other magic that exists in the world."

"How do you think she'll take it?" Dario asked.

"That I don't know." Penny half-turned to face him. "Our mother never told us the monsters under our beds didn't exist. If we were scared of the monsters in our closets, she'd put up a talisman to ward it off. That's probably why I thought I recognized the talisman Milo found in the attic."

"Your mom knew magic and monsters existed?" Dario asked. This might be easier than he'd feared.

"Maybe she did. But we just thought she was a little crazy." There was that sympathetic look in Penny's eyes. "If anything, our mom's behavior made Helena resentful toward anything supernatural. She even hates watching fantasy shows or movies."

Dario's heart grew heavy. This might all be a lot harder than he'd ever expected.

But Helena was his mate, and they were destined to be together. Somehow, he'd make her understand that magic was wonderful and shifting was a gift.

And that he would love her to the end of time.

Now, doesn't that sound like something a stalker might say? His horse chuckled.

Growing up, Dario had learned to be strong. He'd fought and played with his predator brothers, never giving in or backing down. But nothing had prepared him for the challenge his mate posed.

And the stakes could not be higher.

3

HELENA

"You really do like it here, don't you?" Helena asked her nephew as he stared out into the snow-covered formal gardens through the large restaurant windows.

"Yes." He dragged his attention away from the pond and the birds that visited it to drink from the icy water.

"And your mom seems happy." Helena needed to know her sister and nephew were going to be okay if they stayed here in Wishing Moon Bay.

When Penny called and asked Helena if she and Milo could come and stay with her, she'd immediately said yes. She loved Penny and Milo, they were her family. But that decision didn't come without some reservations. Her apartment wasn't exactly big. Sure, it was fine for a woman who lived on her own. But Milo would have gone stir crazy with no outside space to play in.

"Mom loves it here." Milo sidled back toward the table, his eyes sliding sideways to look out at the snow. "She likes Logan a lot. And I like his brothers. They are going to take me into the mountains and down to the beach. In the summer I'm going to swim in the ocean and ride on the back of a dolphin."

"Ride on the back of a dolphin?" Helena studied Milo's serious face. He wasn't joking. "I like the idea of that."

"Then why don't you stay, too, Aunt Helena?" Milo plonked himself down on the seat in front of her and reached for a pastry from the plate. "You would like it here, too."

"I suppose I would. But I have a life elsewhere, I have a home and a job." Helena rested her elbow on the table and cupped her chin in her palm. "But it sure is tempting."

"Helena." Penny came back into the restaurant, she'd gone to speak to Logan in the kitchen but hadn't said what about. Helena had presumed it was about the sleeping arrangements. However, Penny's serious expression said otherwise.

"What's wrong?" She immediately tensed, on her guard as Logan and another man followed behind her. Logan's tense jaw and pinched features said he shared Penny's apprehension, the other guy had a different look on his face. One that confused Helena.

"We need to talk to you." Penny glanced sideways. "There are some things we have to explain."

"Explain." Helena glanced at Milo, who half-turned in his seat while still chewing on his pastry. Had her sister gotten herself into trouble with these men? Would Helena have to force Penny to leave and take them home with her?

"Yes. There are... Wishing Moon Bay isn't a normal town." Penny opened her mouth to say more but her cheeks tinged with pink and she looked at Logan for help.

"Magic is real and Logan and his brothers plus a whole bunch of other people can shift into animals," Milo gushed.

"Now the cat is out of the bag," the guy with Penny said.

"Milo." Penny sent her son a warning look.

"Isn't that what you were going to tell Aunt Helena?" Milo took another bite of his pastry.

"Yes. But I was going to break the news a little more gently." Penny came to the table and sat down. Reaching across the polished wood surface, she took Helena's hand. "Are you okay?"

"Aside from the fact that my sister is crazy." Helena inhaled deeply. "Have these guys brainwashed you into believing this crap?"

"It's all true, Helena. I've seen it with my own eyes."

"Tricks and make-believe. You know that." Helena curled her fingers around Penny's hand, not wanting to let her go. If she had been brainwashed, getting her to leave town would be difficult.

However, she owed it to her sister to get her out of there.

"It's all true," Milo said. "Logan is a white wolf and Rift is a snow leopard. Oh, and Ivan is a dragon. We rode on his back last night after we were rescued from the witch who wanted to take control of Mom's body."

"Penny. This isn't healthy for Milo. Damn, you know what it was like for us growing up with Mom believing in spells and talismans..."

"It was all real. All of it."

"Okay, you are scaring me. This isn't like you." Helena stood up and locked eyes with Logan. "I don't know what you have been telling my sister and nephew, but this is wrong. And it needs to stop."

"Helena." The second guy stepped forward.

Penny smiled softly at the guy. "Helena, this is Dario. He is the horse that you saw on the road outside of town."

"A horse." Helena let go of Penny's hand and strode toward the Dario. "He's a man. Look at him. He's a man." She reached out and touched Dario's arm, wanting to show her sister that he wasn't a horse, he wasn't magic, he was simply flesh and blood. But as her fingertips touched his skin, a spark of electricity shot up her arm.

She jumped back, her eyes fixed on his, seeking an answer to the question in her head. Had he felt that, too?

"Helena, I am a horse shifter. When I saw your car on the road outside of Wishing Moon Bay, you caught me by surprise. I needed you to find the town, I needed you to come here."

"Why? So that you can brainwash me, too? Is that how you guys get your kicks?" she asked hotly.

"No, I needed you to come here so that I could meet you. You and I are mates." He was deadly serious, and Helena could see exactly why Penny would fall for this con trick. They pretended to believe it so thoroughly that it was hard to deny it wasn't the truth.

But Helena knew better, she knew this road led to crazy. This road led to your daughters practically having to raise themselves. She wasn't going to let that happen again. Not to Penny, not to Milo.

"I know this is hard to believe and if you weren't Dario's mate and if you hadn't told me someone had broken into your apartment then I wasn't going to tell you."

"What does this have to do with someone breaking into my apartment?" She put her hand to the side of her head. "I don't even know if anyone did break in." Her eyes widened and she turned her fury onto Dario and Logan. It all made sense now. "That was you? This was all planned. What is your game?"

"No game." He held her stare and she believed him even though she didn't want to.

"Then what the hell is going on?" She tore her gaze from Dario's and faced Penny.

"We don't know. Not about the intruder in your apartment at least. But what we do know..." Penny glanced at Dario and then closed the space between her and Helena, reaching for her hand. "Is that Dario is your mate. And he is a horse shifter, whether you want to believe it or not."

"Penny, this isn't what I want." She cast a glance over her shoulder. "What does it even mean? What does being a person's mate mean?"

"It means that we are meant to be together forever," Dario replied, but he didn't draw closer, even though she sensed he wanted to. Or maybe that was her overactive imagination.

"Together forever. We've only just met, and you think I'm yours forever?" Helena scoffed at the idea yet there was a part of her that wanted to give herself to Dario right now. It didn't matter that they didn't know each other. Destiny was on their side and fate had set up their first meeting on the road outside of Wishing Moon Bay.

She shook her head. That would mean she believed he could shift into a horse and that was just not possible outside of TV shows and movies.

"Listen, why don't I show you?" Dario came closer, talking quietly as if he were trying to calm a startled pony.

"Show me?" She covered her mouth as she shook her head. "You mean so you can make me believe in all of this mumbo jumbo. I don't believe you."

"You won't even believe your own eyes?" Dario asked.

"No. I think this is all smoke and mirrors. You'll show me but really it's just a projection, a trick, like stage magicians use."

"It's not a trick, Helena. I promise." Penny chewed the inside of her cheek, her expression pained.

"Aunt Helena." Milo came to her and threaded his small hand into hers. "It is real. We rode on the back of a dragon."

"Milo, it was a trick."

The small boy shook his head. "I know what's real and what's not. I know that last night I sat on the back of a dragon and flew through the sky, just as I know that Sophie is a witch and she used magic on us."

"Can I have a few minutes alone with Helena, please?" Penny nodded at Logan who had kept out of the discussion.

"Come on, Milo. Shall we go and play in the snow?" Logan held out his hand and Milo skipped toward him, his face burning bright with happiness. Even if this was all a bunch of lies, there was no denying the love Logan had for Milo. Milo who had been through so much. Who had lost his home because of his asshat of a father.

Dario lingered for a few moments longer before he turned and walked away as if it pained him to put any more distance between them. And damn it, Helena hated the idea of him being out of her sight.

"What is this?" Helena hissed at Penny. "Do they put something in the water?" She spun around and stalked back to the table. "Is there something in the coffee? Or the food?"

"Helena." Penny followed her sister and touched her arm lightly. "Listen to me because this is important. Really important."

"Don't try to convince me that all that stuff about shifters, mates, and magic is real." She rounded on Penny. This was her one chance to make her sister see sense.

"Okay, let's backtrack a little. Forget for a moment that I told you about magic and everything. This is about you and me." She reached out for Helena's hands. "When I first came to Wishing Moon Bay, when I walked down the street toward this hotel, I had a sense that I'd been here before."

"We have *never* been to this crazy town before," Helena insisted.

"Okay. Now this intruder in your house. Do you think it's a coincidence that he was in your house the day that Milo and I were supposed to arrive? You'd told him that we were coming that day, didn't you?"

"Yes, in conversation." Helena's face paled and her stomach lurched. "I don't understand. Do you think you know the guy? His name is Barry Matthews."

"I don't know. I certainly don't recognize the name. But what I do know is that we both found this place. What if we arrived here so we would be safe? I've driven along that same stretch of road before, ten times or more, and never seen the signs for this town. You drove along there how many times this morning before you saw Dar...the horse, and then saw the road?"

"You really believe in all of this, don't you?" Helena brushed her sister's hair back from her face. Her heart ached for her. After being so let down by her husband, Penny was desperate to be loved. So desperate that she was willing to believe in magic and a man who would love her until his dying breath.

"I've seen it. I've touched it. I felt the power of the witch last night. And I know deep in my soul that Logan is my mate, the man I am supposed to spend the rest of my life with. And I know that he would protect me and Milo with his life if he had to."

"That's some kind of love, no wonder you are hooked."

"Would you do one thing for me? Because you know how much I love you."

"Don't ask me to believe," Helena shook her head at Penny. "You can't ask me to believe. You know how I felt about Mom."

Penny nodded. "I know how much you hated the way she got sometimes."

"And now you're asking me to believe what she said was true." Helena trembled as her throat constricted. "If I let go and believe then it means all the things I said, all the things I thought were wrong." Her voice caught in her throat.

"I know, honey." Penny slipped her arms around Helena and held her tight as she sobbed on her shoulder.

"Are you sure?"

"As sure as we are standing here now. As sure as I love Milo with all my heart. This is real, this is true, and I think that what happened with this guy and him being in your apartment are all linked."

Helena held Penny tightly as her head throbbed. "Okay. If you believe in this. If you think this is all connected..." She lifted her head and looked Penny in the eyes. "I'm willing to believe if it means keeping you and Milo safe."

"I want you to believe because Dario will make you happy."

"Penny, the days of me thinking I need a man to make me happy are long gone, believe me."

"Don't knock it until you've tried it." Penny smothered a smile. "Honestly, Logan is the best thing to happen to me in a very long time. I love him and I know he loves me and more importantly, he loves Milo." Her eyes misted with tears.

"I'm so happy for you. You and Milo deserve the best."

"And so do you, Helena. I want you to believe that."

"All I can promise is that I'll keep an open mind." She hugged Penny again. "Okay, so what happens next?"

"Next?" Penny shrugged. "We figure out what the hell is going on and then deal with it."

Helena nodded. "So, a horse shifter."

"You always did badger Mom to go horseback riding. Now you have your very own horse." Penny giggled.

"Oh, this is so weird."

"I am learning that weird is good."

"Didn't you nearly get taken over by a witch?"

"Yes, but we defeated her. And if we can defeat Sophie, whatever is out there trying to mess with us does not stand a chance."

"I hope you're right." Helena shuddered. When she got home and realized Barry had been in her apartment, she'd felt violated. She'd also figured he was some sicko who had gotten inside her apartment to check out her underwear drawer.

But if magic were real then it could be something much deeper and darker.

The monsters in the closet were real.

I'm sorry I never believed you, Mom. Helena glanced out of the windows, her eyes were drawn to the clear blue sky. Was her mom up there somewhere looking down on them? If so, did she know how sorry her eldest daughter was for ever doubting her?

"Come on, Helena. Let's go outside. I can't wait to see Dario shift." Penny held out her hand to Helena and she took it. Together they would get through this.

4

DARIO

She's coming, his horse told him, as if Dario couldn't sense her for himself. Yet he didn't begrudge the thrill of excitement coursing through his horse. They had both waited long enough for this day. The day when they met the woman who would complete them.

"Dario. Helena and I have talked and she's willing to suspend her disbelief." Penny linked arms with Helena who was wrapped up against the cold. Her cheeks were flushed pink and a woolen hat covered her raven dark hair, but nothing could hide or diminish her beauty. It shone through her.

"I can't tell you how happy and relieved I am to hear that." Dario approached the two women, leaving Logan playing with Milo in the snow. They had been building a snowman, rolling large snowballs across the hidden lawn, just as they had when they were children.

"Don't get too excited," Helena warned him. "I said I would suspend my disbelief. That doesn't mean I am willing to believe you, without proof."

"Proof." Dario grinned and backed away a couple of paces. "That, I can do."

"Here?" Helena asked, looking around. "Anyone could see you."

"That's the thing about Wishing Moon Bay," Penny explained. "No one hides who they are."

"Wait!" Helena held up her finger. "So this means that magic and shifters and everything else are real in here and out there. Like you can just travel in and out of Wishing Moon Bay, but in here you don't hide what you are while out there you do?"

"A quick learner, I like that." Dario tilted his head to one side. "I was coming home when I passed you out on the road. If you believe in anything, believe that fate brought us together at that exact moment in time for a reason."

"Yeah, you couldn't have appeared and shown me the way to town when I drove along there the first time. Or the second." Helena arched an eyebrow.

"Timing has nothing to do with me." Dario held up his hands.

"Okay, do your thing." She waved him away but still glanced nervously up at the windows of the hotel.

Dario stood still for a moment and stared at his mate before he let go of the world around him and slipped away. In a blink of an eye, his horse replaced him. A rich ruddy brown with a black mane and tail, he tossed his head and snorted as he inhaled the scent of his mate.

"Are you a believer now?" Penny whispered in Helena's ear.

"I might be."

"Wow!" Milo came running toward Dario's horse, but Logan was fast and caught hold of the little guy.

"Slow down there, Milo. You shouldn't run up behind a

horse. You might get kicked." Logan scooped Milo up into his arms.

"Dario wouldn't kick me," Milo protested.

"It's good practice to treat all creatures you see in and out of Wishing Moon Bay with the respect they deserve. There are wild horses and wolves and bears in the mountains. I need you to take care and always presume any animal you meet might be a real animal and not a shifter."

"Okay, I get it." Milo settled in Logan's arms and Dario's heart ached for a child of his own. Logan would make a great dad for the boy and Dario couldn't help the pang of jealousy that pierced his gut.

"Just pet him gently on the face. That's right." Logan held Milo while the boy petted his nose and Dario's horse lifted his head and snorted, blowing warm air over his hand. Milo collapsed in a fit of giggles as he imitated the horse.

"Why don't you pet him, too?" Penny encouraged but Helena hung back.

"Isn't that weird?" Helena asked. "I mean petting his face." He pointed at the horse. "I mean, that is Dario in there, isn't it?"

"Yes," Logan answered. "That's Dario, but the other side of a shifter, it's connected but not exactly the same. It's hard to explain. We're like two separate entities with a linked consciousness."

"And there is only ever one of you in this world at the same time?" Helena asked.

"Yes. One side must give up its hold on this world so the other can come forth. When my wolf isn't here, it's like he's inside of my head. We can talk and communicate, he can sense things..." Logan shrugged. "It's like trying to explain how we eat or breathe. It's just a natural process."

"But if I pet him." Helena looked at Dario's horse with longing. "Isn't that like invading his space? I wouldn't walk up to Dario and just pet his face. That would be too...intimate."

Logan chuckled. "He wouldn't mind."

"I'll take your word for it." With an outstretched hand, Helena approached the horse.

Dario huffed gently, his warm breath caressing his mate's hand as he stood in anticipation. She could touch him all over, she could jump on his back and ride away into the sunset with him if she allowed him to love her.

Since when did having a mate make you so soft, Dario complained. He was a man who knew his own mind and followed his own path and yet here he was talking about giving himself over to a woman.

She's not just a woman, his horse reminded him. She is our mate.

His horse closed his eyes as Helena's fingers touched his nose. Tentative at first, as her confidence grew, she stepped closer and cupped his large head in her hands. "You are sweet."

His horse closed his eyes and rested his head against her as Logan chuckled. "I don't think Dario has ever been called sweet."

"But he's so gentle." She rested her forehead against him and inhaled his scent. "I always dreamed of having a pony when I was younger. But we never had enough money."

"Are you okay?" Penny slipped her arm around Helena's shoulders.

"Yeah. At least I think I am. I'm in shock, to be honest. When I came to meet you, this is not how I saw things playing out. Since it's your birthday tomorrow, I figured we'd have a few drinks and maybe dance..."

"Isn't this better?" Logan asked.

"Yes." Helena nodded and Dario sighed in relief. "Although, I think I'm still going to need a few drinks."

Penny laughed. "You and me both."

Dario pulled away from the small group of people and walked away, before shifting back into his human form. "Will you come with me for a ride?"

"Me?" Helena asked. "On your back?"

"Yes. I won't let you fall. We could go to the mountains and spend some time getting to know each other. I'd have you back before sundown." Dario held out his hand to her.

"Why don't you go up to my cabin?" Logan suggested.

"Yes, you could go up there and take all the stuff back inside. We left Logan's food and bedding out in the snow last night."

"You want me to go to your cabin and clean up..."

"We'll do it," Helena said quickly.

"This is our first date, in a way, and you are happy to spend it doing someone else's chores?" Dario didn't understand why his mate would volunteer them for such a job but if that's what she wanted, he would not deny her.

"I'll need to dress warmly. And maybe we could drive some of the way there. My car has snow tires. We could drive some of the way, couldn't we?" Helena's eyes lit up as she looked at Dario.

"Sure." He nodded.

"Great, then let's go." She backed away from Penny and Dario followed.

"Why are you so eager to go?" Penny asked suspiciously.

"I need some time to process all of this and I'm sure you and Logan need time to talk." She smiled brightly and Dario suspected there was more to this than Helena was saying.

"We do, and Milo needs a bath and some rest." Penny held up her hand when Milo protested. "You need a bath and some time in the warm. After lunch, we can come back out in the snow. Deal?"

"But I wanted to go with Aunt Helena. I want to ride on

Dario's back, just like I rode on Ivan's back." Milo's pleading puppy dog eyes were almost too much to deny.

"Another time." Penny's firm tone was met with a resigned sigh.

He's a good kid, Dario's horse said.

He is. Dario went to the boy and placed his large hand on his shoulder. "I will give you a ride soon. I promise."

"Into the mountains?" Milo asked hopefully.

"We'll go over the mountains when the weather is warmer." Dario nodded and then released the boy. "We will be back before sundown."

"We'll see you then." Logan guided Milo back inside.

"Take care," Penny hugged her sister before turning away and running to catch up with Logan and Milo.

"That just leaves us." Helena held up her car keys. "Shall we go?"

"After you." Dario inclined his head and turned to follow his mate as she went around the side of the hotel. When they reached the parking lot, she pressed the button on her keys and a set of lights flashed on a blue SUV.

"Recognize it?" Helena asked.

"Of course." He placed his hand on the roof. "That first glimpse of you will be etched in my mind forever."

Helena groaned. "Really? I suspect I had my mouth open in shock as you ran out in front of me and tossed your mane as you reared up."

Dario laughed. "To me, you looked completely serene and beautiful."

"Oh, I see how it is, you have a silver tongue." She cocked her head to one side. "I am going to need a filter, so I get to see the real you."

"This is the real me." He held his hands out to his sides. "I won't ever lie to you, Helena."

She turned to face him, the humor was gone from her expression. "You're serious."

He nodded. "It's part of being a shifter. I want you to be happy and I'll do whatever it takes to make you happy. And if there's one thing that is guaranteed to ruin happiness between two mates, it's lies. Trust is important to me. I know only too well that once trust is lost, it's impossible to regain. Not completely."

"Trust can be rebuilt," she told him.

"But never fully restored." He pinched his thumb and fingers together and held them up. "There will always be that seed of doubt and I never want you to doubt what I feel for you. I never want you to need to question my words or my actions."

"I like the sound of that."

"I have lived among horses more than humans for the last couple of years. Do you know horses never lie? They can't talk, they communicate with body language and there is an honesty there that has taught me so much."

"You have lived with horses more than humans?" Helena asked, then blinked. "Sorry, I know that wasn't the point."

"Don't worry, I am house-trained." He winked and went around to the passenger door. "I would rather travel on four hooves than four wheels."

"I thought the car made more sense because we don't know how much of Logan's stuff we will have to bring back down with us." She slid into the driver's seat.

"Why did you agree to do this? It wasn't just to help Penny and Logan. There was something more. I could see it in your eyes."

"Okay, since you have sworn never to lie to me, and I am all about honesty..." She inserted the key in the ignition and started the engine. "We're going to the place where the witch was yesterday. We're going to the place where she tried to take Penny's body."

"Yes." His forehead creased. "Why is that important?"

"Because..." She drove out of the parking lot. "You'll have to give me directions."

"Left." He held up his hand to the left. "Because..." He prompted as the car followed the worn tracks in the snow.

"Because it's proof that what Penny told me happened." She glanced sideways at him. "I have seen you shift. But that's not really magic, is it?"

"Isn't it?" Dario asked. "What is it, if not magic?"

"I don't know." She shook her head. "I just need to go to Logan's cabin and for all the bits and pieces Penny told me happened to be there laid out in the snow."

"And that will be proof that there is magic?" His forehead furrowed then he leaned back in his seat. "I don't understand why you need this proof, but if that's what you need."

"That's what I need."

"Turn right here."

"There's one other thing I need." Her fingers flexed on the steering wheel.

"Ask me." Whatever it was, she was nervous to ask. Was she worried he would say no?

"Okay. Penny told you about what happened at my apartment."

"Yes, she did. She told me about the man who bumped into you on the street and then the smell in your apartment."

"I need you to come back with me. I want you to help me track down this guy and force him to tell me what he knows and why he did it." Her jaw tensed.

"I had already made up my mind to do so."

"I figured as much. But here's the thing." She inhaled deeply. "I want us to go alone. I want you to persuade Logan that Penny and Milo are safer here. I don't want them in any danger. Penny deserves the happiness she's found here."

"And don't you deserve the same happiness?" Dario asked.

"I don't know." She pressed her lips together. "Penny has been through so much. Her ex-husband broke her heart, he chewed her up and spat her out. Logan can put her back together again."

"You think because you haven't suffered like your sister that makes you less worthy of being happy?" Dario shook his head. "That's not how happiness works. You don't have to suffer to experience it."

"I know. But Penny and Milo are the only two people in this world that I love. And in the same way that Logan wants to protect them because he is their mate, I want to protect them because they are my family. I figured you'd understand."

"I do." He nodded. "Left up here and then follow the road into the mountains."

"So we're agreed?"

"We're agreed. As long as you also understand that the same fierce love and protection Logan feels for his mate and you feel for your sister and nephew...that is how I feel for you, Helena. It's unconditional."

Helena swallowed hard. "I think I'm just beginning to realize that."

5

HELENA

Despite Helena's new snow tires, the car couldn't maneuver the road leading into the mountains. One steep curve left her wheels spinning as they tried to gain traction in a deep pocket of snow.

"This is where we get out and walk." Dario looked sideways at her and half-smiled.

"You mean ride." She switched off the engine and pocketed the keys. "You couldn't wait for me to get stuck, could you?"

"I can't deny the thought of your legs wrapped around me as we climb the mountain is exciting." He cracked open the passenger door and shoved it open against the snow. "Is there anything you need from the car?"

"I was going to grab my purse plus some snacks and water." She turned around in her seat and reached into the back seat. "It's always better to be prepared in case you get stranded in the snow."

"I wouldn't mind getting stranded with you," Dario told her before he straightened up and slammed the door closed, leaving her to simmer in the warm glow he coaxed out of her body.

Each look, each word he spoke to her, ignited a deep desire to know him more, to learn about him and what made him tick. He wasn't like any man she'd ever met. He wasn't driven by money or a career, he certainly had no desire to climb the corporate ladder, unlike most of the other men she'd dated.

She yanked a small backpack off the back seat, it contained her emergency kit. The dangers of driving in adverse weather conditions were all too real. Before she left her snug warm apartment, she'd checked the weather forecast and seen the threatening snow. Usually, she'd have put off traveling but this journey was too important.

Determined to get to Penny, and away from the danger that might lurk in her apartment, she'd gone to the local outdoor sports store, bought a small backpack, and filled it with a small medical kit, plus food and water. Adding in a flashlight, and a thick sleeping bag, Helena was satisfied she could survive for a couple of days if she got stranded in the snow.

"Coming?" Dario called, he stood a couple of feet away from the car, watching her.

Heat flared in her belly and fanned out as tendrils of desire unfurled, warming her like no fire ever could. There was a connection between them. This was as close to love at first sight as she was ever going to get.

Helena paused, her hand on the car door. If Dario was her mate, this was it. This was the man she was destined to be with for the rest of her life. There would be no other man. There would be no other lover in her bed.

She swallowed down that thought, ignoring the thrill of excitement that threaded through her veins. The idea that there was some higher power who had decided that Dario was her mate scared her. She liked to be in control of her life. Helena wasn't the kind of woman who went with the flow, she wasn't happy to sit back and let life happen to her.

Yanking on the handle, she opened the car door, a blast of cold air reminding her they were at the mercy of the mountain and the weather.

"Are you sure this is a good idea?" She got out and looked at her car. "How are we going to get back down?"

"When we get to the cabin, we can find some rope. When we come back down, we can make a makeshift harness and I'll pull the car around." He grinned as her eyes widened. "You'd forgotten you had a stallion at your service."

She put her hand to her face and shook her head. "I didn't exactly forget you were a horse. It's not the kind of thing you can *un*see. But no, it didn't even occur to me that you might be able to pull the car around. It's going to take a while for my brain to think in terms of shifters."

"Well, we'd better get started on that." He beckoned to her. "Come on, there's a boulder over here you can stand on. If I get really close, you should be able to swing your leg over my back."

"Can't we walk from here?" Helena was having second thoughts about riding Dario's horse. "I've never been on a horse before." She turned around and looked down the steep mountain road. They'd been lucky her car had gotten them this far.

"I'll keep you safe." He held out his hand to her. "Come on. Trust me."

Helena shuffled through the snow, when she reached him, she placed her hand in his and he drew her toward him. "Trust doesn't come easy."

"I know." He stroked her cheek with the back of his hand and warmth flooded her skin.

"You're so hot."

"I know." A small teasing smile flickered across his mouth.

"You are extremely disturbing." She kept hold of his hand as she surveyed the boulder. "You're going to need to..."

Before she finished the sentence, he scooped her up into his arms and lifted her onto the boulder. "Steady."

"Some warning would have been nice." She shuffled her feet around on top of the boulder until she found level footing and then straightened her clothes. He'd robbed her of her breath, and she took a moment to compose herself.

None of this went unnoticed by Dario. It was as if she were a fascinating bug he wanted to study.

"Ready?" he asked when she stood still, the pack on her back and her gloved hands by her sides.

"As I'll ever be." She sighed. "Go shift."

He took a couple of steps away from her but didn't take his eyes off her face. Everything about him unnerved her. She was beginning to enjoy it. Dario was anything but predictable.

For a woman who had spent her life clinging to being normal, he was a revelation. He opened the world up and filled it with wonder, filled it with potential.

Filled it with danger. The monsters in the closet were real.

Was the man who entered her apartment and filled it with his scent a monster? She shuddered, a sense of dread filling her.

But then the air around Dario sparked and popped and the man faded from the world to be replaced by a horse. A magnificent freakin' horse, with a long flowing mane that cascaded down his neck. The horse threw his head up and down and snorted, his breath a cloud of steam on the cold air.

The horse stared at her and she stared at it. The connection between them was undeniable. This was Dario, only now he took the form of a horse.

"Okay, let's get this over with." She swallowed her nerves as the horse circled around before sidling up to the boulder, his back as close to the rock as he could get without risking injury to his legs.

Helena leaned forward and grasped hold of his mane before letting it go. "Sorry, I don't want to pull your hair."

The horse looked around at her, his eye patient and kind. Helena took this as permission to hold his mane and she grasped a large tuft, before raising her right leg and sliding it over the horse's broad back.

It wasn't exactly dignified, and she'd do better next time, but with some wriggling, she ended up seated behind the horse's shoulders, one leg on either side of his broad back with both hands holding clumps of his mane.

The horse turned to look at her again, tossed his head, and then took a step forward.

The movement came as a surprise, she'd never experienced anything like it. A real living creature beneath her. As he took one more step and then another, a deep sense of regret settled in Helena's chest.

"I wish I'd ridden a horse before," she told Dario and let go of his mane with her right hand. Patting his shoulder lightly, she stroked the soft hair covering his shoulder. "Thank you."

The horse looked around at her one last time before he forged forward through the virgin snow, following the half-hidden road up the mountain.

The horse's muscles bunched beneath her as he climbed higher. Helena relaxed, her body working as one with the beautiful animal who had captured her heart in the same way Dario's human form had. They were one and the same, both caring and capable of loving her.

When she was a girl and her mom was acting strange, Helena hated the idea of magic, she wished her mom would just be normal, like all the other mothers. With each stride the horse took, Helena celebrated the knowledge that shifters were real and there was magic in the world.

"I'm sorry, Mom," she whispered on the mountain breeze. Dario's horse's ears twitched as they heard her speak. It didn't matter, there would be no secrets between them. If their lives were going to be built on more than fate, they would both need to open up about who they were and where they'd come from.

Dario must have stories of his own to tell. He'd been adopted by Valerie, that was a story in itself. What had happened to his parents? How had he ended up under Valerie's care?

Helena switched off her analytical brain. The journey up the mountain was incredibly special, she needed to learn to live in the now. The future might be filled with hidden danger, secrets of her past might be revealed, clues as to who her mother really was.

But for now, the cold on her cheeks, and the warm body between her thighs was all that mattered, all that was real.

Tears trickled down her cheeks, drying instantly, leaving salty trails. She was blessed.

They crested a small rise and Helena caught a glimpse of a small cabin, surrounded by bare trees. In the spring and summer, the place must be surrounded by new life and birdsong but today it was a barren snow scene. Except the snow looked different here. As they drew closer, the branches of the trees weren't weighed down with snow.

She shivered and Dario half-turned his head, his eye on her for a moment before he turned his full attention to the area around the cabin. Beneath her, he tensed, his muscles bunched ready to run. Or maybe he'd stand and fight if danger approached.

Helena placed her hand on his shoulder, soothing him. He tossed his head and slowed his pace, snorting as he lowered his head and sniffed the ground.

"What's that?" Helena swung her leg over his back and slid to the ground. Her feet didn't sink, it was as if the snow here had been turned to thick ice.

She ran toward the large indent in the snow and stopped dead. As she stared at the ground the cold air popped and fizzed as Dario shifted back to his human form. But Helena could not tear her attention away from the icy ground.

"It's a dragon footprint," Dario said from right behind her. "Ivan was here."

"So there really was a witch and they did fight her here." Helena swayed on her feet and Dario put his arm around her and held her close. She leaned into him, welcoming his presence and the warmth of his body.

"Did you really think they'd made it up?"

"No. But to see proof." She turned to face Dario. "Ivan is a dragon shifter?"

"He is. And no, he's not one of a kind, there's a whole bunch of them over the ocean but they keep to themselves." He wrapped his arms tightly around her. "Believe, Helena. Let down the barriers you've put up and believe, see the world with new eyes and embrace the wonder of it all."

"I can't *not* believe, can I?" She pulled away from him. "Do you know what happened here?"

"Ivan told me Sophie melted the snow to destroy the talisman Jeremy had drawn in the snow to protect him and Milo."

"Milo." She put her hands to her mouth. "He was in so much danger."

"He's safe now."

"You want me to believe in the wonder of magic and yet it's not just about wonder, is it? There's danger and horror." The monster in the closet. She closed her eyes and pulled away from him, taking big gulps of air and forcing it into her lungs.

"Danger and horror are not unique to magic," Dario replied. "And magic is not to blame for the danger and horror. It's the people who bend it to their will. Just as outside of Wishing Moon Bay, a person might choose to use a gun, or their fists to hurt another. A bomb to cause untold damage to people's lives or start a war in which millions suffer."

"You're right." She wiped the tears from her cheeks. "I think I'm in shock, that's all."

"Which is completely understandable. Your whole belief system has been turned upside down."

But it was more than that. The knowledge that magic was real, that the supernatural existed around her had awoken something deep inside of her, stirred distant memories.

The monster in the closet was real.

6

DARIO

"I should have been here." Dario stared down at the snow-covered blankets and food items strewn among the runes carved into the snow.

"You couldn't have known what was happening." It was Helena's turn to give comfort, which only made Dario feel worse.

"I could have been here early yesterday morning, but I didn't hurry." He lifted his arm and wrapped it around his mate. Her presence calmed him, soothed him, and he hoped the feelings were reciprocated when he touched his mate.

"Hey, it's done. Don't beat yourself up over it."

"I didn't hurry because part of me was jealous that Logan had found his mate first. How self-centered is that?" He let go of his mate and leaned down, grabbed hold of the fabric, and yanked it out of the snow. Helena caught hold of the other end and together they shook the snow and ice from Logan's bedsheets.

"It's understandable. When finding your mate is such a big thing to you, then it's understandable you were jealous. I know I was when Penny told me Logan was *the one* with such certainty. She'd just come out of a toxic relationship with Milo's dad, her heart was beaten and bruised, and yet there she was telling me she was in love again." Her shoulders sagged and she looked tired as they folded the sheets and placed them on the ground before methodically searching through the snow for the discarded food.

"Why were you jealous?" Dario asked. "Because she had a new love or because she was brave enough to open her heart once more?"

Helena wagged a box of cookies at him. "Can you see inside my head?"

He half-smiled. "Maybe a little." He picked up a couple of bottles of water, the liquid inside frozen solid. "You don't strike me as the kind of person who resents her sister's happiness. You care for her deeply. So, I presumed that you were jealous of her courage to open her heart."

"It's not as if I've closed myself off from love and relationships..." Helena's expression grew more troubled. "I thought that Barry... I thought when he bumped into me in the street and then got my phone number..."

"You thought he might be the one for you, that fate had brought you together?" Now he understood her reaction. His temper flared, he wanted to track down this Barry and kick him in the groin, with both hind hooves.

"Yeah." She laughed and her mood lightened. "I mean what kind of crazy is that? Just bumping into a guy like that?"

He chuckled. "Now, our meeting was fate, pure and simple."

"See, you expect me to believe that our meeting is fate but that my meeting with Barry wasn't. How do you know which was which?" Her mischievous grin didn't have the desired effect.

"How do you know they were *not* both fate?"

Helena stood still and stared at him, her brow furrowed. "That hadn't occurred to me."

"As I see it, it's like a chain reaction." He gathered up the rest of the food, dumped it on the bedsheets, and then gathered the corners of the fabric together and lifted it off the snow. "Let's get inside. I'll light a fire and we can eat and make coffee. We'll have to boil the water over the fire since there's no power unless we use the generator."

"We can manage without power, instant coffee is fine." She followed him into the cabin where Logan had lived for the last few years. Dario wasn't the only brother who had stepped away from society for a while. Logan had come here seeking peace and solitude. He'd only returned to town to run the hotel when Valerie asked him to while she had an operation on her leg.

Dario stamped the snow off his boots and stepped inside. The place looked like it had been ransacked. A fresh wave of guilt covered him. Last night could have gone terribly wrong and his brother might have lost his mate before they'd even had a chance to get to know each other.

If Logan had lost his mate, there was a chance they would all have lost Logan to a bitter deep depression that took hold of shifters who lost their mates. Dario had seen that depression before and would not wish it on anyone.

"So this chain reaction," Helena began, as they set the items from outside in the snow on the counter. Together they sorted through them, placing them in *keep* or *go* piles. Some of the food was ruined, they would take it back with them and put it in the trash. If not, it might attract wild animals to the cabin.

"Yes. I believe that there was a series of events that occurred. Those events led you to be on the road this morning at the exact time I was there. Fate." He waited for her to counter his words.

"I see it. If Barry hadn't bumped into me and broken into my apartment, then I would not have decided to come and meet Penny. If Sophie hadn't been such a witch, then Penny would not have been attacked and she would have met me on the road, and I would never have met you." She held out her hands, looking pleased with herself.

"It's all connected. We're all connected." He paused before continuing. "When you run with a herd, they move as one, we can sense the other horses next to us, a subtle change in direction and we all move. It's like we communicate on a deeper level, a shift in speed, a change in terrain."

"Like a shoal of fish in the water." Helena knelt on the floor and started picking up the canned food that had been dragged out of the cupboards.

"I'm glad Logan doesn't have to see it like this." Dario gathered up a discarded package of dried beans.

"I can't even imagine how scared Penny must have been. Trying to save herself and Milo in the dark." Helena stood up. "Why don't you go and light the fire? I'll finish up here. Although I doubt everything will go back in the right place."

"I don't think Logan will care too much. He won't be living up here anymore." Dario backed away, aware that his life was about to change in the same way Logan's had.

"He has responsibilities now." She glanced up at Dario from under her lashes. "What about you?"

"You mean what about *us*?" He gave a wry smile. "As two strangers, we have to figure out how our lives fit together."

"And we haven't even known each other for five hours."

He closed the distance between them, and she squeaked like a startled mouse. "We have known each other our whole lives, we just didn't know it."

Wrapping his arms around her waist, he pulled her close, their lips inches apart as their eyes locked together. He wanted to kiss her with every fiber of his being, but this was so new to Helena and after what Barry did to her, Dario didn't want to push too far too soon and scare her.

Helena slipped her hands around his neck and cradled his head. "Are you going to kiss me?"

"I want to more than anything." His eyes lingered on her lips and her tongue snaked out and moistened them. She wanted him, he was certain. But suddenly his ability to read body language with such certainty slipped away.

"What's stopping you?" She inclined her head, her lips closer, so close he could taste her.

"Nothing." He tightened his arms around her and closed the space between them. He brushed his lips against hers, a questioning kiss, giving her the chance to back off if that's what she wanted.

It wasn't. She nipped his bottom lip, teasing him until he groaned and deepened their kiss, his tongue brushing her lower lip. Helena opened her mouth and their tongues entwined. She tasted of coffee and Ivan's pastries.

As they stood together in Logan's cabin, he wished that they could stay there forever, just the two of them. He didn't want to go back to town this evening, he didn't want Helena to go back to her apartment and confront whatever darkness awaited her there.

And he was certain there was darkness. Each time she mentioned Barry, a shadow crossed her face. Did Helena know more than she was saying, perhaps keeping details to herself so Penny didn't worry?

Or perhaps it was deeper, darker than any of them realized. Their mother knew of magic, but she'd kept it hidden aside from a few slip-ups. Why?

"I lost you for a moment there." Helena broke their kiss and inched her head away for his. "What's wrong?"

Dario shook his head. "Nothing is wrong, everything is perfect. I just wish we could stay here, the two of us, forever."

"You would soon grow tired of me."

"Never."

"And we both have families, people we care about." The darkness crossed her face. "And I have to find out what Barry wants. I need to know if he's just a plain old human stalker or if there's more to it than that. He came to my apartment on the day Penny and Mio were due to arrive."

"The day their car broke down and they wound up in Wishing Moon Bay."

"There's that coincidence again. If we're all connected then there's a reason he was there that day, don't you think?"

Dario nodded. "I just want to keep you safe, but you need to keep Penny and Milo safe. I get it." He pulled her close again. "But a man can dream, can't he? Dream of us and a simple life."

"Oh, I am all for dreams." She kissed his lips and shivered in his arms.

"You're cold, I'll go get the fire lit." He crushed her to his chest before letting her go.

"I'll fill the kettle and rustle us up something to eat." She watched him as he left the kitchen area and went to the living room. He could feel her gaze on his back but even when he was out of sight, he could still sense her. She was a part of him, they were linked for all eternity.

Dario sank to his knees. As he built the fire, he did the unthinkable, he opened the part of his mind he'd closed off when he came to live with Valerie in Wishing Moon Bay.

It's time we faced our anger, his horse told him. But the anger he held for his father was dimmer now, fading. Now that he'd met Helena, Dario had a new understanding of his father's behavior.

I can't imagine a life without Helena and we've only just met. How did our father feel when he lost our mother? Dario gripped the kindling so tightly he crushed the twigs in his hand.

Like his heart had been ripped out. His horse hung his head in sorrow.

Maybe it's time we let go of our sense of betrayal, Dario said. *It's time we learned to understand our father and forgive him.*

But never forget, his horse replied. *If we are ever blessed with children, then we must promise to never follow the path our father followed. Death is not the answer when others love you and depend on you.*

As the fire crackled into life, Dario stared into the flames and pictured his father, the most incredible black stallion he had ever seen. In that moment Dario was a child once more, who adored his father and worshiped the ground he trod on.

Dario had been so young when his mother died that he barely remembered her. He'd been eight when his father decided he could no longer live in a world without his mom and took his own life.

A year later he'd come to live with Valerie. Before Valerie, he'd counted himself as one of the unluckiest children alive. But being taken in by Valerie and raised alongside his adopted brothers had changed his outlook.

Now, meeting Helena reinforced the idea that he wasn't the unluckiest man alive but the luckiest. He had everything and more any shifter could hope for.

And Barry was not going to rob him of that. History would not repeat itself. Dario planned to live into old age and beyond with his mate at his side.

7

HELENA

"This is cozy." Helena sat on a cushion, her legs crossed as she sipped a hot cup of coffee and crunched potato chips.

"I promise our next date will have real food." Dario ate a cookie and looked up at her. He was stretched out on the rug in front of the fire, reminding her of a primal beast as the fire cast a red glow across his features.

"I am enjoying having junk food forced upon me." She grinned. "I expect if we cracked open some of the cans of food in the cupboards, we could have rustled up something healthy and nutritious, but where's the fun in that?"

"I like your way of thinking, although usually I treat my body as a temple and eat healthily."

She sniggered as she eyed his body. "I could certainly worship at your temple."

"Then my efforts to keep myself trim and toned have been worth it." He rolled onto his back and lifted his shirt to reveal a toned six-pack. "Of course, I had plenty of free time on my hands to focus on myself and my body." He pulled his shirt down and turned onto his side. "Now I have you to care for and provide for."

He reached out and brushed her hair off her shoulder, his fingertips lingering on the exposed skin of her neck. Her nipples hardened and she was glad she hadn't stripped off her sweater. As beads of perspiration formed on her brow, she fanned herself.

"The fire is making me hot."

"And I thought I was responsible for the flush across your neck." He trailed his fingers lower, skimming the neck of her sweater.

"I do not usually sleep with men on the first date." She sighed heavily. "I have never slept with a man on the first date. Not in the first month."

"I do not want to be responsible for you lowering your standards." He raised his hand and stroked her cheek before breaking contact with her.

Helena placed the bag of chips on the coffee table and slid down onto the floor, her body pressed against his. "Everything about you raises my standards."

"I don't want you to regret anything about our relationship," he whispered as he leaned forward and brushed his lips against hers.

"I think I might regret it more if we don't..." She licked his lips, before kissing him harder, her hand sliding across his chest, lingering on the hard buds of his nipples.

Dario groaned. "You are a temptress, threatening to break my resolve."

"You don't want me?" she purred.

"More than you could ever know, but so much has happened in the last few hours, your beliefs have been rocked. I don't want this to be something...something you *think* you want. A distraction."

"You have been distracting me since I first saw you on the

road." She lifted his shirt and stroked his toned abs, her fingers lingering over the ridges of his six-pack muscles.

"You know what I mean, Helena. I want our first time to be special. I want you to want me for me, not just because I'm here." He raised his head and looked at her, his eyes smoldering hot. "Not because I'm insanely attractive and incredibly sexy."

Helena chuckled. "You sure know how to break the mood." She pulled her hand back and slid his shirt down over his stomach. "You're probably right. Although, believe me, I don't think I would regret sleeping with you."

"You wouldn't. But I might."

"Why? Don't you want your mate? Isn't the whole point of us being made for each other so that we can make love and procreate?" Her jaw tightened. "Okay, I get it. We know nothing about each other. I don't even know if you want children. You have wandered the world running with horses for the last couple of years, so you have no job, no way of supporting a family..."

"Okay, maybe we should have just made love and dwelled on my good points rather than getting hung up on my bad ones." He sighed and sat up. The spell was well and truly broken.

"Hey, I was not taking a shot at you." She reached out for his hand and pulled him down beside her. "I'm just trying to look at it objectively." She placed her hand over his heart. "You want us to have a connection beyond the physical. Which you already have. I don't. If we made love now, it would be purely physical for me."

She leaned forward and pressed her lips to his.

Dario slid his arms around her. "That's pretty much it. I want you to want me for me. I guess I'm old-fashioned. Making love should be special, I'd like us to get to know each other a little better first."

"I agree. So tell me about yourself. Let's start with you being adopted by Valerie." Her eyes locked with his. "Unless you'd rather not talk about it. I completely understand if it's too personal, too difficult."

His lower lip trembled and for a moment Dario reminded her of Milo when he was upset. "I've never really talked about it. Not even with Valerie. She knew my history when she adopted me, and even though she encouraged me to talk about my parents, I never did. I shut them out. I shut out the pain."

"I'm sorry." She took hold of his hand and kissed the back of it. "Why don't you tell me about Wishing Moon Bay. Or your favorite place in the world."

"No, I want you to know about my parents. It's part of who I am. It's part of the man you are going to spend the rest of your life with." His voice hitched.

"Hey." She pressed her body against his, cupping his face in her hands. "Take your time and if it's too much, just stop. I'm not going anywhere."

"My father was a shifter. A horse shifter. The gene gets passed down from parent to child." He held her gaze. "So, if we have children, and yes, I want children. More than anything I would love to have a child with you."

"Good to know." She threaded her fingers through his.

"I don't know much about my mother. She died when I was very young, too young to have any memories of her, and my father never spoke of her."

"I'm so sorry." Helena wanted to hold Dario in her arms and make everything all right for him.

"How do you miss someone who barely existed?" He gave a sad half-smile.

"I don't know who my father is," Helena admitted. "I only ever remember my mom and she never spoke about our father. All we know is that Penny and I share the same father. What happened to him, we don't know."

"It's hard, it's like there is a piece of you missing." He kissed her cheek and inhaled her scent as his breath shuddered through his body.

"When you grow up, you expect the pain and the hurt to go but it doesn't, does it?"

"No."

"What happened to your dad?"

"He raised me. At least he fed me and clothed me, but he was never there for me. He was emotionally absent. I didn't understand why until today."

"I don't understand."

"Now that I've met my mate, I realize just how much he lost when his mate, my mother, died. I can't imagine what my life would be like without you now. And we've only just met."

"And that connection between us will grow stronger and deeper." She could sense it inside of her, it was as if there was an invisible tether connecting them, binding them together. And if that snapped, if life was torn from one of them... "He died of a broken heart."

"He took his own life." Dario's voice broke and she held him, cradling him to her.

"I'm so sorry." She rocked him like a baby, this grown man who stirred something inside of her she never dreamed existed.

"I've shut off the hurt and betrayal for so long but today the barrier I put up collapsed."

"I'm sorry." This was her fault.

"Don't be sorry, you coming into my life is the best thing to ever happen to me. I should have faced up to my past before, I should have dealt with the feelings I have. Instead, like a coward, I hid from them."

"There is nothing cowardly about shutting off the pain inside. I know I have. When my mom passed, I felt the same pain and betrayal. She'd always been kind of absent when we were growing up. It was as if she were with us but also somewhere else." She pushed herself to a sitting position and stared toward the window. "I always thought she was a little crazy. Now I'm beginning to think there was more going on than we could ever have imagined."

"I can't change what happened to my parents. There is no mystery, there is just death. But I can help you find out about your mom and maybe we can put the demons to rest."

"The monster in the closet." She half-turned to look at him. "When I was a child, I had nightmares. I was convinced there was a monster in my closet. My mom would hang a talisman in the closet and the dreams would stop for a while. Most other moms would have sat on the bed and told their daughter the monster wasn't real. But what if it was?"

"Lots of children dream of monsters," he told her.

"I know, but this was different." She looked down at her hands. "My mom acted as if it was real, as if her talismans would keep me safe."

"She might have simply had her own way of dealing with it. Instead of telling you it was nonsense and just a dream, she hung a talisman. It's like a placebo."

"I thought that, too. After she died, I thought about her a lot. I realized that she was doing her best for me." Helena's eyes glittered with tears. This realization had brought a whole dose of guilt with it. "But today I learned that monsters are real. What if Barry is a monster? You can shift. What if he's not human? What if he's just in human form? What if my mom knew there really was something stalking us?"

"You mean Barry." Dario sat up, his arm pressing against hers. "You think it's all connected?"

"Barry was in my apartment the day Penny was due to arrive. The day she found Wishing Moon Bay." She inclined her head toward him and gently nudged him. "You are the one who told me there were no such things as coincidences. Penny is certain she's been to Wishing Moon Bay before. So what if it is all connected? What if she is in danger?"

"We should go back to your apartment as soon as possible." Dario got to his feet in one lithe movement and held out his hand to her.

"The day after tomorrow." She slipped her hand into his and he pulled her to her feet. "I want to stay for Penny's birthday and then we leave. Alone. No matter how much Penny insists she's coming, she is going to stay here where Logan and your brothers can keep her safe."

"Why don't you stay with her and I'll go alone?" he suggested.

"No, this is my problem." She slid her arms around his neck. "And I'll be safe enough. I have this big, insanely attractive, and incredibly sexy man to watch over me. And I trust him with my life."

8

DARIO

After a couple of hours ensuring Logan's cabin was tidy and secure, they began their descent down the mountain. Dario shifted into his horse and stood next to the porch steps so that Helena could climb on his back.

"Okay, hold still. This is a little more awkward because of the packs." Helena slipped her right leg over his back and hung on to his mane as she wriggled into position behind the makeshift saddlebags they had fashioned from the wet sheet. They had packed the spoiled food on one side and any other dirty laundry on the other.

As she shifted position on his back, his horse absorbed her warmth and the sense of closeness between them. He longed to carry her across wild grassy plains and swim in the ocean with her on his back. There were so many places he'd love to show her, places he'd explored alone.

We will never be alone again. His horse tossed his head and stepped away from the porch, carefully following the snow-covered trail leading down from the cabin.

Once they had left the clearing in front of the cabin where the battle with Sophie had taken place, the snow was a couple of feet deep, with drifts of three feet or more. Dario's horse lifted his legs high before stepping forward and plunging his hooves into the snow.

A cold wind swept down from the higher peaks and his horse shivered in delight. If he didn't have such precious cargo on his back, and he didn't mean Logan's dirty laundry, he would gallop down the mountainside at breakneck speed.

Soon he would teach his mate to ride at a faster pace. He wanted to share the thrill of the wind in his mane and the ground disappearing under his hooves. The freedom was incredible. But sharing it with his mate would increase his joy beyond measure.

His ears twitched as he listened to his mate. She spoke to him in a soothing voice, encouraging him when they reached a deep drift that came up way past his knees. Then she would fall silent as she looked out over the majestic view of the mountain behind them and the town nestled in the valley below.

All too soon they were back at her car. Their close connection broke as she slid down off his back.

"Are you sure this isn't going to hurt?" she asked as she looped the rope over his head and pulled it back against his shoulders.

The horse tossed his head and snorted, pawing the ground as she removed the saddlebags and unlocked the car. He had pulled heavier loads than this. Plus, he wanted to show off his strength to his mate.

Helena opened the trunk and deposited the saddlebags inside before slamming it shut. Going around to the driver's side, she opened the door and slid into the seat. Inserting the key in the ignition, she started the engine and turned on the heater before getting back out. Her cheeks were white from the cold, her features pinched as she took the end of the rope and attached it to the car.

"Are we ready?" She gave him a thumbs-up and he tossed his head in response. "Okay."

She hurried back to the car and got inside. Helena let off the brake and put the car in reverse, as the wheels spun, Dario took the strain of the rope and pulled the car. It slid slowly out of the snowdrift, the tires finally getting a grip.

Dario quickly shifted into his human form and removed the rope from the car. Running to the edge of the road, he guided Helena forward and back until she had turned the car around.

"Thanks, I couldn't tell where the edge of the road was, the snow is too deep." She put her foot on the gas and they slowly crawled forward down the steep section of the road.

"The snow makes everything look different. Do you like the snow?" Dario needed to find out everything about her. What she liked, what she didn't like, what she wanted from life. He might not have much to offer her right now, but he was determined to make all her dreams come true.

"I like snow, but I don't like the cold. And it's very cold up here." She glanced at the heater which was making a valiant effort to warm the air inside the car.

"You should see the mountains in the summer when the trees are in full leaf. It's an incredible place, filled with birds and small animals making the most of the long days."

"You love it here." She glanced at him and he nodded. "But you've spent so long away."

"I needed to see the world to understand what I was missing." He chuckled. "I went out into the world in the hope that I might find my mate. I knew she wasn't in Wishing Moon Bay and not many new folks come here. I was being proactive."

"And you found her on your return. Who says fate doesn't have a sense of humor?" She laughed. "Do you regret any of it?"

"No. I have seen so much and learned so much about myself and the world around me. It's given me time to think and to appreciate what I have. Of course, that was before I found you. Now I have so much more to appreciate."

"What happens now? I mean after we figure out if Barry is a bad guy."

"I don't know. What do you want?" Dario was dreading her answer. Now that he'd come home to Wishing Moon Bay, he could not bear the thought of leaving and living somewhere else. If they were going to have children, this was where he wanted to raise them.

"I want to be happy." Her simple answer resonated with him.

"That's all I want. But where is happiness for you?"

"I don't know. I don't know if I've ever been happy." She inclined her head toward him. "How sad is that?"

"It's not sad at all. I've had fleeting moments of happiness, and long periods of contentment. But I don't believe I've ever been happy. I've lost myself to a world where happiness didn't matter, where it was more about survival, finding food, and keeping the herd safe. But even then, I wasn't happy."

"When I look at you, it's as if I'm holding up a mirror to myself." She reached for his hand as she steered the car with one hand. "We are meant to be together and make each other happy."

"You're a believer?" He arched an eyebrow at her.

"Yes, I'm a believer." She shook her head. "All this because a horse ran out in front of me."

They reached the town and he directed her back to the hotel. As she switched off the engine, neither of them moved.

"Thank you for today. I know you came to town to see your sister but I'm glad we spent the day together."

"Me, too." She leaned across and kissed his lips. "I'm going to spend the evening with Penny and Milo. Then tomorrow we'll celebrate her birthday."

"And the day after that we'll leave." He sighed. "I'll make the arrangements and make sure my brothers know what's going on. My guess is, if Penny is anything like you, she is not going to like being told to stay here."

"No, she won't. But she will if it's to protect Milo. My sister will do anything for her son. And I'll do anything to keep them both safe."

"That's not something I need to hear." Dario placed his hand on the car door. Perhaps he should leave tonight while Helena was spending time with her sister.

She will never trust us again if we do leave without her, his horse told him firmly. I don't like the idea of putting Helena in danger any more than you do. But this isn't a choice we can make for her.

And we have no way of tracking down this Barry person. If we're going to deal with him, we're going to need Helena.

We'll keep her safe. His horse sighed heavily. I just wish we knew what we were up against.

Maybe he's just a creepy human and we just have to impress on him that Helena is out of bounds and if he ever gets within twenty feet of her again or invites himself into her apartment then we will deal with him.

At least we know he's not a vampire. His horse shuddered. He wouldn't have been able to get into her apartment uninvited if he were.

Vampires. Dario shared his mistrust of the creatures of the night. Although most vampires who lived in Wishing Moon Bay were peace-loving and drank donated blood. He couldn't remember the last time there was a vampire-related death in Wishing Moon Bay. You had more chance of being hit by a lightning bolt sent from the hands of an inexperienced witch or wizard.

Dario grabbed the makeshift packs from the back of the car and carried them inside, with Helena walking behind him, checking her phone for messages. As they walked through the main door, he sensed Logan and another man in the reception area. And Valerie.

"Mom." He grinned as the woman who had raised him after his father's death and the only mother he had ever known turned to look at him.

"Dario." Her forehead creased and she wagged her finger at him. "You come home after all these months and then disappear out of the door without even a hello."

"Sorry, I had something important to do."

"More important than seeing your mother?" Valerie put her hands on her hips. "Is that dirty laundry?"

"It's the stuff from Logan's cabin, we went up there to clean up the mess."

"Well, you're here now." Valerie held out her arms to her son and he hugged her close. "I missed you." Even at forty-two, Dario still missed Valerie when he was away. He missed her hugs and her wisdom, she was home to him. "And who is *we*?"

Valerie patted his back and pulled away from him as Helena entered the hotel.

"Logan didn't tell you?" Dario shot Logan a questioning look.

"We agreed it wasn't our news to tell," Logan said in defense.

"Didn't tell me what?" Valerie's expression cleared and her mouth fell open. "No!"

"Mom, this is Helena, my mate. Helena, this is Valerie, my mom." He grinned like a fool as the two most important women in his life met.

"Your mate!" Valerie covered her face in her hands, her voice choked with emotion.

"It's good news, Mom, no need to cry." Dario winked at Helena as he slipped his arm around Valerie's shoulders.

"They're good tears," Valerie insisted as she cleared her throat and wiped her tears from her cheeks. "I just can't believe it. After all this time, two of my sons find their mates. We're truly blessed."

"I figured you had been down on the beach throwing all the wishing stones into the ocean under a full moon," Dario said drily.

Valerie playfully slapped his arm. "I have been doing that since you boys first shifted. It's sure taken long enough."

"But the wait has been worth it." Dario guided his mom toward his mate. Something he'd never dreamed would happen. Just like his mom and his brothers, he'd figured that fate had passed him by, that he'd used up all his luck when Valerie opened her door and her heart to him.

"I'd reserve your judgment there." Helena blushed as she glanced from Dario to Valerie and back again. She looked like a cornered animal as she licked her lips and smiled.

"I know you must be special if you are lucky enough to be the mate of one of my boys." Valerie looked up at Dario. "They are all special in their own unique way."

"Isn't that what every mother says?" Dario said drily.

"It is, but this mother means it. I've always been honest with you all." Valerie broke away from Dario and opened her arms to Helena. "And we're doubly blessed that you are Penny's sister."

"There's nothing like keeping it in the family, is there?" Helena hugged Valerie back. "It's good to meet you, I think you're incredibly brave to adopt six boys."

"I see it as incredibly blessed." Valerie inched back and put her hands on Helena's upper arms. "As I've gotten older, they have come in very useful. I always have someone to fix things around the hotel."

Helena laughed. "I see, they were an investment."

"Like a retirement fund." Valerie laughed. "You know I'm only joking." She half-turned to look at Dario and Logan, her voice cracking as she added, "Although they are the best investment I have ever made. If you pour in enough love, then you get an immeasurable return."

"I think the amount of stress we caused you growing up might make us a very bad investment," Logan replied. "But we're all incredibly grateful for everything you did."

"Oh, I didn't do it for your gratitude," Valerie told her son. "I did it because you all needed a home and someone to care for you."

"You're too modest, as always, Mom." Dario shuffled his feet. Valerie always did see the best in them all, no matter their faults and they all had faults. No one, not even Ivan, would argue about that.

"Okay, Logan, we have some trash from your cabin and some laundry that needs washing. We've put everything away, although we can't guarantee it's in the right place." Dario held up the sheets he'd fashioned into bags.

"Thanks." Logan came around the reception desk and held out his hand. "I'll deal with this. Jeremy, can I leave you in charge here for a couple of minutes?"

"Sure," Jeremy answered nervously.

"Jeremy?" Helena stepped closer to the desk. "You were on the mountain with my sister yesterday? You protected Milo."

"I did." Jeremy tensed as he glanced at Dario, who stared at the warlock, a warning carved into his features.

Relax, his horse told him. Not every man we meet is a threat to our mate.

"Thank you." Helena's sincerity brought a smile to Jeremy's face.

"It was nothing. And technically, Penny saved me from

Sophie, too. I suppose I was returning the favor." His cheeks flushed pink.

"Still, it was brave to hang around, knowing what you were up against." Helena nodded at Jeremy. "So, thank you."

"You're welcome." Jeremy's smile broadened.

"Okay, I should go find Penny and Milo." She spun around to face Dario. "I'll see you later, if not tomorrow."

"I'll organize everything," Dario told his mate.

"Thank you." She reached out, her fingers curling around his lower arm as she leaned forward and kissed his lips. "I've had a wonderful time."

She looked up at him from under her lashes before she turned and walked away, taking his heart with him.

"You're a lucky man," Jeremy told him as he tapped the computer keyboard.

"I know," Dario replied.

9

HELENA

"How did your day go?" Penny asked Helena as she stripped off her outdoor clothes and hung them up.

"Good." Helena glanced around the hotel room. "This is cozy."

"While you were out, Logan and Rift set up a small bed for Milo, so you can sleep in his bed. The hotel is pretty full, or else they would have given you your own room." Penny ran her hand over the freshly made bed. "You didn't answer my question."

Penny sat down on the bed and Helena padded across the room to join her. "Ooh, comfy."

"Are you avoiding the question?" Penny asked in concern.

"No, I'm not avoiding it." She sighed. "It went well, I like Dario, I like him a lot. Maybe too much since we have only just met."

"Why is that a bad thing?" Penny asked.

"It just proves that..." She cupped her face in her hands. "I don't know..." She half-turned to face Penny. "Don't you ever feel as if your life isn't your own? That some other force decided who you were meant to be with?"

Penny chuckled. "You are asking me?"

"Yes, you must have felt the same way. Didn't you?"

"Not really. Remember I have got one failed marriage behind me. I like the idea of knowing that Logan is the man for me. I like that I'll never have to question if he's going to look at another woman or betray me." Her bottom lip trembled but then she blew out a breath. "Sorry, I'm a little emotional."

"Hey, is everything all right? Milo's all right?" Helena assumed her nephew was with one of Logan's brothers.

"Yes, more than all right." She drew in a shuddering breath. "That's the problem. It seems *too* right." Penny placed her hand over her heart. "Do you know what I mean? It's like I'm just waiting for the world to smack me down again."

"You don't have to worry. I think everything will work out just fine for you if you stay here in Wishing Moon Bay." Helena's jaw clenched and she fought back her own emotions which threatened to overwhelm her. Penny deserved happiness, after all she'd endured.

"You're right." Penny nodded. "Finding Logan wasn't just a chance meeting, we are meant to be together."

"And Milo adores him. It's good that the little man has other males around who will be wonderful role models for him. Unlike his father." Helena couldn't have wished for her sister and nephew to get a happier ending.

But was this their happy ending or merely a happy interlude? Penny was right, it did feel as if this was a brief pause, a glimpse at happiness before...

"Once we've dealt with your intruder, we can both come back here to live." Penny nudged Helena. "You will come and live here, won't you?"

"Helena, I have a life, a job, out in the real world. What

would I do here?" She shook her head. "You know that Dario hasn't worked for a while, he's been running around with horses in the wild." She held up her hand. "And while I am the last person who would ever dictate a person's life choices, that's not going to put a roof over our heads."

"Our heads. At least it sounds as if you are thinking of building a future with him."

"When we're together, yes. I can't think of anything else I'd rather do. But what future do we have together? Do you think he'd be happy living in my apartment when he's used to being wild and free?" Doubts darkened her horizon. Being with Dario was just a dream, the sooner she faced up to that, the better.

"He'd live wherever you wanted to live," Penny assured her. "He just wants to be with you."

"And I want him to be happy. I certainly don't want to be responsible for him being miserable. But he wants children, and I won't... I can't have a child unless I feel secure, financially as well as emotionally." She wiped her hand across her eyes.

"Helena, don't make swift judgments without thinking this through and talking it over with Dario. You don't know what his plans are. He might be able to get work in town. If you sublet your apartment, you might be able to afford a house here."

"I know what you're saying." Her mouth turned down at the corners. "I'm scared. Aren't you scared?"

"Scared of what?" Penny asked.

"Mom believed in magic, didn't she? We thought she was a little crazy. Kids at school used to tease me about her, tell me she was away with the fairies. And she was."

"What does that have to do with Dario and being scared?" Penny asked.

"I don't want that for my child. If I was blessed to have a child with Dario, I want them to have a normal life."

"I still don't understand. They would have a normal life here in Wishing Moon Bay. Not the same normal life as if you lived out of town, sure. But this place has so much to offer a child. So much to offer you. If you'll let it. I know how you felt about Mom. I know how betrayed you felt when she died."

"Betrayed." Helena sobbed. "I just missed her. But when I look back, I don't think she was ever really there. It was like she was half in our world and half in another world."

"Do you think she was something else?" Penny asked quietly.

"Something else?" Helena's forehead furrowed. "What do you mean? She can't be a shifter, she would have passed the gene onto us. She can't be a witch, or we would have inherited her power. Wouldn't we?"

"I don't know, there's so much we don't know." Penny looked down at her hands then raised her head to lock eyes with her sister. "I still have the box of her things."

"Here?" Helena's eyes rested on Penny's luggage which was piled neatly under the window.

"Yes." Penny nodded. "I wondered if there might be some clue that we missed. Well, not *missed*, but now we know more about...all of this."

"I think we should take a look." Helena got up from the bed and wiped the tears from her cheeks.

"It's in here." Penny went to her belongings and grabbed a large suitcase. She paused before she unzipped it and flipped open the lid.

"It's a good thing you kept the box with her stuff in it, I would have thrown it out by now," Helena said bitterly.

"No, you wouldn't." Penny slipped her arm around her sister's shoulders. "I know you try to convince yourself and others that you didn't have time for her strange ways, but you loved her. You would have kept her things."

"Don't be too sure."

"You are still wearing her favorite earrings." Penny arched an eyebrow at her sister as Helena put her hands to her ears and covered her lobes.

"I like them. They're pretty."

"Of course that's the only reason you have worn them every day since she died." Penny stared down at her sister. "There's nothing wrong with that. There's nothing wrong with wanting to remember her every time you look in the mirror."

"I was so cruel to her. Some of the things I said when I was a teenager. I didn't make life easy for either of us. I just wanted to be normal. To fit in."

"She hurt you. I know she did. Mom should have been the person you could depend on most in this world and she let you down, she let us both down when we were young. But I truly believe she did her best." Penny inhaled, her breath shuddering through her chest. "Now that it's just me and Milo, I think I can understand her better. She had two daughters to raise. She had to provide for us. There was no child support check each month. No backup. We had no other relatives. She was alone."

"I tried to trace our family tree once. You know, on one of those ancestry sites." Helena sat down on the bed. "There's nothing. It's as if Mom just appeared. She didn't have parents, she didn't have a family. There was no birth certificate in her belongings. I searched and searched after she passed."

"You never told me." Penny sat down with the box of their mom's belongings on her lap.

"I didn't think it was worth troubling you over. There could be so many reasons that she didn't keep any record of her past. Our father might have been abusive. She might have been on the run. She might not have wanted to leave behind any clue in case we tried to find him."

"I never thought about it like that." Penny placed her hands on top of the box. "But you might be right. If Milo's father had been abusive, I would do whatever I could to protect him."

"So maybe this is all coincidence." Helena held her hands up. "Barry might simply be a jerk. Mom might have decided to believe in magic and talismans because they made her feel better."

"And the monster in the closet might have been our father." Penny leaned her head on Helena's shoulder. "Maybe we should leave the lid on this box. Maybe we shouldn't pursue any of it. If Mom wanted the past sealed from us, then we should respect her wishes."

"Could you live not knowing?" Helena asked.

"We've lived this long without questioning any of it. Why not just carry on?" Penny had a point. A really good point but not one Helena could embrace.

"I need to know. More now than ever. It's like you coming to Wishing Moon Bay has pulled the stopper out of a bottle and the genie is on the loose. Dario thinks everything that's happened is connected and I'm beginning to agree with him." She reached over and opened the flap of the box. "Why not let me take a look? You can keep out of it, stay here with Milo, and let me deal with the fallout of what I might find."

"You really think I'm going to let you do this alone?" Penny asked as she flipped the flap of the box open.

"Yes." Helena looked her sister right in the eye.

"What do you mean?" Penny's expression darkened.

"Whatever we do or don't find in the box won't change the fact that I want you to stay here in Wishing Moon Bay with Logan and his brothers while Dario and I go track down Barry, or at least figure out what he wanted."

"You want me to stay here while you put yourself in danger?" Penny shook her head, her expression firm. "No way."

"Yes, way." Helena covered Penny's hand with her own. "Dario will go with me and he'll keep me safe, you know he will."

"Just like Logan would keep me safe if we came with you." Penny's jaw tightened.

"And what about Milo? He only has one decent caring parent. If anything did happen to you, he'd have to go and live with his father. Is it really worth the risk?" Helena's tone pierced her sister's resolve. "You are safe here and you are happy. I can't remember the last time I saw Milo so carefree, he's not worried about your future, he doesn't even miss his father." She held up her hand. "And I am not saying that is a good thing, I'm just stating it as fact. Logan is a better man than Kelvin could ever be, we both know that."

"I hate it when you make so much sense," Penny grumbled.

"I know. And I know how much you want to get to the bottom of this. And I promise I will do whatever it takes to find out what, if anything, is going on. But it'll be easier if I'm not constantly worried that something might happen to you."

"Damn it, Helena. You certainly know how to make people do exactly what you want." Penny's words stung.

Despite Helena taking her sister's words to heart, she smiled and closed her hand over Penny's, pulling the flap of the box open. "This is important to me. You and Milo are important to me. You know that you two are the only people in the world that I love."

"I don't think that's true anymore," Penny reminded her.

"You have Dario, he is your mate, and you'll love him. You might not realize it yet, but you will."

"Just like you love Logan." Helena sighed as they opened the box and stared into the familiar contents. They had been through this box of sentimental items many times over the first few years after their mom's death. Even though it had been a long time since Helena had looked inside, she didn't expect anything to jump out at her as a clue for what Barry might have wanted.

The more she thought about it, the more she wasn't sure that the whole thing with Barry might have been a coincidence and that Dario was wrong. Everything wasn't connected. Life was made up of isolated fragments that were a jumbled-up mess.

The horse shifter wanted to see order in events because it would tie everything up with a neat bow. But life didn't work that way.

"Does anything look out of place to you?" Penny asked as she took the objects out of the box and set them down on the bed.

"No, they all look the same as before. Mom's ivy brooch, her silver comb, and hairbrush." Helena stroked the soft bristles. "Do you remember when we used to sit at the mirror and Mom used to brush our hair, over and over again? It used to put me to sleep."

"Me, too." Penny ran her palm over the soft bristles. "I miss her. I miss the smell of her and the sound of her voice."

"Me, too." Helena slid her arm around Penny's shoulders. "She did her best for us, didn't she?"

"She did. No matter what she felt, no matter how painful her past might have been, I do believe she did her best." Penny placed the hairbrush down on the bed and picked out a silver frame containing a photograph of the three of them.

"We were happy. Most of the time we were happy, weren't we?"

"We were," Helena agreed. "It's strange, looking through these things, it makes me feel closer to her, it makes me forget the bad times and focus on the good."

Penny leaned into her sister as she held the frame in both hands. "That's why I kept them. So we could feel closer to Mom and remember the good times. There's no point dwelling on the bad. My failed marriage has taught me that."

"I love you, Penny, I probably don't say it enough, but I love you and that crazy, funny son of yours."

"I love you, too, Helena." Penny placed the photo down on the bed and turned to hug Helena, the rest of the contents forgotten as they took a moment to celebrate their sisterly love.

10

DARIO

"Here he is." Ivan waved his spatula in the air as Dario entered the kitchen.

"How are you, Ivan?"

"Since this morning?" Rift asked as he gathered up a couple of plates of food and headed for the restaurant.

"You have Rift working here now?" Dario asked.

"He's covering for Penny, who is covering for Melanie. I think we'll be looking for a new server if you're looking for a job." Logan looked hot and bothered as he headed back into the kitchen.

"I don't exactly see myself waiting tables for the rest of my life. Not now that I have responsibilities." His expression clouded and he went to the open kitchen door and stared out at the stars.

"Responsibilities, that sounds ominous," Ivan exchanged a glance with Logan.

"What?" Dario swung around to face them. "If you have something to say, say it."

"You and Helena have just met, you need to give yourself

some time to get to know each other before you get into the heavy stuff," Ivan replied.

"The heavy stuff?" Dario ground out. "Like the fact that she might have a stalker?"

"Logan mentioned this Barry person. But don't jump to conclusions, don't go looking for trouble that isn't there."

"But what if there is trouble there?" Dario's troubled mind wouldn't let go of his fear for Helena. "Logan, back me up on this. Do you want to risk there being some unknown threat out there? Do you want us to bury our heads in the sand and just believe everything will work out?"

"I think you should take a breath and then we should go find Barry and have a calm, rational talk with him." Logan waited for Ivan to pour a sauce over chicken fillets.

"I am going to have a calm talk with him, but you are going to stay here with Penny and Milo. That's what Helena wants."

Logan's brows furrowed. "Penny asked me to go with her when you leave."

"It makes sense for you to stay here with Penny and Milo," Ivan agreed. "If this does end up being something, then we are here to protect you."

"I can protect Penny," Logan insisted.

"How do you know that?" Ivan asked. "Only last night we had to defend against a witch. There's no way you would have defeated her on your own." He tapped his temples. "Be smart."

"Thank you," Dario said.

"And you need to think smart, too. Don't go making up trouble where there is none to prove yourself to Helena." Ivan's eyes flashed as his temper rose.

"Why would I do that?" Dario asked churlishly.

"Because you have grown up in the shadow of five predators

and you always think you have something to prove." Ivan waved his spatula at Dario. "I stand by my first statement. Give yourself a chance to breathe and get accustomed to having a mate in your life. Let yourself adjust to that before you go running off to defend her honor, which might not need defending."

"What if by delaying leaving Wishing Moon Bay and finding this guy, it gives him a chance to act, a chance to hurt Helena?" Dario's gut instinct told him they needed to act fast or things might get out of control.

"I just don't want you or Helena to get hurt out there." Ivan glanced in the direction of the tunnel that led to the world outside of Wishing Moon Bay. Ivan had spent the least time in that world. He was a true creature of the supernatural, as a dragon, he could never blend in with a herd of horses or meander across remote mountain ranges as a white wolf or a bear.

He's afraid of the unknown and he is right to be, but we know that world, his horse reminded Dario.

"I appreciate your concern," Dario said gently. "But if I don't go with Helena then she'll go alone. I don't think I could talk her out of it."

Ivan sighed. "It was worth a try."

"And I appreciate you trying to help, I appreciate your wise words and you might be right." Dario went to his brother and hugged him.

"And I might be wrong," Ivan said quietly. "There is no right or wrong, only hindsight."

"You are the wisest man I know, Ivan." Dario ignored the small voice inside his head that told him his brother was rarely wrong. This was different, it concerned his mate and he had to follow his gut.

"And you are one of the luckiest. You have an incredible mate." Ivan let go of his brother. "Now, if you give me some space to work, I can get all the meals prepared for the last of the diners, and then we can go for a run."

"A run?" Rift came back into the kitchen with dirty dishes and began loading them into the dishwasher.

"I thought since we are all together for once that we could go for a run in the snow. Maybe along the beach." Ivan added a handful of onions to a pan, they crackled and sizzled in the hot oil and a delicious smell filled the kitchen.

"I like the sound of that." Logan picked up two plates and headed out of the kitchen. "I'll just tell Valerie we're going out. Jeremy is working the late evening shift since it's quiet then. I'm sure with Valerie keeping an eye on him, he'll do just fine."

"Who would have thought one of the most annoying guests we've ever had would wind up working here." Ivan chuckled.

"He's still on a trial," Logan rumbled. "But he really wants the job."

"A motivated employee. Just what you need." Ivan locked eyes with Rift who chuckled.

"What?" Logan asked as he paused before entering the restaurant.

"Well, Sophie was motivated, too. But for a whole different reason." Rift closed the dishwasher. "She wanted your body. Jeremy just wants a paycheck."

"We hope." Ivan turned away from Logan and focused on cooking his onions.

"Jeremy knows, in no uncertain terms, that if he screws up, if he is working here for any other reason than because he needs a job, I will personally chew his head off. And I do not mean verbally." With that, Logan left the kitchen.

"Okay, I am going to go get some fresh air," Dario said. "I'll meet you all out in front of the hotel when you've finished up here and we can go for a run."

"I'll give Aiden and Caleb a call. I think they're out somewhere already." Ivan added chicken to the pan.

"Okay, thanks. For everything. I appreciate your advice."

"Even if you don't take it." Ivan's jaw tightened but he didn't say anymore as Dario went outside.

The air was cool, the snow crisp beneath his feet as he strolled around the outer edges of the formal gardens behind the hotel. There was no one else outside, but he could sense the people in the hotel.

He could sense his mate. He stood in the deep shadows of a weeping willow tree and stared up at her window. She was inside the room with Penny and Milo. Was she happy? Were they talking about him?

His horse laughed. I'm sure they have a lot of catching up to do and we are only a small part of that. Penny is probably telling Helena about Logan and everything that's happened since they arrived.

Trouble sure has been seeking them out, Dario remarked. Is that a coincidence?

From what Logan said, at first Sophie was after him, not Penny. She wanted to put Rad the Bad's spirit inside of his body. Penny and Milo got caught in the crossfire. This has nothing to do with Helena's intruder.

Someone is coming. Dario lifted his chin and inhaled deeply. *Bears.*

Aiden and Caleb entered the garden and crossed the lawn in bear form before shifting into their human forms. They were broad-chested and tall, almost identical in every way. At least to those who didn't know them.

"There you are skulking in the shrubbery," Aiden said as the two brothers joined Dario under the willow tree.

"Can you sense her?" Caleb asked. "I mean, out of all the other people in the hotel, can you tell which one is Helena?"

"I can." He nodded. "It's like there's a connection between us, as if our souls are joined together."

"Congratulations, by the way," Aiden said. "We're hoping a little of your good fortune might brush off on us." His brother enveloped him in a bear hug.

"You and Logan." Caleb hugged Dario, too.

"I hope you both get lucky," Dario's sincerity brought tears to his eyes. "I wish we could all feel this happy."

"One day." Caleb stood back and followed Dario's stare. "You're going to track down the guy who broke into Helena's apartment."

"I am."

"Do you need backup? We know you've told Logan to stay here with Penny and Milo, but we're free to come with you," Aiden told him.

"Thanks. I appreciate the offer, and I'd appreciate you as backup. But I think we should go alone. We'll draw less attention that way."

"If you're sure." Aiden didn't sound sure.

"I am, but I'd appreciate it if you could be on standby. I know it's a four-hour drive..."

"But we have a dragon who could fly us there in an hour or less if it's dark," Caleb reminded him.

"No, I'd never ask Ivan to take that kind of risk," Dario said firmly.

"What kind of risk?" Ivan asked as he approached with Logan and Rift.

"The kind of risk that might expose you to the outside world," Dario replied.

"You know I'd risk everything for you and Helena," Ivan's gruff voice caught in his throat.

"I know." Dario inhaled deeply. "Enough of the future, let's celebrate the present and the six of us being together. It's been a long time."

"Too long." With that, Aiden and Caleb shifted into their bears and loped out of the garden. Logan and Rift followed while Dario lingered behind, waiting for Ivan to shift into his dragon.

Struck by the awesome sight, he stared as the dragon took off, his wingbeats thrumming the cold air as he rode up into the night sky and flew toward the beach.

Dario took one last look at the hotel where his mate sat oblivious to the shifters outside her window. Then the air popped and crackled as he shifted, and his horse trotted out of the garden and onto the street.

With a toss of his head, he ran after the others, the snow crunching beneath his hooves as he galloped down the street toward the beach. When he reached the beach, he leaped the wall and galloped across the sand, reveling in the freedom.

But ready to face a future with his mate. Wherever that might lead.

11

HELENA

"Happy birthday, Mommy!" Milo's excitement beamed across his face as he slid out of his bed, rummaged in a backpack, and then ran to his mom.

Penny sat up in bed and helped her son as he wriggled up next to her. "Can I have a birthday hug?"

"Yes." Milo threw his arms around her as Helena got out of bed and padded across the carpet to her purse. "I have a present for you, too."

"Just having you both here is enough for me." Penny's eyes glistened with tears as she held her son tightly.

"It's not exactly where I expected to celebrate your birthday. I'd planned to take you both out to dinner. Somewhere really fancy." Helena perched on the side of Penny's bed.

"Logan has arranged for us to eat in Valerie's apartment this afternoon. It's an odd time because Ivan's fitting it in between lunch and dinner." Penny accepted the card Milo handed to her and a small box wrapped up in pretty paper.

"Logan helped me wrap the box and Rift took me to choose a card yesterday." Milo shuffled as he watched his mom open the card. "Do you like it?"

"I love it." She held the card up so that Helena could see the picture of a beautifully decorated birthday cake sitting on a table, surrounded by ribbons and balloons and champagne glasses.

"Ivan is making you a cake." Milo moved his hands as he talked. "It's going to have icing and sugar flowers and candles."

"I'm very lucky." Penny hugged her son again.

"Open the box." Milo stared at the box as Penny carefully unwrapped it.

"I wonder what it is?" Penny kissed Milo's cheek.

"You know what it is," he told her. "It's all the things I collected on the beach when we went for a picnic. Don't you remember?"

"I remember, I was teasing." Penny set the unwrapped box on her lap and then carefully lifted the lid. "Wow, these are beautiful."

"This one is my favorite." Milo picked up a spiral shell that glittered in the light. "It's so sparkly."

"It is sparkly." Penny picked up a large conch. "You found this on the beach?"

"I did. Logan helped me." Milo sat back thoughtfully. "Logan helps me a lot."

"He does." Penny picked out a smooth, flat, gold-colored pebble. "Is this a wishing stone?"

"It is. I wanted you to have a birthday wish." Milo stared at it for a moment and then asked, "What are you going to wish for?"

"Oh, I think it might be for us all to be happy." Penny reached out for Helena's hand. "And safe."

"Is that two wishes?" Helena swallowed down her emotions.

"Mommy already has a wish stone so she could make two wishes," Milo informed his aunt. "And I have one, too." He got off the bed and went to his backpack. "Here. Logan said we have to throw them in the ocean on a full moon and make a wish and it'll come true."

"Although, wishes can sometimes take a while to come true," Penny added a voice of reason.

"I know." Milo came back with a small flat stone of a similar shape to the one in the box. "We should go to the beach and find a wish stone for Aunt Helena."

"When I get back, we'll do that." Helena didn't meet Penny's eyes as Milo placed his stone in her hand. She turned it over and over, the small smooth stone was warm as she held it. "These look too good to throw in the ocean."

"But that's how you make a wish," Milo told her firmly. "And there are plenty of them on the beach."

"I can't wait to make a wish." Helena handed the stone back to Milo.

"You can keep it." He closed her fingers around the stone. "Logan will help me find another one next time we go to the beach."

"Are you sure?" The stone felt warm in her palm.

"Yes." He nodded firmly.

"Thanks, Milo." She kissed her nephew on the cheek. "What's your wish going to be?"

"I shouldn't really say in case it doesn't come true," Milo said seriously.

"Then why not keep it to yourself," Penny advised. "Because I want all of our wishes to come true."

Milo nodded and took the stone back to his backpack. "What present did you get for Mommy?" he asked Helena.

"My gift to you isn't as exciting or as valuable as a wish." Helena handed Penny an envelope. "And I got this for you before I knew about Wishing Moon Bay and Logan."

"What is it?" Penny's brows furrowed together as she slid

her finger under the envelope and pulled out a card. "Oh, that's too much."

"I know you don't have much in the way of money so I thought this would ease things for you a little bit." She handed a large rectangular box to Penny. "And these are for you to enjoy now."

"Helena, the check is too much." Penny grabbed hold of her sister and hugged her. "It's much too much."

"I have some money saved away. And I wanted to do something special for you and I figured this was it. You could have put it down as a deposit for a place of your own. Or bought some furniture, since you left everything behind. Or you could use it to start your own business."

"My own business?" Penny asked. "I wouldn't know where to begin."

"Then maybe we should get our heads together and figure something out. If I move to Wishing Moon Bay, I am going to need a job. Since that mate of mine has spent the last couple of years running around in the wild." She pressed her lips together, she'd said too much.

"Dario will find a job. If there is one thing I have learned about shifters, it's their need to provide for their family," Penny assured her.

"That's the thing, we aren't a family. Not like you and Logan and Milo." Helena stroked Milo's head. "You'll make a beautiful family."

"And so will you and Dario. You're not too old to have children. Or to even adopt a child."

"We'll see."

"Helena, if that's your dream, and I always thought it was, then you should go after it with the same drive and determination you went after your career." Penny clasped Helena's hand tightly. "Don't ever give up on your dreams."

Helena wiped a tear from her cheek. "Look at me, I'm crying on your birthday."

"I love you." Penny pulled her sister close. "And thank you. The check is more than I could ever have expected but don't you need it now? What about you and Dario setting up a business or something?"

"No, it's yours. It was a decision I made before I arrived in town and it's one I plan on sticking to. So put it in your bank account until you know what you want to do with it." She wiped her cheeks and chuckled. "They do have banks here, don't they?"

"I have no idea," Penny admitted. "Milo and I only explored a very small part of town before we were kidnapped by Sophie. Maybe when you get back, we can go explore together." She chewed the inside of her cheek. "I'd like to know if there's any part of town that you recognize."

"When I drove through town yesterday to get here and then when we went into the mountains, there was nothing familiar at all," Helena told Penny.

Penny sighed and stared at the window. "Not even the library? I know I have seen it somewhere before."

"Maybe you saw it in a photo. It could have been one of your friends. We know there are shifters and all other kinds of magic users outside of Wishing Moon Bay. What if one of our friends had been here?"

"That would explain it," Penny agreed but didn't sound too convinced.

"We'll get to the bottom of it," Helena assured Penny. "But first we need to get dressed and go down to breakfast."

"We usually have breakfast in our room." Milo was sorting through the box of shells he'd given to Penny.

"Ah, but today is special and Logan and his family want to do something special. They're all waiting for you downstairs." Helena glanced at her phone. "At least they will be in ten minutes."

"Ten minutes." Penny dragged her fingers through her hair. "It's going to take more than ten minutes to tame my hair and put on some makeup."

"You know Logan doesn't care what you look like. You could go downstairs like that, and he'll think you are adorable. As for the rest of his family, they are so happy he's got a mate they don't care either." Helena laughed as she got up off the bed. "I guess the same goes for me, too. Why don't we go down like this and test that theory?"

"It's a good thing I know you well enough to realize you are joking," Penny told her sister.

"I am. But, since it's your birthday, why don't you go jump in the shower and I'll help Milo get dressed," Helena suggested.

"I can get myself dressed," Milo said firmly.

"No," Penny wagged her finger at her son. "Let Helena help you. I remember what happened when your dad let you pick what to wear. You picked out a T-shirt when the temperature was hardly above freezing."

Milo shuddered. "At least my clothes matched, I had flip-flops on my feet, too." He sat down on the bed and held up his feet, wiggling his toes.

"I think we can figure out something between us." Helena shooed her sister into the bathroom. "Go on, make yourself beautiful while we muddle through out here."

"If you are picking my outfit, does that mean I get to pick yours?" Milo asked hopefully.

"No, it doesn't." She chuckled. "I do love you, Milo."

"I love you, too, Aunt Helena."

A little over ten minutes later, they were leaving the hotel room and heading downstairs. Penny was dressed in smart black slacks and a thick gray-blue fleece jacket, with her newly washed and hastily dried hair framing her face.

Helena had opted for jeans and a green woolen cardigan that covered her thighs. As for Milo, he wore a dinosaur sweater and jeans, plus a big smile as Logan met them at the bottom of the stairs. The wolf shifter looked a little nervous, but his eyes filled with love and admiration as he saw Penny.

"Happy birthday." Logan rushed forward and wrapped his arms around his mate. The warmth of his expression and the way he held his mate dispelled any fears Helena might have that these two people were not meant to be together. Their love was real, it was as if she could reach out and touch it.

"We are eating breakfast in Valerie's apartment. Ivan won't be joining us, but everyone else is there." He let her go, albeit reluctantly.

"Morning, Logan." Milo ran up to the shifter and wrapped his arms around Logan's knees.

"Morning, young man." Logan leaned down and picked the boy up. "Have you grown overnight?"

"No," Milo laughed as he slipped his arms around Logan's neck.

"Are you sure? You feel heavier, and you look taller." Logan looked up at Milo, whose eyes were level with the top of the shifter's head.

"That's because you are carrying me," Milo laughed and reached up into the air. "I'm nearly tall enough to reach the ceiling."

"Then you'll need to duck as we go through the door." Logan swooped Milo down so that his shoulder skimmed the floor.

"Whoa, do that again."

"It looks as if you have two kids," Helena teased as she reached for Penny's hand. "That must be the best birthday present ever. To see Milo and Logan together."

"Don't," Penny warned as she dabbed her eyes. "I'll ruin my makeup." She sniffed and composed herself. "I can't believe how lucky I am after the way Milo's dad treated us."

"You deserve happiness." Helena squeezed her hand. "And cake, lots of cake."

"Are we having cake for breakfast?" Milo asked over Logan's shoulder.

"Not for breakfast," Penny answered.

"Pity." Helena laughed, feeling light and happy. If the specter of Barry didn't hang over them then she would be happy to never leave Wishing Moon Bay.

The thought struck her in the solar plexus, and she took a deep breath. Did this mean she was ready to settle down here with Dario? Yes, she was. As they entered Valerie's apartment and the sense of love and affection washed over her, she felt at home. As if she belonged, something she had never experienced before. Living with her mom had always felt like living on the edge.

The edge of what, she had no idea. But it was as if they were teetering on the edge of oblivion, one wrong step and they would fall into a deep dark pit.

Her mom's depression. That was the deep dark pit that had threatened them as they grew up. Their mom couldn't help it, Helena understood that now, as an adult. But as a child, she'd never been able to understand what her mom was going through.

"Happy birthday!" A chorus of voices welcomed Penny and Valerie hugged her like she was the daughter she'd always wanted.

"Thanks, Valerie." Penny kissed Valerie on the cheek. "It's kind of you to let us take over your apartment."

"Don't be silly, you are family." Valerie reached out for Helena's hand. "You both are. The daughters I never had."

Helena took Valerie's offered hand. Growing up, Valerie

was just the kind of mom she'd wished for. Kind and caring, she exuded warmth and confidence.

Guilt came swift and sharp as if she'd pierced her heart. Helena loved her mom. Really loved her, and deep down she knew her mom had done the best she could. However, that knowledge didn't make any of it easier.

"Happy birthday." Rift grabbed Penny's hand and pulled her into his arms. "I'm trying to make your mate jealous, I think it's working."

"He knows you are only trying to bait him." Penny hugged Rift.

"Here's your gift." Rift handed Penny a box, decorated with the same paper as Milo's gift.

"Thanks. And thanks for helping Milo with my birthday card." Penny held Rift's gift in her hands.

"Morning." Helena felt Dario's presence before he entered the room, but she dared not turn and look at him, her cheeks were flushed pink as heat crept across her skin.

"Morning." She stared at Penny, her eyes unseeing as every fiber of her being focused on the horse shifter.

"There you are, Dario. I thought you were going to miss breakfast," Valerie kissed her son on the cheek. "But since your mate is here, I should have known better."

"Mom." Dario rolled his eyes at his mom as Helena glanced up at him from under her lashes. Damn, he was so handsome, in a rugged mountain man way. He was as wild and free as his horse and her throat constricted as she swallowed down her desire.

Yesterday, when they were alone in the cabin, they'd been close, not just physically, but emotionally, as if they were on the same wavelength, but here surrounded by other people, it was as if that closeness had evaporated. There was a distance between them. One she wanted to close.

"I thought Dario had come for the food," Helena joked, and his mouth curled up at one corner in a half-smile.

"Ah, my mate knows me already." He winked at her and she smiled back at him. "Food used to be the most important thing to me until I met you, Helena. And old habits die hard."

"I'm not surprised food is so important to you when you have a brother who can cook like Ivan can. He has quite the reputation." Helena slipped her hand into Dario's, needing to feel the touch of his skin and the warmth of his flesh.

His eyes darkened as his fingers closed around hers. "One day soon I'll make you breakfast. I'm not as good as Ivan, but my eggs are good, and my oatmeal is legendary."

"Dario is right, his oatmeal is legendary," Valerie agreed as she took a step away from them. "I am going to give my gift to Penny and hug Milo. It's been too long since there's been a child in the hotel."

"I thought you had enough of children after raising the six of us," Dario said lightly.

"Never enough," Valerie answered. "Children can show you the world anew and I'm getting old. I'd like to get one last glimpse of the world as a child sees it."

"She's incredible," Helena whispered to Dario. "Just seeing you all here together, it's obvious she loved raising you and she's been so kind to me and Penny."

"Valerie is one of the kindest and most generous people I have ever met." Dario pulled Helena toward the long dining table filled with freshly baked pastries, eggs, bacon, toast, and fruit. Her stomach rumbled in appreciation as he handed her a plate.

"I hope I can live up to her standards." Helena swallowed down her nerves.

"What's wrong?" Dario's hand on the small of her back calmed her and she turned into him, pressing close.

"Nothing's wrong. It's just..." She looked around the room

at the happy faces of Dario's brothers. And Penny, who had slipped seamlessly into this family. "I've never been part of a family, not like this. It comes naturally to Penny, but me... Even when I was young and went to play at my friends' houses, I always felt like the odd one out. Like the girl at a dance who was always left on the sidelines."

Dario took hold of her hand and raised it to his lips. "You'll never be left on the sidelines again, Helena. As for my family, just be yourself, we all come from different backgrounds, we're all a little broken. But we're good at putting each other back together."

Helena nodded. Perhaps when she'd dealt with Barry and the possible threat he posed, she'd come back to Wishing Moon Bay and spend the rest of her life learning to be part of this loving family.

12

DARIO

After breakfast, he'd helped Helena clear the table while the others left the apartment. All except Valerie who looked tired after standing on her feet for too long.

"Sit down, Mom, and I'll make you some tea. You should rest before this afternoon." His lips were a thin line as he ordered his mom to sit in her recliner.

"I'll make the tea," Helena offered. "Why don't you spend some time with your mom, and I can go ask Ivan if he needs some help in the kitchen?"

"No, you two spend the day together," Valerie insisted. "As much as I would love to spend a couple of hours with you, Dario, I think I need a nap before this afternoon. I'll sit and watch my show, *Doctors of Haversham County* is on in ten minutes, and after that, I'll doze in my chair for an hour or two."

"Okay, do you want us to set out the table while you watch your show?" Dario asked. He didn't like seeing his mom tired, her expression pained.

"Rift is coming to help lay the table at two. Why don't you

come back then and help him? We're eating at three." She sat down heavily in her chair and pressed a button on the side. The footrest rose slowly while the back of the chair reclined until Valerie was almost horizontal. "That's better."

"You didn't need to go to so much trouble," Helena told Dario as they made tea for Valerie. "Penny would have been happy with you all wishing her a happy birthday."

"She might be, but my mom wouldn't. This is a big thing for her. She's waited so long for us to have mates." Dario cracked a grin. "When's your birthday? I'd better start making arrangements to do something special or my mom will have something to say about it."

"I don't think your mom ever gets cross with you. I bet you are a golden boy who never got into trouble."

"You're right. But not because I'm a golden boy." He turned on the faucet and half-filled the kettle before setting it on the stove to boil. "I was so grateful to Valerie for letting me come live here that I promised myself I would never cause her trouble."

"And did you stick to that promise?" Helena asked.

"I tried." He grinned. "But I have five brothers. Do you know how hard it is to keep out of trouble when you have five brothers?"

"I can imagine." She chuckled. "You have a good heart, Dario. I'm certain Valerie knows that. And whatever trouble you and your brothers got yourselves into, she knew it wasn't malicious."

"Never." His expression sobered and his eyes wandered toward the doorway and the sound of the TV beyond. "I just hate to see Valerie in pain. She looks so old. Maybe the six of us were too much for her."

"Your mom doesn't think so. She knows you would do anything for her, and she will always live on through you." Helena pushed herself away from the counter and went to him as the kettle hissed on the stove. "She loves you and she's incredibly proud of you all, I can see it whenever she looks at any of you."

"We owe it all to her." He slipped his arms around her waist and pulled her close. "I just hope that we have children one day soon and those children get a chance to meet their grandmother."

"I'd like that. I'd like that a lot." She leaned forward, her lips pursed as she pressed them against his.

Dario's arms tightened around his mate and he held her close as their kiss deepened. She nipped his bottom lip, his arousal kicking up a notch as her tongue soothed the bruised flesh. Damn, he wanted her. Why hadn't he claimed her yesterday in the cabin?

The shrill whistle of the kettle broke the spell cast over them and Helena pulled away from him. "Where are the cups?"

"The second cupboard on the right." He pointed to the cupboard where Valerie had always kept the coffee mugs. Nothing much had changed in the apartment since they had all lived here. Sure, the decor had been updated several times over the years, but the apartment still reminded him of his childhood, of sharing a room with his brother. Just like any other teenagers, they had argued over stupid things, only to make up the next day. No grudges held, after all, they were brothers. Not by blood, but they were brothers all the same.

We will always be brothers, bonded by more than blood. A shared understanding of being abandoned and finding love and security. The same love and security every child should have.

It was that security that would make them track down Barry even though it would be better for them to all stay in town and never leave. But there were so many places Dario wanted to show his mate, so many sights he wanted to share with her. He was not about to allow Barry to make them prisoners in town. Even a town he loved.

"I think you've stirred it enough." Helena put her hand over his and he looked down at the swirling liquid in the teacup. "What's wrong?"

"Nothing." He put the spoon in the sink and folded his arms across his body as he leaned back on the counter. "I'm just eager to get going, that's all. The sooner we leave, the sooner we can figure this all out."

"And the sooner we can put it all behind us." Helena cupped her face in her hands. "I'm hoping I simply picked up a normal, everyday stalker. That Barry let himself into my apartment to check out my underwear drawer or something else...normal."

"A man letting himself into a woman's apartment to look in her underwear drawer is normal?" Dario arched his eyebrow in question.

"More normal than a guy letting himself into my apartment to lie in wait for me or my sister. I certainly know which version of events I prefer." She gave a tight smile that didn't reach her eyes. But it did reach his heart. He would make this all go away.

"Maybe that's all it was." He let his arms drop to his sides and went to her. "If you hadn't come here and found out about shifters and magic, you would have let it go. I know I said there's no such thing as coincidence, but maybe we are reading too much into it and it was just a coincidence that Barry was in your apartment the day Penny was due to arrive."

"I thought you said you would never lie to me." Helena looked up at him through tear-filled eyes.

"I'm not lying." He rubbed her upper arm, his voice low and soothing as her brow furrowed. "We don't know. So maybe until we do know something, we need to believe it was just some mundane coincidence."

"I agree." She sniffed loudly and wiped her tears. "Only because I don't want Penny to worry. It's her birthday, I want her to enjoy it with you and your family."

"And you. You are part of our family now and we are all part of yours." He leaned forward and kissed her cheeks, tasting her salty tears. "You are not alone."

"I know that."

"Do you?" he murmured against her skin.

"You have told me we are mates enough times."

"It's not just me. My brothers and Valerie are part of your family, too. And we protect our own." His eyes darkened and his body tensed as an overwhelming desire to protect Helena from any hurt swept over him. But he knew that wasn't possible. There was no way to shield his mate from every bad thing that might come her way.

She needed to live and breathe, to experience the lows so her heart could soar on the highs.

"I want to protect you, too. This isn't a one-way deal. I might not be as strong as you and I might have no clue about this new world. But I'm smart, Dario, and sometimes it's what's in here," she tapped the side of her head, "that saves people."

"I have no doubt you are a brave warrior. Your heart is pure, and you have a strong will, but often when it comes down to fighting, particularly with shifters, it does come down to brute strength."

"Then we should always stick together. We are two halves of the whole, you have the strength and I have the brains." She covered her mouth and laughed. "I'm sorry, that sounds as if I'm implying you are stupid."

"I know what you're trying to say and on one thing we definitely agree. We need to stick together no matter what. We were brought together now for a reason. A reason we'll figure out together." He picked up the teacup. "Now, let's go and give this to Valerie. Then I'm going to go pack some clothes, you should do the same and spend some time with Penny and Milo. Tomorrow we leave and I can't promise when we'll be back."

"I'm going to do that right now." She kissed his cheek and hugged him before she headed for the door. "Tell Valerie I'll see her later."

Dario nodded and watched her leave before he took the cup of tea into Valerie who was watching her show on TV. "Here we go, Mom."

"Thanks, Dario." She held out her hand to him. "I've missed you."

"I've missed you, too." He kissed his mom on the cheek and held her close.

"Has Helena gone?"

"She's gone to spend some time with Penny and Milo before we leave tomorrow."

"Good." Valerie looked up at him, her eyes sharp. "You're a lucky man."

"I know that." He held her hand. "And I don't just mean because I met Helena. I was lucky that you took me in and raised me. I've been blessed to travel the world and see things from a different perspective thanks to my other side. I just hope my luck holds."

"I believe we can create our own luck. You've always strived to be good, to be the best you can be."

"I never wanted to cause you any trouble." He gave her a sheepish look. "I've had a blessed life since the day I walked through that hotel door. It's only now that I have a mate that I'm beginning to see I should have worked harder and gotten some cash behind me. I feel like a failure with nothing to offer Helena."

"You have your heart, Dario." Valerie placed her hand over his heart. "If a man had ever offered me such a good heart, I wouldn't have cared about his bank account balance. And neither does Helena."

"I'm not so sure. She has worked hard all her life and built a career. Would she give all of that up for a man like me?"

"In a heartbeat." Valerie patted his chest. "She might not see it right away. We hold onto our beliefs and don't ever want to let them go. And I suspect part of Helena's belief system, part of why she's worked hard to build a life for herself, was to try to please her mom."

"Her mom has been gone a long time," Dario reminded Valerie.

"I know. But being a child is a strange business. No matter if our parents are living or dead, we want them to look at us and be proud." She smiled sadly, her eyes fixed on his face, her TV show forgotten.

"Is that why you adopted us all?" Dario asked the question that had often popped into his head as he ran across vast plains with a herd of horses. Being in a herd and galloping free brought him to an almost meditative state where his mind would pose a question and his subconscious would try to figure out the answer,

One of his most frequent questions was why Valerie adopted six boys. Or more specifically, why did she adopt Dario? Out of all the children she could have adopted, why a small orphan horse shifter?

"I adopted the six of you because I know what it's like to be raised in the system, to believe that no one is there for you, that no one has your back." She smiled sadly. "Of course, I had planned on stopping at one child, but then the next came along and the next. I only stopped at six because I couldn't squeeze another bed into the apartment."

"You were in the system?" Dario asked. "It's funny, I've

never thought about it before, but that would explain why you never talk about your family, you have never once mentioned your mom and dad."

"It's not that I don't know who they are." She looked down at the teacup in her hands. "When I was eighteen, I began my search for them. Not because I wanted anything from them but because I needed to satisfy my curiosity."

"And what did you find?" Dario asked quietly.

"What I was searching for." She took a sip of her tea, her eyes straying to the TV screen, but Dario doubted the images on the screen were the same ones playing in her head.

"Were they bad people?" Dario asked gently, not wanting to push his mom where she didn't want to go.

"No, not really. My mom had been very young when she found out she was pregnant. I was an accident. My mom said she wasn't sure who my father was." She smiled sadly. "I'm grateful that my mom decided to ignore the child growing inside of her rather than tell anyone and seek an abortion. Instead, she didn't tell anyone until she went into labor."

"Wow." Dario's shock caused him to pull back and he sat down heavily on the carpet. "That must have been incredibly scary for her."

"Yes. Now, I can look back and feel sorry for the woman who gave birth to me. From what she told me, her parents insisted on her giving the child up for adoption. After all, there were plenty of couples who wanted a baby."

"But you weren't adopted?" Dario asked. "You said you grew up in the system."

"No, I was adopted. A lovely couple, they had been trying for a child for ten years with no luck. So they adopted me. I can only imagine my early years were happy, but I was too young to remember."

"What happened?" Dario reached for her hand and held it tight as Valerie's eyes filled with tears.

"I was four when my mom got pregnant. It's all they ever wanted, to have a child of their own."

"But they had a child, they had you." His hand tightened around hers and he wanted to take her pain and make it his own. The woman who had raised him deserved happiness.

"Their child was born with a heart defect. It meant several rounds of surgery. It drained them physically and emotionally until they didn't have the time or the energy for the little girl they had adopted. I was placed into foster care." Her voice trembled. "Can I blame them?" She shrugged. "I didn't remember them. If I do, those memories are wrapped up in a whole string of foster homes and failed adoptions. It was as if I was jinxed, as if there was something at work stopping me from being adopted again."

"Do you believe that?"

"I've taught you to make your own luck, Dario. And that lesson comes from the heart of a child who made her own luck. But that luck was bad. It was as if I messed up every chance of being happy and having a permanent family." She sighed. "I've had a lot of time to think it over. I believe I was too emotionally scarred by losing my family to ever let anyone else in."

"Then why decide to adopt us?"

"Because I realized that if I didn't take a chance on love then I would die lonely and bitter, and I didn't want that. I'd spent too long alone already. I'd been in relationships, of course I had. But the guys never stuck around or else I got bored of them. I certainly didn't love any of them."

"So you chose to adopt children."

"I decided to adopt a girl." She gave a short laugh. "I have no idea what went wrong there. I figured I'd be okay with a girl because, well, I was a girl and knew how to do girly things."

"Ah, girls would have been boring." Dario rolled his eyes.

"You might be right. And I wouldn't have raised the best chef in Wishing Moon Bay if I hadn't adopted Ivan." She laughed. "That said, I'm proud of you all. You're all special in your own unique way."

"Said like a loving mom." He kissed her cheek. "Did we get in the way of you finding love?"

"No!" She shook her head firmly. "There was never any way to get in. The right man never came along, and I think I'm too old for that to change and maybe I'm too old to even care."

"You're never too old for love, Mom." He hugged her, aware her old bones were no match for his muscled arms. "I just want you to be happy."

"I have been happy since I first set eyes on Logan. I knew then that adopting a child was the right decision for me. He fulfilled me in a way I can never explain. But that set me on the path I traveled."

"Just don't tell me I have to tell him we're grateful to him, please." Dario inched away from his mom and then stood up. "I have to pack and get ready for tomorrow."

"I didn't know if you've even unpacked, you travel very light for a man of your age."

"I live off the land, I work for what I need," he told her.

"And now it's time for you to set down roots." Valerie reluctantly let go of his hand. "Just make sure the two of you come back in one piece. And that means physically and mentally. You know what lurks in the darkness."

"I do."

"You know what lives in the closet." She fixed her eyes on his. "You need to teach Helena about the possible threats she may be exposed to."

"There are some things I'd rather she didn't know about."

"And what gives you the power to pick and choose?"

"You're right."

"I know that you want to protect her. But the best way to protect someone is to give them the power to defend themselves against whatever might come at them." Valerie's eyes flashed. "She's strong. But you can make her stronger." Her hand gripped his lower arm and her fingers dug into his flesh. "And together you are invincible."

Dario hugged his mom before he got up and left the apartment. He had a lot to think over before he and Helena left town.

Then he had decisions to make. Decisions that would affect his future with his mate.

13

HELENA

"It seems like you've only just gotten here and now you are leaving." Penny's eyes widened as if she'd had a eureka moment. "Oh, you *have* just gotten here."

"Don't tease, you know exactly why I'm leaving town so soon. Believe me, I would rather stay." Helen grabbed her sister and hugged her tightly.

"This is my way of covering my emotions," Penny admitted. "I don't want you to go. Not without me. Not if this my fault."

"How can it be your fault?" Helena asked sharply. "You haven't done anything." She brushed her hand through her hair. "Sorry, I didn't mean to be sharp. It's just that even if this about you, it's not your fault. You didn't tell creepy Barry to let himself into my apartment, did you?"

"No, I did not. That doesn't mean he wasn't there because of something I've done."

"Like what?" Helena's question was answered by a shrug from Penny. "Exactly. There's nothing you have done. And there's still a chance that Barry's story is true. He might have bumped into me by accident and then been overcome with the need to possess me that he made an error of judgment and broke into my apartment."

"That's true."

"Not that he won't get his head ripped off either way." She sighed. "I'm stupid really, I should have dealt with it before I came here. But it freaked me out a little. You hear all these things on the news about obsessive people and the crimes they perpetrate."

"There will be no perpetration from Barry once he knows you have Dario at your back."

"And that is my second fear," Helena admitted. "That Dario might do something that we'll all wind up regretting."

"Logan said he's not a violent man unless severely pressed. In which case I hope he does do something worth regretting. Barry needs to be stopped. Even if he broke into your apartment just for kicks, it's still very, very wrong."

"I suppose we'll see when we find him." Helena hugged Penny and carried her luggage to the door. "I have to go. Give the sleepy man a hug from me."

"I'm assuming you mean Milo and not Logan." Penny grinned.

"You can give them both a hug from me, I've told them both to keep a close watch on you. If Barry is up to no good, I want to make sure you're safe here." Helena opened the door and stepped out into the hallway. "I'll keep in touch. And you need to call me if anything happens here. Okay?"

"Okay." Penny leaned on the door and watched Helena as she carried her luggage along the corridor toward the stairs. "Take care of yourself, and Dario. Shifters have a strong need to protect their mate. I only hope Dario can rein in his anger if you are threatened."

"We'll be okay. Just enjoy being here and spending time with Logan and Milo. Before you know it, Milo will be starting school and you three won't have time to bond."

Helena shrugged. "That's my argument against you coming anyway. But I know you can see through it. I just need to know the two of you are safe."

"And I want you to be safe. Even if Barry is no more than a lecherous stalker, that still makes him dangerous. We've lived in the world outside of Wishing Moon Bay to know that you don't have to be supernatural to be dangerous." Penny ran along the corridor to Helena. "Come back soon."

"As soon as we can." She looked down at her hand holding the suitcase. "I was thinking of going into the office and quitting my job."

"You were? You didn't say." Penny stepped back, searching her sister's face for answers. "Is that what you want? I know I would love for you to move here and I'm sure Dario would be more than happy if you relocate here. But what about work? I know you've worked so hard to get to where you are. You've made sacrifices in your personal life for promotion at work."

"And for what? So I can go home each evening and sit on the couch alone?" She inhaled deeply, fear filling her chest as she took a deep breath. "I want to be happy. Seeing the family together yesterday, everyone around the dinner table, talking, laughing..."

"You want a slice of that, too. I know exactly how you feel. We grew up with just the three of us. You, me, and Mom. We had no one else, no aunts, no uncles, no cousins. Mom never had any close friends." Penny held both of Helena's hands but didn't meet her eyes as she added, "When you have dealt with the Barry situation, I want us to track down any information we can on Mom and where she came from. I want to find out about our father. There must be some clues somewhere. People don't just appear."

"Witness protection." Helena had been giving the whole thing a lot of thought ever since they went through their mom's things. "Isn't that the only explanation? Whether it was official or whether Mom was in hiding on her own, it just feels as if she purposely kept our family history from us."

"Witness protection? Really? Why?" Penny wasn't buying into the idea. "Was it even a thing when we were kids?"

"I just think she was on the run...from something." Helena gave a short laugh. "Now I'm hoping Barry is more than just a stalker so we can get all the information from him. It would be a whole lot easier than trawling through archives trying to figure out who we are."

"Maybe that's where we should start." Penny pointed her finger at Helena as she started to back away. "The best place to start is with the two things we know for sure. Where we were born."

"Neither of our birth certificates have our father's name on them. So, I don't know how that will help to find him."

"I know, but I could scour the newspapers for...anything. Those are the only two fixed points we have." Her shoulders sagged. "I know it's like a needle in a haystack, but it'll give me something to do while you're gone."

"Spend time with Milo and Logan. Leave the rest until we come back." Helena watched Penny go back into the hotel room. "At least leave it until you know what information we get from Barry."

"Okay," Penny answered but Helena didn't believe her.

"Focus," she told herself as she turned toward the stairs and headed down to the reception area where Dario was waiting.

"I thought you were never coming." He came to meet her at the bottom of the stairs and grabbed her luggage. "I'll carry that."

"I can manage," she told him firmly but resisted the urge to grab her suitcase back.

"I know. But Valerie raised us to be what most people

would call old-fashioned." He opened the door leading out into the parking lot and held it for her. "Courtesy costs nothing."

"You know, Valerie could simply have been training you to be a bellboy." Helena grinned as he followed her out of the hotel.

"My mom had ulterior motives. How to destroy a childhood."

"You know I'm joking. Valerie raised six good men. And I like a little old-fashioned courtesy, just don't expect me to have your shirts ironed and a hot meal on the table every night."

"And I thought you were my perfect mate." He waited by her car as she unlocked it and popped the trunk.

"Are you having second thoughts already?" Helena asked.

"Never." Dario lifted her suitcase and placed it in the trunk, then deposited his backpack next to it. "I'm used to traveling light."

"I suppose you are." She slammed the trunk shut and went around to the driver's side. "Have you ever learned to drive?"

"I have, I even owned a car once." He slid into the passenger seat.

"So you choose not to drive?" She started the engine.

"Is that a subtle way of asking me if I lost my license?"

"No, it's me being curious. We have a long journey ahead of us. I thought it might be a good opportunity to get to know each other." She drove away from the hotel and headed down the road that had brought her into Wishing Moon Bay only two nights ago.

"Ask me anything, I have nothing to hide."

"Everyone has something to hide, even if it's just their most embarrassing moment."

"Okay, you have me there."

"Now I'm intrigued as to what it is. If you don't tell me,

I'm sure I can get an embellished version from your brothers."

"Ah, there are some things we are sworn to secrecy."

"I expect if Penny asked Logan, he would tell her. Does a mate trump a brother?" She chuckled as he shook his head in defeat. "I told you I was clever."

"I'm beginning to realize I am doomed." She laughed and switched on the radio as he said, "Maybe we should talk about less personal things, like our favorite music or favorite color."

"Are you backing down?" she asked. "Avoiding the question?"

"Oh, don't think you're going to trick me into admitting my most embarrassing moment." He wagged his finger at her and chuckled.

"You will." She shuffled smugly in her seat.

"You sound confident, but there is no way I am going to tell you." He leaned back in his seat looking relaxed and incredibly handsome.

"I thought you'd do anything to make me happy." She pouted but couldn't keep a straight face when he rolled his eyes at her. "Oh, this is it, the tunnel."

"The tunnel. What's wrong with it?"

"There's nothing wrong with it, it's just... Once we go through the tunnel, we leave Wishing Moon Bay behind us. What if I can't find it again?" She breathed in through her nose and out through her mouth as she tried to control her panic. "What if Penny and Milo are lost to me forever?"

"Hey." He touched her hand and she jumped, her foot easing off the gas before they entered the long tunnel. "You belong here now. This is your town, I am your mate."

"You know Penny thought she'd been here before." She glanced at Dario.

"Yes."

"What if we came here before and for whatever reason the town closed itself off to us?" The question had been spinning around in her head along with a handful of others as she lay in bed trying to sleep last night.

"Even if that was true, the town revealed itself to you after you saw me. That's because you belong to me." He leaned across the car and wrapped his arm around her shoulders. "And anyway, I'm with you. There's no way the town will seal itself off from me."

"Are you sure?" She leaned on his shoulder while staring into the mouth of the long dark tunnel. "What if you leave with me and the town seals itself off from you?"

"There's only one way to find out." He kissed her cheek and then pulled away from her. "Put your foot on the gas pedal and drive. Once we're out of town, we can check if we can see the signs and the road. Okay?"

She blew the air out of her cheeks. "Okay."

She put her foot on the gas and the car slid forward, the darkness enveloping them. Switching on the lights, she kept her eyes fixed on a point in the distance. It was a pinprick of light that grew steadily bigger as she drove.

As the darkness surrounded them, her senses seemed to heighten. Her connection to Dario strengthened, she became more aware of him, of his presence, his scent, the warmth of his body. It was as if he were a beacon, keeping her from drifting off into the darkness.

Then the light at the end of the tunnel was bigger and her sense of him faded. Yes, he was still there, and she was very aware of him, but it wasn't the same.

They left the tunnel and Helena glanced in the rearview mirror, relieved that the tunnel hadn't disappeared. "It's still there."

"Of course it is." He smiled and warmth flooded her veins as if the sun had come out to chase the chill of winter away.

Helena drove to the junction and turned left, heading toward the large town where her apartment waited for her. As she accelerated, she glanced in the rearview mirror once more, relieved to see the signs leading to Wishing Moon Bay. It would still be there for her when she came back.

"At least if the town is hard to find, Penny and Milo will be safe there." Helena adjusted her position in the driver's seat, there was a long journey ahead of them so she might as well get comfortable.

"They are safe with Logan and my brothers." He glanced at Helena and she noted his concern.

"What's wrong?"

"I'm worried this has nothing to do with Penny and Milo and it's all about you."

"Okay."

"I need you to be aware of that. Don't take chances because you believe that Barry was only interested in Penny."

"I won't take chances," she assured him.

"Good. Because I need you. Penny and Milo need you." He gave her a half-smile. "Sorry, I had to say it."

"I understand." She ran her hand through her hair and rested her elbow on the door. "I'm scared that Barry has something to do with the monster in my closet." There, she'd finally admitted it. She'd never tell Penny. Her sister worried about her enough as it was, and the idea did seem kind of crazy.

"That had crossed my mind, too."

She gave a hollow laugh. "When I was a little girl, and I told my mom about the monster in my closet, I never understood why she never just told me it wasn't real like other moms would."

"She might have been trying to protect you. We just have to figure out what from." He took out his phone and tapped the screen. "Hypothetically, at least."

"If it's real, what is it?" She shook her head and groaned. She was even beginning to sound like her mom. "This is crazy talk."

"No, Helena. Crazy is pretending that the monster isn't real. Once you know they are then all you are doing is lying. Your mom didn't lie to you, she told you the truth and hung a talisman to keep it away." He put his phone back in his pocket. "Do you still put a talisman in your closet?"

"Oh, I should have known that question was coming."

"You do?"

"Yes."

"Then deep down, you always believed your mom when she told you the monster was real." His expression changed as he studied her.

"What are you thinking?"

"That if we really want the truth, it's time to take down the talisman and let the monster out."

"I had a feeling you were going to say that. And there I was thinking Barry was the worst of my problems."

"He still might be. There's only one way to find out."

"I'm glad you are by my side, Dario."

"Don't worry, I am never going to leave. Not ever."

14

DARIO

"This is where you live?" Dario stood next to Helena, facing a door that looked just like all the other doors in the apartment building.

"No, I brought you to someone else's apartment." She rolled her eyes. "Sorry, I'm on edge."

"You have every right to be." He looked over his shoulder, pushing his senses out as he checked for danger. "I can't sense anyone lurking in the corridors. Only the people in their apartments."

Helena sighed. "The problem is, I have no idea if Barry lives in this apartment building. I assumed we met by accident on the street and I'm certain I'd never seen him before that day, but for all I know, I might have passed him in the corridor or stood next to him in the elevator. It's easy to not see people. I mean see them for long enough to remember them."

"Let's get inside." He glanced around one last time while Helena unlocked her door and opened the door slowly.

He could sense the tension in her body, her fight-or-flight

mechanism had cut in and her nostrils flared a little as her breathing quickened and her heart rate increased.

I think she'd fight, his horse remarked.

So do I, Dario agreed. Even if the safest thing would be flight.

We would fight by her side, his horse added.

No, we would fight in front of her and shield her from whatever danger might be present. Dario's jaw tensed as Helena stepped inside her apartment.

"I can't smell him," she whispered.

Dario nodded, using his senses to check for danger both inside and outside of the apartment. He was certain the apartment was empty, otherwise, he would not have let his mate enter first. However, a swift-footed shifter could spring an ambush from behind, so until the apartment door was closed, and the lock was in place, he was taking no chances.

"Definitely no smell." She led him to the small kitchen area. "Can you smell anything?"

"I can smell coffee and bleach." He half-smiled. "I can smell you."

"I mean can you smell him?" She sucked in a deep breath. "It's a spicy scent. Leathery."

He shook his head. "I can't smell a male cologne and I can't smell the scent of a male who might use cologne to mask his true scent."

Her face paled. "Is that why you think he wears a strong cologne? To mask what he is?" Her eyes flickered toward the bedroom.

She's thinking of the closet and the monster inside, his horse told him.

That would be my guess. Dario stepped out of the kitchen and headed down the narrow hallway. "The bathroom and bedrooms are this way?" His eyes swept the living room as he opened the bathroom door first, it was empty, he knew it was empty, but he had to check anyway.

In a world filled with magic, it might be possible for someone to mask more than their scent.

"That's my bedroom." Helena was at his shoulder as she pointed to a closed door.

He reached out and turned the door handle, pushing the door open but not entering the room. He searched the bedroom with his senses, inhaling the scent of his mate as his eyes searched the room for anything out of place.

The head of Helena's bed was pushed against the wall on the right, the pretty cotton sheets, decorated with delicate pink flowers were smooth as if freshly made. The floor was clear, with no scattered clothes, no traces of dirt. The furniture, a dresser, and a matching free-standing closet were against the opposite wall to the bed.

"Does anything look...wrong?"

"No," she whispered.

He let out the breath he'd been holding and entered the room. "Everything looks exactly as you left it?"

"Exactly." She nodded.

Dario went to the window and looked out on the streets below. They were busy, rush-hour traffic filled the roads while people walked the streets to catch buses and trains to take them home.

He turned his back on the urban streets and went to the closet. "Can I open it?"

She swallowed hard. "Yes, of course."

He flicked the door open to reveal neatly arranged clothes. "No monsters in there."

"It's the wrong sort of closet," she answered as naturally as if she were talking about the rain.

"The wrong sort of closet?" His forehead creased.

"Yes." She gave a short laugh.

"What is the right sort of closet?" He had to ask.

"The one in the other bedroom." She left the room and

went along the hallway. "It's in there."

He opened the door and went inside. There was a double bed and a small single bed, both made. The double bed had similar pretty covers, while the smaller bed had a train bedspread. "This was where Penny and Milo were going to sleep?"

"Yes, it's the bigger of the two rooms. Most other occupants use it as their main bedroom." She held her hand out to indicate the built-in closet, but she didn't directly look at it. "I wouldn't be able to sleep."

"Okay." He strode toward the closet. "May I?"

She nodded, chewing her bottom lip and hugging herself as he reached for the small doorknob and turned it. The door creaked as it opened, revealing an empty space. "I never use it."

Dario stepped forward to inspect the closet. "It's empty, there's nothing in here."

"I know." She gave a low laugh. "Monsters only come out of closets when it's dark."

"Of course." He checked the closet once more. He was wrong, the closet wasn't empty. Hanging on the empty rail was a small talisman, a ward against monsters.

"My mom used to hang one up in the closets. I was sure she only did it to make me feel better. Of course, I know different now." She stepped closer but not too close. "When I moved here, I hung it there."

"Does it help?"

She shrugged. "I've never had the dream but that doesn't mean it helps. I might just have grown out of my dreams."

"But you've never taken it down." He closed the door and turned to face her.

"Why would I?" She took another step forward. "Whether it works or not, I have had no bad dreams with it hanging there. If it's a placebo, it works; if it's real, it works."

"Good answer." He grinned and slipped his arm around her shoulders. "I don't know about you, but I could really do with a cup of coffee and something to eat. Then we figure out what we're going to do."

"I suppose that's something we could have done on the drive here." She led him back to the kitchen area where he made coffee while she checked the scant contents of her fridge. "I have some pasta and tomatoes in the cupboard. I make a mean garlic and tomato sauce."

"That sounds good." His stomach rumbled in anticipation. "My stomach agrees."

"I'm afraid it won't be anywhere near as good as Ivan's food."

"I'm used to a simpler life and simpler food." He placed a cup of coffee down on the counter next to her food preparation area. "Is there anything else I can do to help?"

"No, thanks. The kitchen is small, and I'm used to working here on my own." She filled a pan with water.

"If Penny and Milo had come here, you'd have learned to cook and live together." He sat down and stretched his legs out in front of him. He hated sitting around so much, first the car and now the apartment.

"We both knew them moving here would have been temporary. Either they would have moved out on their own when Penny got a job, or we would have needed to find a bigger place together." She waved a spoon toward the bedrooms. "You saw their room, there's no way they could have shared a bedroom for long. It's not right."

"And children need outdoor space. Especially active kids like Milo."

She chuckled. "You are not wrong there. I think he'd have gone stir crazy living here. It all worked out for the best really, didn't it?"

"The best any of us could have hoped for," Dario agreed.

He sipped his coffee and watched his mate work. "What about you?"

"Me?" She glanced over her shoulder.

"Yes, what do you see yourself doing?"

"Translated to, am I expecting you to go stir crazy in this apartment?"

"We should discuss our future." He sat up straight. "But first let's concentrate on the present. There's no use complicating things any further. We need to find Barry and find out if he is a danger to you or Penny."

"I agree." She wiped her hands. "Why don't I text him and see if he'll reply?"

"Have you spoken to him since you thought he'd been in here?" Dario's shoulders tensed and he forced himself not to ball his hands into fists as he thought of Barry being in his mate's apartment.

"No. I didn't want to let him know I thought he'd been in the apartment. I certainly didn't want him to know I was leaving town for a few days to visit Penny. I was scared he might follow me." Her mouth tightened into a thin line. "Honestly, if I never saw or heard from him again, that would be fine with me. I have no idea what I saw in the guy." She brushed her hair back from her face.

"Understandable. Now you've found the real thing." He smiled and she picked up a dish towel and threw it at him. "I guess I deserved that."

"You did. Although, you are probably right. I was chasing a dream when I started dating Barry. He came along and made me feel better about myself. He was interested in me." Her fingers paused as they typed out a message.

"What's wrong?" Dario sprang out of his seat and went to her side, guiding her into a chair.

"He was *really* interested in me." She placed the phone down on the table and stared at the screen.

"Isn't that usual, when people start dating?" Dario had little experience of normal human dating but when he did go out with a woman, he was always interested in getting to know her. He liked making a connection with people.

"Not really. Most men I've dated tend to be more interested in talking about themselves, especially to begin with. It's like they are trying to impress you." She covered her mouth with her hand. "Barry asked about my family, about my childhood. Where we'd lived. He was interested in Penny, concerned when I told him she was at the end of a messy divorce. That's how come he knew she was coming to town."

"There's nothing wrong in being open about yourself," Dario assured her.

"I fell for him because I liked that he was attentive. When really he was just digging for information." She shook her head and clenched her hand around her phone.

"We still don't know that," he reminded her. "He sounds like any other obsessed stalker."

She tapped out her message and pressed send. "Whichever way I look at it, I'm a poor judge of character. The guy is a jerk."

"You're lucky you have a sure thing in your life now." He hunkered down beside her chair and wrapped his arms around her. "I'm the real deal, Helena."

"I know. In my heart, I know." She cupped his face in her hands and leaned forward, her lips an inch away from his. "And in answer to your earlier question. I'm happy to live wherever you are. Even if that's in a tent in the middle of a grassy plain."

He gave her a lopsided smile. "I love you."

Her eyes widened but he claimed her lips before she had a chance to answer.

15

HELENA

"Can you think of anywhere else he might be?" Dario's attempt to hide his frustration failed.

"No, we've been all across town looking for him. We checked out all the places we ever met and all the places he ever mentioned." Helena pressed the button for the elevator and stepped back. She'd gone over every conversation she'd had with Barry in minute detail several times since she suspected him of breaking into her apartment. "I'm absolutely certain."

"What about work?" Dario stared up at the numbers as they counted down.

"He told me he worked from home. He never mentioned who he worked for. I, stupidly, never asked." She shook her head and rubbed her forehead as the elevator doors pinged open. "I'm sorry. I should have questioned him more."

Dario slipped his arm around her shoulders as they stepped into the elevator. "It doesn't matter, he would only have told you what he wanted you to know."

"Right now it's looking as if he sure didn't want me to be

able to find him." She jabbed the button for the fifth floor and the doors closed.

"I suppose, if we can't find him and he doesn't answer your texts, we can assume he got what he wanted and now he'll leave you alone."

"Do you really believe that?" She hugged herself as the elevator climbed to her floor.

"Yes, I do. Maybe when he broke into your apartment, he got what he wanted or realized that he'd made a mistake. We might never know his motives. And that's okay. If he leaves you alone then we just move on." The doors opened and they stepped out into the hallway.

Dario paused, his eyes out of focus. Helena had learned through the afternoon searching for Barry that this meant Dario was pushing his senses outward. He could see more than any normal human, he could smell more and sense more. He truly was supernatural.

How could she ever have thought her mom crazy to believe in something so incredible? Helena had anchored herself in the mundane world when tiny miracles were happening all around her every day. While they had been out, Dario had sensed at least five other shifters in the area they covered.

Five. How many more were there out there?

"Is it safe?" She looked right and left, her eyes on her apartment door. Since the break-in each time she approached the door, her stomach tied in knots as her head filled with all kinds of crazy ideas of what might be behind the slab of wood.

Her nightmares were no longer contained to what might be in the closet.

"It's safe," he assured her, and she believed him. The more time she spent with Dario, the more she appreciated his hidden talents and the more she depended on him.

And the more she wished she had shifter powers, too.

Helena took out her key as they reached her apartment door and inserted it in the lock. She took a breath before turning it and pushing the door open. "In here?"

"There's no one in your apartment," he assured her as he followed her inside. "Do you want me to check each room?"

She shook her head. "Before I went to Wishing Moon Bay, I wasn't this jumpy. I figured if Barry was in here, I'd be able to deal with him. Now, well, I have no idea what exactly Barry might be."

"I can upgrade the security locks on your door," he offered.

"I already had the locks changed." She glanced at the closed front door. "I have no idea how he got hold of my keys and made a copy."

"You might have left your purse unattended while you went to the bathroom. If this guy is good, he could have gotten what he needed in less than a minute." Dario smiled sympathetically. "But that's not going to happen again."

"I guess I could get a second lock and keep the keys in separate compartments of my purse."

"Now you're thinking." He kissed her cheek and moved past her, heading toward the front door. "Why don't I go back out and grab some takeout?"

"I can order in?" she offered.

"No, I'll go out. It'll give me a chance to take a look around." He opened the door and let himself out. "Stay here, don't go out without telling me. Please."

"I won't, I promise." She closed the door behind him and checked that it was locked before she went to the kitchen and made a fresh pot of coffee, more to give herself something to do than because she needed caffeine. Her nerves were already on edge, which was ridiculous since she was safe here in her apartment with the door locked.

But what if Barry had gotten into the apartment some other way? What if he were a shifter and could turn into a mouse and squeeze through the air vents? Or he might be a snake that could slither through small gaps, maybe up through the drain in the shower.

Stop it, she told herself sharply. This was not helping. She'd spent her life fearing the monsters in the closet, she didn't need to see monsters everywhere, that was a one-way ticket to crazy town.

Taking out her phone, she occupied herself with texting Penny. Helena wanted to check in and make sure everything was okay with her sister. A couple of text exchanges set Helena's mind at rest. Penny had spent the afternoon with Valerie rummaging through the hotel attic for some toys and clothes for Milo.

Glad you've had fun, speak tomorrow xx

I hope you're enjoying some alone time with Dario. Goodnight xx

Helena wasn't about to tell Penny that she wasn't alone with Dario, just alone. *Goodnight xx*

He'll be back soon, she reminded herself, then shivered as the hairs on the back of her neck prickled against her sweater. She shivered and rubbed her neck. She was safe, Dario had checked the apartment, there was no one else here.

She tensed at the knock on the door.

Relax, it's only Dario.

Or was it? He must have been fast to leave the apartment, grab a takeout and get back here so soon.

But he was a shifter, shifters were fast.

He wouldn't risk showing off his enhanced abilities for just anyone to see.

The knock came again.

Helena tiptoed toward the door. If she called out to ask if

it was Dario, then whoever was out there would know she was in here.

She stopped five steps away from the door. Five steps away from opening it and meeting her fate.

Was that fate her mate, or Barry?

"Helena, if you're in there, please open the door." A softer knock accompanied Barry's voice.

She covered her mouth with her hand.

"You texted me. I thought we could go to dinner." Another knock. "Helena."

If she just let him walk away believing she wasn't home, then what? They'd spent all afternoon looking for him, this might be her one chance at finding out the truth from him.

"Barry, I thought you'd text me back, not show up on the doorstep." She winced as her voice wavered.

"I thought I'd surprise you."

You have. She glanced at her phone. "Give me a minute."

Barry is at the door. I'm going to let him in and then leave the door open. She sent the text message to Dario and then set her phone to mute.

"Are you okay?" Barry's voice held the right amount of concern. If he wasn't genuine, he was certainly a good actor.

"Yes, I just needed to switch something off in the kitchen," she lied smoothly. Could she match his deceit?

What if he was genuinely concerned for her? He might genuinely like her, and she'd gotten this all wrong. But the smell. He had been in her apartment, of that she had no doubt.

Don't let him in. Dario's reply came through as she reached for the lock. With no time to answer, she opened the door and shoved her phone in the back pocket of her jeans.

"Hey, Barry. What are you doing here?" Helena kept her voice level.

"I wanted to see you." He smiled warmly and took a step

forward, but she didn't move, blocking his entry. Dario would get back here super-fast, she was certain. All Helena had to do was stall Barry at the door.

"I mean how did you know I lived here?" She cocked her head to one side. "I don't recall telling you where I lived."

"Sure you did." He gave a low laugh. "You told me you lived in Tower Heights Apartments."

"I didn't. I certainly didn't ever tell you my apartment number." Her jaw tensed. This was a mistake, she should have let him walk away. Dario could have picked up his scent and tracked him down.

Unless he got in a cab. Then he'd be lost to them again. She'd done the right thing.

Her heart, hammering in her chest, told her otherwise.

"Okay." He held up his hands. "I admit it. I heard you tell the cab driver where you lived."

She pressed her lips together, her eyes narrowed as she shook her head. "Again, you would know my apartment building but not the number of my apartment. I don't tell that to any cab driver."

He sighed and reached out his hand, placing it on her upper arm. When they'd first met, his touch used to send tingles of excitement through her. Now he left her cold. "I found out the same way I found out your telephone number at work. I'm good at finding things."

"That's no explanation." She stepped back and his hand fell to his side. "Can you just be honest with me, Barry, please? What is going on here?"

"Can we talk inside?" He smiled his most disarming smile.

"I don't think that's a good idea, do you? At least not until you give me an explanation. Most men don't stalk women and that's what this is. Was you bumping into me really an accident?"

Her direct question made him jerk back, his mouth opening and closing. “Yes. Of course.”

“I don’t believe you.”

“Helena, where’s this coming from?” he asked in hushed tones.

She took a deep breath. “It comes from the fact that I know you have been in my apartment.”

He put his hand to his temple, his shoulders heaving as he looked down at the floor. “Damn.” He looked her directly in the eye, his stare as cold as his touch. “How did you know?”

“Your cologne.” She inched forward and inhaled. “Yep. Very distinctive.”

“Bravo!” He clapped lightly. “Okay, the game is up. I didn’t expect you to figure it out. Now that you have, we need to talk.” He went to walk into her apartment, but she shook her head.

“We can talk here.”

“You do not want to hear what I have to say standing on your doorstep,” Barry said firmly, his eyes darting up and down the corridor.

“Just tell me, Barry. If Barry is even your real name.”

“You really don’t trust me at all.” He turned his head as if looking at her from different angles. “Something has changed. What is it?” He spoke as if he were talking to himself, as if he were musing over an abstract problem.

“Me.” Dario appeared by Barry’s side, grabbed him by the collar, and shoved him into Helena’s apartment.

Helena dodged out of the way, her throat constricted in panic as she closed the door behind them, sealing them in the apartment with Barry. If the guy were something other than human, they could be in a whole heap of trouble.

“Helena? What’s going on?” Barry squawked as Dario let go of him. They were in the living room, surrounded by her furniture, surrounded by her life, that until she’d met Barry, was normal. Too normal. She'd wanted a change, to get out of a rut, but she wasn't sure she wanted this.

"Barry, you let yourself into my apartment. You admitted as much. I need to know why. What did you want? Were you looking for something?" Helena folded her arms across her body.

"I just wanted to..." He put on his puppy dog eyes and she sighed and shook her head.

"Don't play me, Barry. Not anymore. I fell for it before, but I know things now. And I think you do, too." She took a gamble, attempting to push Barry into admitting the truth.

Barry straightened his shoulders, his expression cool as he turned his attention to Dario. "You do know things, don't you?" He laughed and shook his head. "Well, look at that, after all these long, lonely years, you bagged yourself a shifter, Helena."

"You know what I am." Dario kept his eyes fixed on Barry as if he were a slippery eel who might attempt to slide out of there.

"I can smell you." Barry wrinkled his nose.

"What else do you know?" Helena asked.

"I know more than you." He twisted around, his cold eyes on her. "I know where you come from. I know you were born in Wishing Moon Bay. I know your father was murdered there."

Stunned, she froze, her eyes wide, her breath caught in her chest as the news she'd always dreaded hit her.

"How do you know all this?" Dario asked.

"Because the same person who killed Helena's father killed mine and I want to get back there so I can finally find some peace." Barry's expression softened. "You've been there, haven't you?"

Helena shook her head. "I don't believe you."

"Of course you don't. You've spent your whole life imagining that your daddy would just appear and make some sense of your world, of your mother and her delusions." Barry shook his head, his expression sympathetic. "I didn't want to be the one to break the news to you, Helena." He reached out to her, but Dario snarled, and Barry's hand snapped back.

"What is your game here?" Helena forced herself to ask. "Why are you toying with me?"

"That day I bumped into you outside of your office, that was a coincidence. Although I like to think of it as serendipity. When I looked up and saw those earrings." He touched his earlobes. "I knew you were connected to Wishing Moon Bay."

"My earrings?" She mimicked his action.

"They belonged to your mother. You told me that. But I already knew. I met your mom when I was young. I expect I met you back then..." His voice drifted off.

"So you bumped into me, saw my earrings, and then decided to stalk me?"

"No. You make it sound so sordid. When I saw your earrings, I admit that I asked you on a date because I wanted to know what you knew. But when I realized you had no idea about any of it, I just wanted to be with you." He glanced at Dario. "But it's too late for us now, I understand that."

"What happened to my father?"

"Helena, I'm sorry. All I know is that he was murdered by the same man who murdered my father." He pressed his lips together, the puppy dog eyes back in place. "The answers we both seek are in Wishing Moon Bay." He stepped forward but then froze as he caught a glimpse of Dario out of the corner of his eye. "Why don't we go there together and find the answers."

"Okay." She went to the kitchen and grabbed her purse. "Let's go."

"Really?" His eyes brightened.

"Yes, tell me where to drive and I'll drive us right now." She dangled the keys on her fingers.

Confusion crossed Barry's face. "I thought you knew. I thought that's where you met your shifter."

"No, we met in a bar across town. O'Malley's, you know the one." She sidled close to Dario. "We've had a wild couple of days."

"So you don't know where this Wishing Moon Bay is?" Dario asked.

"No."

"Does it even exist?" Dario asked incredulously.

"Yes, it exists." Barry leaned forward, his focus on Helena. "You really don't remember a thing?"

"No. If what you say is true, I have no memory of the town. I can't help you, Barry." Helena shook her head. "Are you sure about my dad?"

"Oh, yes. Very sure." His cool tone left Helena in no doubt that this part of his story was true.

"I'd like you to leave now." She went to the front door and yanked it open.

"Helena, please, I'm not the bad guy here." His eyes said otherwise, but Helena controlled her emotions and kept her thoughts firmly in her head. "I want us to find Wishing Moon Bay together. I want us to find answers together."

"You've just told me my dad is dead. I need time to process this. Don't you understand?" Her voice cracked and tears threatened but she swallowed them down. She wouldn't break until this horrible man was out of her apartment.

"Of course." A flicker of a smile crossed his mouth before he nodded and left.

Helena closed the door behind Barry and locked it. Her breath shuddered through her body as she inhaled deeply, unsure if her legs could support her. Then Dario was there, his strong arms wrapped around her, his warm body pressed against her, his words of comfort in her ears.

"I'm here, Helena. Let it out, let it all out." He lifted her and carried her to her bedroom, where he laid her down on the bed, then slid down by her side, holding her while she cried for the man she'd never known. Yet where she now believed this all began.

Her father.

16

DARIO

"Do you think he was telling the truth?" Helena's hoarse voice broke his heart.

"Not entirely." Dario's arms tightened around her as she sobbed.

"But you think my father is dead?" Her fingers dug into his lower arm as she fought for control of her breathing.

"Yes." He kissed the top of her head, wishing he could take her pain away. But the pain and loss of a parent was not something he could shoulder, even for his mate.

"And the rest of it? Do you think the same person killed his father?"

Dario hesitated. In the hour or more since Barry had left, he'd gone over and over the conversation. He'd explored every angle and come up with some disturbing scenarios. "Yes."

"But?" Helena turned to face him and propped herself up on one elbow.

"I don't know." He raked his hand through his hair, his eyes were gritty with unshed tears, tears for his mate.

We need to keep calm and keep control of our temper, his horse warned him.

I know, but right now I want to hunt Barry down and wring his neck until he tells us the truth.

You don't think he already has? His horse had come to the same disturbing conclusion.

"We should get back to Wishing Moon Bay." He sat up. "Do you think you can drive?"

"We're going to lead Barry back to town?" Helena shook her head. "We don't know what he truly wants. We don't know if he's a threat to Penny and Milo."

"Which is why we're going to drive in the opposite direction. We'll ditch your car and travel across country to Wishing Moon Bay."

"Okay. That's a good plan. A really good plan." She sat up and leaned back on the headboard. "Did you get any sense of what he might be?"

"No. He either knows how to hide himself really well, or else he is just a normal person. The one thing I'm sure about is that he isn't a shifter. I'd know."

"He knew you were a shifter." She leaned her head on his shoulder. "How did he know that?"

"He said he could smell me." Dario lifted his arm and sniffed it. "Maybe we do give off a scent."

She sniffed his neck and he shivered as her breath caressed his skin. "You smell just fine to me."

"Thanks." He lifted his arm and slid it around her shoulders.

"And thank you for being there for me and having my back. I don't know if I would've had the guts to lie to his face like that without you there to back me up." She placed her hand on his chest and his heart thumped so hard he was scared it might break through his ribcage.

"You would have done what you had to do. You're stronger than you think, believe me." He looked down at her red-rimmed eyes, noting the salty tracks down her cheeks. "But I'm here, whatever you need."

"I need you right here right now." She nestled closer to him. "Just being next to you makes it all seem a little less bleak."

"I'm here for you. Always." He kissed the top of her head and she tilted her chin back and stroked his cheek with her hand.

"What did I do to deserve you?" She inched closer and licked her lips as she kissed him.

Dario groaned, his arms tightened around her as their kiss deepened. "We deserve each other, remember?"

"I do." Her breath was warm across his skin as she smiled through her tears. "I want you, Dario. I want to be with you and forget all about the rest of it for a while."

"Are you sure? You're upset, I don't want you to do something you might regret."

"We're here for tonight, we're not going anywhere until the morning. I want to make the most of this night. You and me together. It's what I want and it's what I want for the right reasons." She slipped her hand under his sweater and caressed his stomach. His muscles clenched, he'd denied his mate yesterday at the cabin. He was not going to deny her again.

Helena knew her own mind, she'd proved that when she'd controlled her reaction to the news her dad was dead. Dario wasn't going to insult her by telling her he knew what was best for her.

He lifted the bedspread and they slid down into the warmth. "You have no idea how much I want you. How much I've wanted you since the moment I saw you in the car." He chuckled as he cupped her face in his hand and brushed his lips against hers. "It was just a flash of recognition, but I knew you were the one."

"I am the one." She tugged his sweater up over his head and he wriggled out of it, before casting it to the floor. "You have the physique of a man half your age."

"I work out a lot. Not in the gym, but outdoors. When I traveled, I didn't only spend time as a horse. I often sought work where I was needed. Building schools, helping the old and frail to stock up on wood for the winter."

"You're a good man, Dario." She sat up and tugged at the hem of her sweater.

"Here, let me help you with that." He swept it over her head in a flash, before he cupped her breast in his hand, his thumb brushing against her hardened nipple through the lace of her bra.

"Are you going to help me with this, too?" She reached for the clasp.

"If you insist." He swallowed hard as he pulled the clasp undone and the lacy undergarment fell forward, revealing her generous breasts. "You are beautiful."

"A little curved around the edges." Color tinged her cheeks as she snuggled back down under the bedspread.

"I like curves." He trailed his fingers across the swell of her breasts, and she gasped as he pinched her nipple between his thumb and fingers. "I like everything about you, Helena."

"You might want to get to know me before you make such a blanket statement."

"I don't need to know you more. I know you enough. Whatever flaws you have will be perfect." He smiled and lowered his head, capturing the taut bud in his mouth and rolling his tongue around and around.

"I think I died and went to heaven." She arched her back, offering herself to him.

"You are very much alive, I can feel your heart beating." He lifted his head and placed his hand over her heart. "A good strong heart."

Helena reached down between their bodies and tugged at his belt buckle. "Why don't we get naked?"

"I am not going to argue with you." He unbuttoned her jeans and pushed them down over her hips before she'd even unbuckled his belt.

"Expert hands." She wriggled out of her jeans and he hooked his fingers in the elastic of her panties and pulled them down over her thighs, too. Then he swiftly unbuttoned his jeans and dragged them off.

"Better?" He hooked his hand under her knee and drew it upwards.

"Much better." Helena curled her fingers around his hard length and stroked him up and down. He closed his eyes and fought for control. When he came, he wanted to be deep inside her, he wanted to fill her with his essence and spark life inside her.

He dipped his fingers inside her, stroking her inner walls as she teased him. Dario bit his bottom lip, fighting to hold on, but it was too much.

Using his weight, he pushed her onto her back and nestled between her thighs. Helena guided him inside her, her own need matching his. With a hard thrust forward, he entered her, stretching her as he moved in and out. Deeper and deeper he moved, until he was fully inside her, her warmth and heat surrounding him.

Dario lay still, reveling in the sensations coursing through his body. It was as if they were one, two creatures joined together. The bond between them was almost tangible, but just out of reach.

Helena nipped his neck, the sharp stab of pain as her teeth dug into his tender flesh sparking him to life. Dario slid his hand under the small of her back and held her in place while he pulled back out of her and then lunged forward, filling her in one hard stroke.

Helena wrapped her thighs around him urging him on. He was not about to disappoint his mate. In a steady rhythm that built slowly, he drove them to new heights.

When he roamed the grassy plains and wide-open spaces with a herd of horses, he experienced freedom, but as he came inside his mate, he experienced a new freedom. Profound freedom because she was there with him, calling out his name as she came around him.

"You're hungry." She lifted herself up on one elbow.

His stomach gave another deep rumble in reply. "I can run back out for food. Our order is still probably waiting for us."

"I don't know if I want you to leave me." She kissed his shoulder and then pulled away from him and swung her legs over the side of the bed. "But we need to eat, and I need to unpack and then repack if we're leaving tomorrow."

Dario slid out of bed and dressed, retrieving his clothes one item at a time. "Pack light but pack warm."

"How long will it take us to get to Wishing Moon Bay?" Helena pulled on a robe and grabbed the suitcase she'd taken on her first trip to Wishing Moon Bay.

"If we leave early tomorrow, we should be back in town the day after. We'll have to camp out for a night, but we can probably find a summer cabin that's been closed off for the winter and sleep there overnight. We'll need to make sure we take enough food and water. Which is why the rest of the luggage will need to be a bare minimum."

Helena paused in her packing, her shoulders hunched forward. "I'm sorry I got you into this, Dario. Whatever *this* is."

"Hey." He crossed the room, with one sock on and one sock off. "This is not on you in any way. This is on Barry." He pulled her into his arms and held her close. "Anyway, I would rather be here caught up in this mess with you than to have never met you. And I mean that. It's not just words."

"Thank you." She rested her head on his shoulder, her arms wrapped around his neck. "I never thought I'd ever be lucky enough to find a man like you. I was beginning to think I was never going to be lucky enough to find a man at all. That's what Barry fed on, I'm certain. I was a poor needy woman who wanted to be loved."

"There's nothing wrong with wanting love," Dario told her sharply. He loosened his grip on her and pushed her away. Looking down at her, he held her gaze. "Love is the most incredible thing. The love of a parent for a child, a man for a woman, and a woman for a man. Family, friends, we're all held together by love. It's one of the most important lessons Valerie ever taught us."

"I know. I feel the same about Penny and Milo. I love them so much, but I wanted more, I wanted the love that would bind me to a man forever, a man I could trust to have children with." She tilted her head to one side. "You're right, we should be thanking Barry for bringing us together because I know when I look into your eyes that I have found that love with you."

She leaned forward and brushed her lips against his. Dario tightened his arms around her, his eyes lingering on the unmade bed. Maybe there was enough time for them to make love once more before they left the apartment.

But Helena pulled away from him and went back to her packing. There would be time for lovemaking later when they were holed up in a cabin somewhere remote.

For now, they had to pack and leave town, making sure

Barry didn't follow them back to Wishing Moon Bay. Dario might not believe everything the man had said, but he did believe Barry desperately wanted to get to town. But why?

The answer to that question would unravel the whole mystery.

17

HELENA

They were packed and ready to go. As she locked the door behind her, she wondered if she would ever see her apartment again.

Of course she would. She'd have to come back here and collect the rest of her things, for she knew in her heart that she would never live here again. Her heart belonged to Dario and living in her apartment would kill him. Not that he wouldn't do it for her. But he would die a slow death being cramped up here with nowhere for his horse to run free. They could move to the suburbs and buy a house with a large backyard, but there was nowhere for him to run wild and free without attracting too much attention.

Deep down, Helena believed Wishing Moon Bay was the right place for her, too. A place to raise their children if they were blessed. Children who would one day shift just like their father and need the freedom to run wild and free while they explored their special gift.

"Second thoughts?" Dario placed his hand on her shoulder.

"No." She'd been staring at the door, but he'd pulled her

out of her reverie and now it was time to go, time to face whatever Barry might throw at them.

Or maybe they were making more out of this than it actually was. Maybe Barry had no intention of following them and they were about to trek across the country for two days for nothing.

But if her mom had taught her anything, it was caution. If you thought there was a monster in your closet, you put up a talisman to ward it off. You didn't just pretend they didn't exist.

A now familiar pang of guilt stabbed Helena in the chest. She'd been so hard on her mom, never understanding the truth of her mom's beliefs and knowledge. Why hadn't she told her daughters about this other world?

"Okay. I think you've checked the door is locked enough times." Dario's gentle voice roused her. She'd slipped back into a dreamlike state without even realizing it.

"Sorry, this has stirred up so many memories and emotions." She brushed a stray tear off her cheek and then turned to him. "Okay, let's go."

She shouldered her pack, even though Dario had insisted on carrying it, she'd told him she could manage. It wasn't heavy, she'd packed very light, just two changes of clothes and some food. Dario carried a second pack that held water and more food, plus a warm blanket. They would attach the straps together and place them over his shoulders like saddle bags once he'd shifted.

They took the elevator down to the ground floor. Nervous energy threaded through her veins as she kept a look out for Barry. Although Dario's senses would pick up on the man first.

"Is he out there?" she asked as they headed down the street to where she'd parked her car.

"Not that I can tell. But now that we're out in the open,

there are too many people for me to pinpoint him." He looked around as she unlocked the car door. "It'll be easier once we get out on the open road to see if there's a car following us. I looked at the map and have a few ideas of how we can flush him out."

"Have you done this before?" Helena slung her pack in the back seat and climbed in.

"Not in a car but my brothers and I used to play games like this out on the mountains when we were younger. It was a good way to learn to track." He slid into the passenger seat, looking too big for her small car.

"Then let's put this plan into action." She started the engine and checked the mirrors, before she put the car in drive and pulled out into the traffic. "I don't know if I'm going to feel a little disappointed if he doesn't follow us."

"I won't be disappointed, but we're going to follow the plan. I'm almost certain Barry isn't a shifter, but that doesn't mean he can't disguise himself as something else." Dario blew the air out of his cheeks. "Hell, he might even be something else."

"Like what?" Helena squawked.

"I don't know." He frowned and shook his head. "Sorry, I shouldn't have said anything. I don't want to frighten you."

"Hey, I can take it. You just caught me by surprise, that's all." She reached across the car and put her hand on his. "Promise me you won't ever keep things to yourself just because you think I might get scared or freak out. Not ever."

"I promise," he answered solemnly.

"Okay, we'll be out of the traffic soon and heading along the highway. Let's see if we can flush out our tail." She giggled. "That sounds so weird."

"You have no idea how much weirder life in Wishing Moon Bay can get," he warned.

"I am tempted to ask you to tell me, but I think I'd like to find out for myself. I like surprises and my life is going to be full of them from now on."

Dario was silent for a moment and then he took a deep breath and asked, "Does this mean you will live there with me?"

"Yes. If we can figure out a way to earn money. We can't live on love." She stared at the road ahead. This was it, she'd committed to living in a new town. There was no way she could change her mind now. Not when Dario was grinning from ear to ear.

"I'm sure we'll come up with a plan. There's plenty of opportunity in Wishing Moon Bay. And since both of us have seen so much of the world outside of town, we could introduce some of those ideas to the town." He relaxed back in his seat, his eyes a little unfocused as his mind worked.

If Helena did have any doubts about her mate, they were swept aside during the car journey. Dario was smart and committed. He proved that as he took her along winding roads, only for them to arrive back on the highway, all the time she drove, he kept a look out for Barry or anyone else who might be following them.

"Anything?" Helena asked.

"Not that I can see. He's either very good or never saw us leave town." Dario didn't look as happy with this news as she expected.

"What's wrong?"

"I thought we'd see him following us and shake him. Since that hasn't happened, I'm worried we just don't see him, or sense him. Or he has another plan."

"Another plan?" Helena hadn't considered this. "What kind of plan?"

"We're assuming that you are the only person he's found from Wishing Moon Bay. But if he's that committed to finding the town, he could be searching for any witch or shifter who knows the location. Most of the townsfolk would never share that information but there are plenty who would, for the right price or in the right situation."

"So we could be wasting our time trying to shake a tail who isn't there." She glanced in the rearview mirror. "And there I was thinking I was special, and that Barry and I shared a connection."

"You mean because he said the same person killed your father and his father?" Dario's gentle voice probed.

She nodded, not trusting herself to speak.

"Perhaps he was lying." Dario's tone told her he didn't really believe that. "He's a bad man. That's my sense of him anyway."

"And not just because he was hitting on your mate?" Helena wiped a tear from her cheek.

"I admit I was already biased. But the more I think about last night, the more I don't trust the guy." He glanced in the mirror and sat up straighter in his seat.

"What is it?" Helena flexed her fingers on the steering wheel and looked in the rearview mirror.

"There's a blue car. It's the Nissan, can you see it?"

She nodded. "It's following us?"

"I've seen it a couple of times. It didn't follow us when we turned off the highway, but it's back behind us now."

"Are you sure it didn't follow us?" Her heart rate increased, and the blood thundered in her ears.

"I've made a mental note of the registration." He pointed to a turnout up ahead. "We can take the next right and then double back on ourselves. Let's see if he follows."

She nodded, following Dario's directions along back roads that wound past small farms and country cottages. "Did he follow?"

Dario shook his head and let out a long breath. "False alarm."

"And there's no other way he can track us?"

"Not unless he's put a tracking device on the car or can track your phone."

"My phone?" Helena pulled off the road and parked in a gateway to a field full of cattle. "There's an app, Find My Phone, but surely he can't use it on my phone."

"We can't take the risk." He pressed his lips together, his eyes flashing with anger.

"Okay, I'll switch it off, but first I'm going to call Penny and tell her what's happening." Helena's hands shook as she took her phone out of her pocket and pressed dial.

"Tell Penny to call me on my cell phone if she needs you. Okay?" Dario's concern was evident as he waited for Penny to answer.

"Okay." Helena nodded, chewing on her nail as she stared into the field of ruddy brown cattle that moved slowly around their field without a care in the world. Helena envied them. "Hi, Penny."

"Helena. I was going to call you later today." Penny sounded anxious and Helena's cow envy grew.

"What's wrong?"

"When are you coming home?" Penny paused. "When are you coming back to Wishing Moon Bay?"

"We're on our way back now, but we're taking a long route, dumping the car and coming in on foot. At least Dario will shift, and I'll ride him." She closed her eyes, not wanting to worry her sister, but she had a right to know they might be in more danger than they ever imagined. "Barry wants to get to Wishing Moon Bay. That's been his plan all along. We aren't sure if he's following us and I'm going to need to turn off my phone."

"Your phone?"

"In case he can track it, we're not taking any chances."

"Is he dangerous?" Penny asked.

"I don't know. But we have to be cautious." Helena wasn't going to tell her sister what Barry had said about their father. Not over the phone.

"Okay. Be careful. Please."

"We will. Why were you going to call me?" Helena closed her eyes, sure she wasn't going to like what Penny said.

"We can talk when you get here. There's something I found..." Penny's voice wavered.

"Now I'm really worried."

"It's better you see what I've found rather than me trying to explain." Penny's voice cracked with emotion.

"Penny, tell me."

Her sister didn't answer for a moment or two. "We went into the attic yesterday. Valerie and I were going through the toys and clothes. Milo was with us, but he was more interested in the stuff in the attic belonging to Rad and the previous owners."

"What did he find?" She covered her face with her free hand, not daring to look at Dario.

"Photos."

"Photos of who?"

"Of Mom and Dad." She sobbed and then inhaled deeply. "We know who they are, Helena. We know that they lived here."

"Do you know any more?" Helena squeezed her eyes shut, willing herself not to break down and cry.

"No, we're going to the library today. We're going to search the news archives for anything we can find on them." Penny sniffed loudly. "I'm scared, Helena."

"Wait until tomorrow. Wait until I'm there with you."

"Why?" Penny whispered.

"I'm scared of what you might find." Helena chewed the inside of her cheek, her throat constricting as her emotions threatened to overwhelm her.

"I think Dad's dead, Helena." Penny sobbed, and Helena wanted to reach down the phone and hug her.

"I think you might be right. And I want us to be together when we find out what happened. Please. I know it's a big thing to ask, I know how much you want the truth because I want it, too."

"I'll wait. Just hurry."

"I will, Penny. I love you." Her voice finally broke.

"I love you, too, Helena. Take care and come home safely." Penny sobbed.

Dario reached for the phone and switched it off, before enveloping Helena in his arms and holding her until she could cry no more.

18

DARIO

Dario noted the blue Nissan once more as they left the highway and turned onto a road that threaded its way through a couple of villages. This was their last planned detour, their last chance to shake their tail.

At least we know he is following us and not using anyone else to get back to Wishing Moon Bay. If we lose him this time, we will have lost him for good. His horse couldn't wait to escape the confines of the car and run free.

It buys us time. But Barry will always be waiting for Helena to come home. We need a permanent solution.

How did the driver find us? his horse asked.

Barry, if it's Barry, must have guessed our route. Perhaps he'd hurried to follow us once Helena's phone was switched off, or maybe he has some other way of tracking us. A location spell? The thought didn't sit well with Dario.

When Barry dated Helena, he could easily have gathered a few hairs off her coat. Or maybe he'd taken them from her hairbrush when he broke into her apartment?

I'll call Logan and ask him to get one of the local witches to cast a temporary cloaking spell. Once we're back inside Wishing Moon Bay, Barry's location spell will be useless.

When the town was founded hundreds of years ago, the witches and warlocks had cast a spell covering the whole town. Those inside were protected from any spells cast in the outside world. Including location spells.

Good idea. Then we'll lose him when we travel across country, his horse said confidently.

We must, there is no way we want that loathsome man reaching Wishing Moon Bay before we have some clue as to what he wants. Dario's jaw tightened as he imagined what he'd like to do to the man who threatened his mate.

I know what I'd like to do to him just for upsetting Helena, his horse said savagely. *How could he just blurt out that her father is dead like that?*

Because he's the kind of man who likes to inflict pain and watch the suffering it causes. Dario had met plenty of people like Barry before. Often, they were people who bought a horse but forgot it was a creature, an animal with thoughts and feelings rather than a machine. There were cruel people in the world, some liked to use their hands as weapons, others used words.

But there are good people, too, his horse added. *We have seen both sides of humans.*

I get the feeling Barry only has a bad side. Dario shuddered. There was something about the guy that was off, way off. He didn't want a confrontation with the man out in the wilds. There was no telling what tricks the guy might have up his sleeve. When Dario finally confronted Barry, he preferred to have his brothers as backup. There were few threats in Wishing Moon Bay that they couldn't face down together.

"So how much farther?" Helena checked the rearview mirror.

"I'm going to call Logan and ask him to cast a cloaking spell. Just to be sure."

"And there's no way he'll be able to figure out where Wishing Moon Bay is even if he followed us this far?" Helena was jittery. Dario couldn't wait to ditch the car and get out into the fresh air where they could both relax a little.

"No way. We're going to leave tracks in the direction leading away from the town and then double back. There's a river that runs through the forest. We can follow it for a couple of miles so that he'll never pick up the track again. Not for a long time."

"It's a good thing there's no snow here or our tracks would be hard to cover."

He grinned. "The snow will reach here tomorrow. Which will hide our tracks even better. Of course, it's going to mean a temperature drop so we need to make sure we are back in town before then. I don't want you to freeze."

"I don't think that's possible if I snuggle up against you." She gave him a sidelong glance. "You are hot in more ways than one."

He chuckled, trying to relax. There was no sign of the blue car or any car for that matter. They'd lost him. "Okay, let's double back around here and onto the highway."

"I thought we were done with all that."

"No, we're going to drive back the way we came and enter the forest a little farther to the north. If Barry was using the signal from your phone, even though he's lost it, he'll know we turned off here. I suspect he's waiting farther up the highway for us to drive past, this way he's going to have a long wait."

"You're sly." She checked a grin. "I like it."

"I've run with enough herds to learn how to lose a predator. If a horse has to choose, he'll usually choose flight. But you can't run forever, so if you can't shake off the danger, you eventually have to fight."

"Like we're going to have to fight Barry at some point."

"Exactly. But we want it on our terms when we know as much information about him as possible. If Penny has discovered evidence of who your father is, we are one step closer to learning what happened and if Barry has anything to do with it." Dario hated the pain etched deep into his mate's features. Barry had already done enough damage.

"Maybe he just wants to use me to get back to town." Helena chewed her bottom lip. "Maybe my dad died in an accident and Barry is just twisting the information."

"Until we know all the facts, we treat him as the most dangerous man in the world. Okay? Don't let your guard down for a second when he's around." He made the call to Logan, who said he'd get right on it.

Helena kept driving. Only when Dario received a text from Logan telling him the cloaking spell was done did he guide her back toward the highway.

"I think we've lost him for good." He glanced in the rearview mirror as they rejoined the highway. "And, if I have my way, he won't be coming anywhere near you again."

"At least not until we know if he's dangerous." Helena gripped the steering wheel tightly and drove back along the highway, hopefully putting some distance between them and Barry.

"Not at all."

"If it turns out he's just some weaselly little guy, I am going to see him again so I can tear a strip off him. What he did, how he tried to use me... Then to tell me so coldly and callously that my father is dead..." The whites of her knuckles showed.

"Will you make me one promise?" Dario asked as they

neared the turnout that would finally take them off the highway and onto the next phase of their journey.

"That depends." She arched her eyebrow at him.

"I want you to promise me that no matter what, once this is over, and it will be over, that you let it go. Everything Barry has done to you, just let it go and don't let it taint our lives together."

She gave a hollow laugh. "You're asking me? A woman who has held a stupid grudge against her mom all her life. I should have let it go and forgiven my mom long ago. I should have healed our relationship while she was still alive."

"I'm sure your mom knew how much you loved her. From what you've said, it sounds as if she wasn't herself."

"I should have been forgiving and understanding."

"I am not forgiving or understanding toward my father," he admitted savagely.

"Then maybe it's a promise we should both make. Let go of the past and embrace the future. Our parents are gone, there's no use holding onto our pain. We should forgive them and accept that they did their best." She turned off the highway and drove toward the forest and freedom. After being in the car for so long, he couldn't wait to get out and run free.

To try to outrun the past. His horse was right. When they were younger, they had often joined herds and run with them just to forget.

Now it's time to let go of the past. His pain was mirrored in his mate's. How could he ask her to let go of her own pain, even though he knew it was for the best, if he could not let go of his own?

"What do you say?" Helena asked. "We jump together into the unknown, where the actions of our parents don't affect our future?"

"We jump together," he agreed. "Side by side and hand in hand, we forgive both our parents and ourselves."

"I think that might be the hardest thing to do. Forgive myself when there's no way to say sorry to my mom." She pressed her lips together. "What would my dad think of me?"

"He'd understand and he'd be proud of you. Proud that you can admit your mistakes. Proud that you flourished despite it all."

"I've never allowed myself to think about him, you know. I thought he'd abandoned us. My mom never talked about him, so I thought he'd just left us. Or that he was cruel to my mom and she'd hidden us from him."

"I felt the same about my mom, that she abandoned me. But she had no choice. She died. Your dad had no choice. Let's stop dwelling in the past and strive for a future together where we can open our hearts to both of our parents and love them for who they were. We need to live our lives together and celebrate us."

Helena turned off the road into a small parking lot in the forest. "Okay. We figure this all out and when it's done, no matter what hideous secrets are revealed..." She paused and took a breath. "I promise to forgive myself and my parents. I can't say I'll be able to forgive Barry. But I do promise not to give him any power over me."

"I promise to forgive myself and my parents. Being with you gives me a fresh insight as to how my father felt when he lost my mom. He did his best. Even though it wasn't enough for his son." He gave a bittersweet smile. "Or maybe I just wasn't enough for him."

She leaned across the car and kissed his cheek. "You are enough for me. Always and forever."

"Always and forever." He hugged her and then pulled away. "As much as I would love to spend the rest of the day here in your arms, we need to get going. We have a few hours before dark and I want to put as much distance between us and Barry as possible."

"Then let's go." She got out of the car and stretched before leaning down and grabbing her backpack.

Dario reached for his pack and shouldered it while she locked the car. "Have you taken everything of value out of it?"

"Why? Don't you think it'll still be there when we come back?" she asked, checking the glove compartment.

"I don't want to take any chances." He stood still, pushing his senses out as far as possible. If they could get away without being seen and then cover their tracks, they would not lead Barry to Wishing Moon Bay.

Unless he is something we cannot sense or has a way of tracking us that we don't know about. His horse pawed the ground in Dario's head, anxious to be away from here as soon as possible.

"I'm ready." Helena handed Dario her pack and he quickly looped the straps together.

"Put these over my shoulders like we did at the cabin. I'll stand next to that big boulder and you can scramble onto my back." He took one last look around.

"Are we alone?" Helena glanced nervously around.

"As far as I can tell. But let's not wait to see if Barry catches up with us." He strode toward the boulder. "We're going to head uphill and then cut down the other side of that hill to the river. Just hold on tightly and I'll look after you."

"I know you will." She dropped the packs and ran to him. "I trust you."

He nodded, kissed her cheek, and then moved away from her. Helena ran back to the packs, picked them up, and then turned to watch him shift. Dario stared at her while the world faded away, wanting his mate to be the last thing he saw before his horse took over.

"Hey, boy. It's good to see you again." Helena hurried toward him and stroked his nose before she moved to his side and slid one of the packs across his shoulders. She adjusted them until satisfied the weight was evenly spread.

After giving him a quick pat, she climbed onto the large boulder, grabbing hold of his mane before sliding her leg over his back. She was more confident this time and she adjusted her seat quickly before patting his shoulder once more to tell him it was okay to go.

Dario's horse took a tentative step forward, Helena rocked to the side but then wriggled so her weight was more central. The horse moved forward at a steady pace, keeping to the trail as they headed into the trees.

Soon they lost sight of the car, and all that surrounded them were trees filled with birdsong and the sounds of creatures scurrying around, looking for food before the sun went down.

We are going to need to move a lot faster if we're going to get through the river and deep into the wilderness before dark.

We must find a cabin, Dario reminded his horse. *We can keep Helena warm to some degree, but I don't know if it'll be enough, even with a fire going.*

The horse looked over his shoulder, Helena had quickly learned to keep her balance over the rough terrain, but now she needed to cope with a faster speed.

"It's okay, I understand." She patted his shoulder and then grabbed hold of his mane with both hands. "I trust you not to let me fall."

The horse nodded his head and broke into a slow jog. Helena bounced around before settling to the rhythm. As smoothly as possible, Dario's horse increased his speed until he was trotting up the trail, his muscles straining as the incline grew steeper.

When they reached the top, a flat stretch of ground

invited him to canter. If he'd been on his own, he would've galloped across the open country, but he wasn't sure if Helena was ready for that.

"This is incredible." She gripped his sides with her legs, her hands grasping his mane as they covered the ground, faster and faster. His blood pumped through his veins and he let go of all thoughts, of all worries. This was a moment between a shifter and his mate that Dario would treasure forever.

Too soon they reached the end of the open space and the trees once more encroached, leaving Dario with no choice but to slow down. If he went too fast, Helena might get knocked off by a low branch or another unseen obstacle.

This is all so new, his horse said. We aren't used to traveling with a rider on our back.

Yet we wouldn't have it any other way, Dario replied.

No, we wouldn't. This is how it should be from now on.

They reached the river, his hooves splashing in the cold water as he headed downstream. Their scent and hoofprints should be masked by the water, only a creature with enhanced senses would be able to follow them.

As Dario left the river and headed deeper into the forest, he hoped they were safe. Darkness would soon be upon them, the ideal time for an attack.

19

HELENA

"There, is that a cabin?" Helena's teeth chattered as she pointed through the trees to what she hoped was a roof, half-hidden by trees.

The horse swung his head in the direction she pointed, his sides heaving as he inhaled deeply. Satisfied there was no danger, he left the game trail they had been following and walked toward the cabin. Helena flattened herself onto his back as they went under a low-hanging branch, when she lifted her head, she sighed with relief.

"It is a cabin." There were no lights from the window, despite the encroaching darkness. No smell of woodsmoke, even though the temperature had dipped low. The cabin must be empty.

It must be. She didn't think she could go on much farther. Her hands were frozen around the tufts of mane she held onto as if her life depended on it. The flesh of her thighs was almost numb.

Dario's horse entered the small clearing outside of the cabin and stood still. She could imagine Dario pushing his senses out in every direction, trying to figure out if they were safe here. If there was anyone close by, he would wheel around and leave the cabin as fast as possible without losing his rider.

She'd experienced the exact reaction when they approached a cabin about ten miles back.

They'd found a cabin that looked deserted, but just as Helena was about to dismount, Dario's horse tossed his head and snorted in warning. Luckily, Helena still had a good clump of his mane in her hands and her leg muscles gripped his body instinctively as he wheeled around and cantered away from the cabin.

In the distance she'd heard voices, a woman laughing, a woman who probably posed no danger to them. But Dario didn't want to be seen, he didn't want there to be any chance of Barry following them. She was glad he was so vigilant, but she really needed to get off his back and stretch her poor aching legs and get warm.

Dario's horse turned his head and looked at her, then nodded. Helena took this as a sign it was safe to dismount and she leaned forward and slowly slid her legs behind her before sliding down to the ground. Her stiff fingers still grasped a clump of mane and this was the only thing that kept her on her feet as her knees buckled beneath her.

She leaned heavily on the solid shoulder of the horse as she moved her feet as if walking on the spot. Painfully slowly the circulation came back to her legs and she uncurled her fingers and stepped away, finally breaking the connection between her and the horse.

Reaching out, she grabbed the packs and pulled them off his back. With no strength to hold them, there was nothing she could do to prevent them from falling to the ground.

Immediately the air shimmered and popped and Dario's horse faded away, only for the man to appear in his place.

"Are you okay?" He scooped her up in his arms and carried her to the cabin.

"I'm fine, I'm just stiff. Sitting on your back is harder than it looks." She rested her head on his shoulder. "But you must be tired, too. We've traveled a long way."

Dario looked up at the sky, his expression clouded. "I'm not sure if we've traveled far enough. We'll need an early start in the morning if we're going to make it back to town before dark."

"Do you want to go on farther tonight?" she asked as he let her go, holding her against him as she teetered to one side. "I'm okay."

"No, we should stay here. We might not find another cabin to rest in and we both need to rest. We'll get a good night's sleep and then set off early tomorrow. We can stop a couple of times along the way, the terrain is easier, and you could walk for small sections of it, so you don't get too stiff."

Helena put her hand on the small of her back. "I always wanted to learn to ride, but I didn't expect my first experience to be bareback over a mountain."

He chuckled as he went to the door and tried the handle. "That wasn't a mountain."

"It wasn't? We went up so high." She shook her legs as the circulation came back fully.

"Nope, it was a big hill, but not a mountain. In the summer I'll take you over the mountains outside Wishing Moon Bay, then you'll know what a real mountain is." He went to a window and looked inside. "I'm going to check all round to see if I can get in without causing any damage."

"Okay, I'll go grab the packs." She trudged back to the packs and bent down to pick them up. What she wouldn't give for a nice soak in a hot bath. But an evening spent alone with Dario would be just as relaxing once they got a fire going.

"There's a small window around the side that's unlatched." Dario came back to her and hooked his hand under her arm while grabbing the packs with the other. "If I give you a boost, you should be able to squeeze through and then open the door."

"I have never broken into anywhere before. You are leading me astray, Dario." She followed him around the side of the cabin. "You want me to squeeze through there?"

"The window is small but if you took off your coat and maybe your sweater, you would fit through it," he assured her then grinned. "Believe me, I know your dimensions perfectly."

"My dimensions?" She unzipped her coat and shrugged it off, immediately the cold chilled her arms and torso. "And my sweater?"

"I think so." He helped her wrestle it off, then pulled the window open as wide as possible. "Ready?"

"Not really, but I don't want to freeze out here, so I guess I have no choice." She put her hands on the windowsill and bent her leg at the knee. Dario leaned down and grabbed her knee, boosting her up so her head and shoulders fit through the window.

With much wriggling, she made a very undignified entrance into the cabin. Sprawling across the floor, she pulled her knees up under her and crawled forward before standing up. At least Dario hadn't witnessed the whole thing.

Dusting herself down, she headed for the cabin door. She needed her sweater and coat since the air inside the cabin was as cold as that outside. At least that meant the cabin was currently unoccupied and they should be able to spend an undisturbed night here.

"Come in." She unlatched the door in the falling light and Dario entered, handing her back her sweater and coat.

"Good job. I'll get a fire started." He hurried past her and knelt by the hearth of the open fireplace. After a couple of minutes rummaging around, he grunted with satisfaction. "I'll replace the wood we use before we leave tomorrow."

"I think I saw a wood store around the side of the cabin. Do you want me to go get more wood now?"

"No, there's plenty here for tonight. Why don't you sort out some food and maybe see if there's a kettle? We should eat something warm and drink plenty." He glanced at her with some concern before he turned back to the fire.

"Okay, kettle. Where are you?" The light was fading fast as she went to the small kitchen area. Luckily there was a kettle sitting on top of a stove. All she needed now was water. "Shall I use the water we brought with us?"

"Yes, for now. We can check to see if there's a well or a pump for fresh water in the morning. If there is, we can refill our water bottles, if not, there's a freshwater stream on the border of Wishing Moon Bay, we have enough water until then."

She filled the kettle and carried it to the fire, which Dario had coaxed into life. "Can we boil the kettle on the fire?"

"There's a hook here." He held out his hand for the kettle and showed her how to hook it over the fire. "I can probably get the stove going, too. But we should be able to manage with just the fire."

"It feels very primitive." She sat down next to him and handed him an energy bar. "Here's the first course of our dinner. You must be starving."

"Thanks. I was okay while we were traveling but now that we've stopped, my stomach is complaining about the lack of food." He unwrapped the bar and took a bite. "Not bad."

"Once the kettle is boiled, we can have coffee. I'll find a pan and we can heat the rest of the food." She held out her hands to the fire. "Oh, that feels good."

"We should grab some blankets and sleep here. I'll bank

the fire up, so it keeps going most of the night." He pointed to his pack. "There's a flashlight in there. We should take a look around the cabin before it gets too dark."

"Did you camp out with your brothers when you were younger?" She leaned against him sandwiched between the warmth of his body and the fire. Helena didn't care if she moved again, it was so cozy here with Dario.

"Yes, we still do. When we're all together in town, we'll spend a couple of nights up in the mountains sleeping under the stars and cooking on a campfire. It brings us together and strengthens the bond between us." He sighed and scrunched up his wrapper. "It's easy to grow apart when you get older. We were super close when we were teenagers not long after we'd all mastered shifting."

"I know what you mean. Penny and I have drifted apart the last few years. She got married and had Milo, they lived their own lives and I lived mine." She snuggled down and rested her head on his thigh, her eyes heavy as she stared at the fire. "I like that we've reconnected. I don't necessarily like the circumstances, but I'm looking forward to being a part of their lives again."

"Why don't you stay here while I go take a look around and gather what we need?" He leaned forward and kissed her cheek.

"I was going to insist I help but I don't know if I can move." She stretched out her aching legs. "I wanted to make you dinner."

"I'm the provider, the hunter-gatherer, you stay there and watch the fire." He stroked her head and then got up in one fluid motion. Grabbing a couple of cushions from the sofa, he wedged them behind her back, propping her up.

Helena watched the flames flicker as she listened to Dario move around the cabin, fighting the urge to go to sleep. But the urge was too strong, and she rested her head on her hands, closing her eyes for a moment.

With Dario close, she was safe. Even out here in the middle of nowhere, he would protect her.

Always.

20

DARIO

"Thank you. For looking after me last night. And today." Helena slipped her hand into his.

"You are welcome. I'll always be there for you." Dario squeezed her hand and smiled.

"And I'll always be there for you. I might not be able to protect you in the same way you can protect me, but I can protect your heart." She leaned on his shoulder and giggled nervously. "That sounded better in my head."

"It sounds just about right to me." He sighed, if the situation were different, he'd be content. After carrying Helena all morning, they had stopped for lunch, a mixture of granola bars, sandwiches made with the scant contents they'd found in Helena's cupboards before they left her apartment, and some potato chips. After they'd eaten, Helena had walked for a couple of miles before Dario shifted and carried her to the borders of Wishing Moon Bay.

He'd moved at a faster pace, and Helena hadn't complained even though her legs must be sore, and her muscles cramped. They both knew they had to get back to

Wishing Moon Bay before dark, neither of them wanted to spend another night out in the wild.

Fresh snowfall was imminent and the chances of them finding another cabin to stay in overnight were slim out here in this part of the wilderness.

Helena needed to get back to Penny. She needed to know what Penny found and then figure out what happened to their father. His horse could sense the tension in their mate as she rode on his back. She was anxious, her emotions feeding into his horse as clearly as if they were one and the same.

"I could ride some more," she told him as they crested the top of a hill.

"I wanted to be here by your side when you saw this view for the first time." He jogged forward and pulled her along with him to the top of the hill.

"Wow, that is quite a view." She shielded her eyes against the low sun.

"We're on the opposite side of town to Logan's cabin. From here you can see the entire bay and the islands beyond. If you go out past the islands, you would reach the landmass where the dragons live." He stared out across the ocean, but even with his enhanced senses, he could not see the dragons.

"Dragons live out there?" Helena stared out to sea. "I know Ivan is a dragon shifter, but I thought they lived among you."

"No!" He shook his head. "They are far too proud to live among the rest of us."

"You're not joking?" Her eyes widened. "So there's a whole land filled with dragons with a superiority complex?"

"Yes, there is." He turned a little to the right and pointed. "The moon will fill the sky tonight. It's a wishing moon."

"A wishing moon?" Helena asked following his gaze.

"Yes, when the moon is full, we call it a wishing moon.

You can make a wish anytime you choose, but there's more chance of the wish coming true if you make it on a wishing moon."

"Then let's get to town. I think I might like to make a wish tonight." She dragged him forward, but he pulled her back. "What's wrong?" Helena tensed and looked around. "Is there someone here?"

"There." He pointed into the distance. Just above the tips of the trees, something was moving toward them.

"Is that a bird?" She leaned forward and squinted. "It's a bird. A big bird."

"It's Ivan. I sent him a text to let him know we were close." He slipped his arm around her waist. "This will cut a couple of hours or more off our journey."

"We're going to ride on the back of a dragon?" She swallowed hard. "What kind of crazy world have I found myself in?"

"The good kind of crazy. Most of the time at least." Dario held her hand tightly, as they watched the dragon grow bigger as he drew closer. Helena's heart rate increased, and she breathed rapidly but she stood her ground.

"Where's he going to land?" she asked breathlessly as the air swirled around them with each downbeat of his wings.

"He can land right here. He's very agile." Dario watched his brother as he pushed his taloned feet forward and then flapped his wings backward to slow himself down. With more grace than should be possible for a creature so big, he landed effortlessly, and folded in his wings.

"How do we get on?" Helena dug her nails into Dario's hand as he led her forward. Ivan didn't shift, they could talk and catch up once they were back at the hotel.

Ivan lowered himself down toward the ground, his foreleg bent so they could clamber on. Dario hadn't ridden on the dragon's back for years, but the thrill was something he never forgot or got bored of.

"Follow me." He let go of his mate's hand for a moment and climbed onto the dragon's forelimb before reaching for a horned spike on his back. Bending his knees, he sprang up onto the dragon's back and slipped his leg over his scaly spine.

"You make it look easy." Helena climbed onto Ivan's forelimb, her actions tentative as if she were scared of hurting the dragon.

"He's pretty tough." Dario leaned down and held out his hand to his mate.

"I'm standing on his leg. It just feels wrong." She patted the dragon's scaly hide. "Sorry."

The dragon turned around and surveyed her with his reptilian-like eyes that were still uniquely Ivan.

"He forgives you." Dario beckoned to her. "Come on, I'll pull you up."

Helena slipped her hand into his and then scrambled onto Ivan's back. "Okay, I'm on."

The dragon crouched down and then sprang into the air, dropping down from the top of the hill with his wings outstretched. They glided silently toward town, the wind rushing at them, bringing the first flakes of new snow.

Dario's heart danced with happiness. Here he was flying on the back of a dragon with his mate's arms wrapped around his waist. Did life get any better?

Yet soon it was over, they were back at the hotel, standing in the parking lot with the two backpacks next to them as they watched Ivan shift from dragon to human.

"Thanks, Ivan." Dario embraced his brother.

"You're welcome. Plus, I figured Helena might appreciate riding on my back after spending hours on the back of that horse of yours." He grinned and winked at Helena over Dario's shoulder.

"Hey, Helena loves riding on my horse." Dario let go of his brother and swung around to face his mate.

"I do. Although, I do appreciate the dragon's speed. It's good to be back here before nightfall."

"She thinks you're slow," Ivan whispered theatrically.

"I did not say that." Helena laughed and wagged her finger at Ivan. "I can see there is a rivalry between you all."

"Always." Ivan hugged Helena. "It's good you're here. Penny is going out of her mind waiting for you."

"Where is she?" Helena asked.

"In Valerie's apartment. They've brought more stuff down from the attic. Penny is convinced they might find more photos and maybe some answers." He clamped his mouth shut as he locked eyes with Dario. "Come on. There might be time for you to get to the library tonight, too. It's been hard for Penny to sit still and not go check out the news articles in the library archives. If you hadn't gotten back today, I don't think she could have waited any longer."

"I'm glad she did." They followed Ivan around the back of the hotel. Taking a left turn, they entered Valerie's apartment by a private outside door rather than the one that led through the hotel.

"Penny said you met this Barry character." Ivan's eyes glowed as he turned to look over his shoulder, his jaw tense. "She told us what he said to you, Helena. If what he said is true, I am sorry. So very sorry. I believe Penny always held onto the hope that your father might still be alive."

"We both did. At least a small part of us did. I suppose it's natural, although as the years went by, we questioned why he'd never tried to find us. But then we explained it away by believing that our mother hid us very well or that she'd asked him to leave us alone and he'd obeyed her wish." She gave a low laugh. "The number of times we've gone around and around in circles trying to reason out why we never met him, or Mom never told us about him."

"There are photos." Ivan closed the door behind them. "He and your mom look happy."

Helena covered her mouth and hiccupped as she swallowed down a sob. "I can't wait to see them. And yet I'm scared."

"Helena?" Penny came out of Valerie's living room and ran toward her sister. "You're back. Thank you, Dario. Thank you, Ivan."

"It's good to be back...home." Helena hugged Penny as Dario exchanged a worried glance with Ivan. Later, after Penny and Helena had shared their news, he planned on talking to all his brothers, they needed to be ready for anything that might threaten the two women. They had to be ready for Barry's next move.

Whether that is inside or outside of Wishing Moon Bay, his horse confirmed.

"Come and look at what we found in the attic. Milo got bored looking through clothes. He was looking for old toys in the farthest corners of the attic when he found a box full of old photos." Penny pulled Helena toward the living room.

"One day we should go through all of the stuff in the attic and see if there's anything useful or valuable up there," Ivan murmured to Dario.

"Or dangerous?" Dario arched an eyebrow at his brother.

"Exactly." Ivan and Dario followed Penny and Helena.

"This is Mom and Dad?" Helena stared at the photo in her left hand, the fingers of her right hand caressing the earrings she wore. The same earrings Barry had recognized.

"Yes, Milo saw the earrings and came to show me. But there's no mistaking this is Mom. You have the same eyes." Penny twirled her finger. "Turn it over."

"Oliver and Amanda Olsen outside Sweet Creations." Helena looked up. "They owned a candy store?"

"Yes." Valerie came into the room with Logan at her shoulder, carrying a tray of coffee and cookies. "I was talking to Jeremy earlier, his family has lived here their whole lives. He said he can remember your parents. Your father used to make magic sweets and candy."

"Magic sweets?" Helena asked. "Dad had magic?"

"No," Penny answered quickly. "Mom and Dad used to buy the spells from the local witches and blend them with sugar and natural flavorings."

"Jeremy said his favorite was a gobstopper that made your voice come out funny. Some would make your voice high-pitched, some would make you croak like a frog. The kids used to buy them and have hours of fun." Valerie smiled, her eyes filled with tears. "He said your parents were well-loved."

"Does he know what happened to them?" Helena asked. "Wait, does he remember us?"

Valerie glanced at Penny. "I'm sorry I didn't tell you earlier. I wanted to wait until you were both here together."

"Tell us what?" Penny folded her arms across her body. "What do you know?"

"Jeremy couldn't remember too many details, he was only six or seven at the time. But he does remember the shop closing and his mom told him your father had been..." Valerie hesitated, her expression filled with pain.

"Barry told me Dad was dead," Helena said quietly. "He was murdered."

"Murdered?" Penny put her hands to her mouth. "No."

"That's what Barry told me." Helena looked at Valerie for confirmation.

"Yes, that's what Jeremy's mom told him." Valerie brushed her hand over her eyes. "I'm so sorry."

"What else did Jeremy say?" Penny asked, her face a mask as she held in her emotions.

"Not much really. He doesn't remember either of you, but you would have been very young, and children don't always take notice of these things."

"So Barry was right." Helena cupped her face in her hands. "Does Jeremy know who did it?"

"No, he called his mom, but she said no one was ever charged as far as she can remember but it's all a bit hazy since it was so long ago." Valerie went to Penny and hugged her. "I'm sorry I didn't tell you right away."

"It's okay." Penny held out her hand to Helena. "You're right, it's better that we learn the truth together." She looked down at Helena's hand as her sister took it. "You are freezing. Have some coffee and warm yourself up. We can always go to the library tomorrow."

"No, let's go today." She accepted a cup of coffee from Logan. "Thanks."

"What do we know so far?" Ivan asked.

"We know that Barry has some knowledge of what happened. He told us that the same man who killed our father also killed his father." Helena cupped her coffee in both hands. Dario wanted to hold her close and comfort her, but she was strong.

"And now we know that Dad was murd... That our dad is most likely dead. But Jeremy doesn't know who did it and neither did anyone when it happened. So how does Barry know?"

"He could have investigated the murders himself," Ivan suggested. "If his father was murdered but no one was charged, then he might have picked up the investigation. He might have linked the two murders. Certainly, Barry might have more information than the authorities."

"Does that mean we should bring him back here?" Penny asked.

"No!" Helena shook her head firmly. "At least until we know for sure he doesn't have some ulterior motive. He broke into my apartment. If he is the innocent party here, why didn't he tell us what he knew?"

"He seemed a little...unhinged to me," Dario admitted. "There was something off about him. When he told Helena about her father, there was no empathy, no concern for her feelings."

"We don't know what life he's had." Penny's voice caught in her throat. "Mom might not have been perfect but at least she was there for us. How do we know Barry wasn't abandoned? What if he was alone in the world and he wasn't lucky enough to have someone as kind and caring as Valerie to raise him?"

"You're right, Penny," Dario agreed. "We shouldn't pass judgment on the man until we have all the facts. When we go to the library, we should look for other similar deaths at around the same time. If Barry's father was murdered at around the same time, that adds some weight to his story."

"There's one other thing we need to know," Helena began. Everyone turned to look at her. "Why can't Penny and I remember any of this?"

"You were young, it must have been very traumatic for you both. You probably blocked it out." Dario moved closer to his mate, his voice tender. "Maybe it's a blessing that you don't remember."

"But I need to," Helena replied. "I need to know. The more I think about it, the more my monster in the closet is the person who killed Dad. I might be a witness. I might be able to solve this for us and for Barry."

"Or your monster might not be connected," Valerie

replied softly. "If this was traumatic enough that you have blocked it out, then maybe it's better not to remember."

"It's like we've been living fake lives," Penny said. "I agree with Helena. It's time we knew the truth, it's time we remembered what happened. I want to remember our father. And I know the memories might be traumatic, but there would be good memories, too. There must be. Our dad made fun sweets that made people laugh."

Helena pulled away from Dario and went to Penny, holding her close. "We'll find a way."

Dario's heart contracted, he hated seeing his mate in pain. But the pain might get much worse if she remembered her past here in Wishing Moon Bay.

She deserves to know, his horse told him. We would want to know about our parents.

Would we? Dario asked. Would our lives have been better if we grew up believing they had both died in an accident rather than knowing that our father killed himself because our mother died?

The truth has made us who we are, his horse replied.

And not knowing the truth has made Penny and Helena who they are. The truth might not set them free. The truth might make a prison they can never escape from.

It's not our decision to make, his horse replied.

On that, they agreed. All Dario could do was be there for his mate.

21

HELENA

"Deaths and marriages are all registered here along with births." The rather bemused elderly female assistant at the library showed them to the archives.

"Thank you, Daisy." Logan and Penny would search through the register for anything containing information on their parents along with Penny's and Helena's birth certificates. Unless their mom had changed their dates of birth, those should be easy to find.

Along with their father's death certificate, once they found the newspaper article with the information in it. Even without it, they could narrow their search down to within a few years.

"And I'll show you to the newspaper archives." Daisy eyed Helena up and down. "You're new in town."

"I am, yes. I arrived a couple of days ago." She took a deep steadying breath. "But I believe I was born here. That's what we're trying to find out. My father used to own a candy store in town."

Daisy's steps faltered and she swung around to face Helena

and Dario. "Sweet Creations. Oh, Oliver Olsen was your father? I'm so sorry, he was such a kind man. My daughter used to love his *jiggle wobbles*. They used to make your tummy jiggle and wobble, had her in stitches. He was such a clever man." Her eyes misted with tears. "So unfair, the way he..."

"I don't know how he died," Helena admitted. "Until a couple of days ago, I had no idea he was murdered, and I only found out today that he owned the candy store." She swallowed down her emotions, fighting the need to grab hold of Daisy's hand and beg her to help them. "Do you have any information that might help? Even just the date he died so we can narrow our search of the archives."

"I'll find the archives for you. It was one of the biggest news stories for years. There are not many murders in Wishing Moon Bay." Daisy beckoned them to follow her and she switched on a computer and sat down at the keyboard.

"Was there only one murder?" Dario asked.

"Only one?" Daisy ducked her chin and looked at Dario over her glasses. "Isn't one enough?"

"We were told that there were two murders. That the same person who murdered Helena's father murdered another man. Are you saying that isn't true?" Dario reached for Helena's hand.

"As far as I am aware there was only one murderer in Wishing Moon Bay in the time surrounding your father's death." She slipped her hand over the mouse and clicked. "Of course, this is a town filled with magic. There could have been a murder that was treated as a suspicious death. We can search the archives around the same time for anything that might fit if you really want to."

"Thanks," Helena croaked and then cleared her throat.

"Is your source reliable?" Daisy didn't take her eyes off the screen.

"He's the same person who told me my dad had been murdered. He said his father had been murdered by the same man." Helena received a startled look from Daisy.

"How could he know that when no one had a clue who murdered your dad? It's one of the biggest mysteries. One of those unsolved cases. They even reopened it as a cold case a few years ago." She dropped her voice and glanced around. "It's like the one that got away. The police officer who was first on the scene went on to become a detective. He sees it as a black mark against his name that he never brought anyone to justice for the murder."

"That's what we're trying to figure out. If you can help us in any way... Or the detective you spoke about. Do you think he would be willing to talk to us?" This could, potentially, be the biggest breakthrough so far. Instead of trawling through past records for new stories, they could go directly to the source.

"I don't know. Oscar Renshaw keeps to himself these days. He lives on the outskirts of town and doesn't entertain many visitors." Daisy stared at Helena over her glasses and Helena held her breath as if waiting for Daisy to pass judgment on her. "But that case did get under his skin and I'm sure he'd like to speak to you." Daisy frowned, her brow wrinkled as she thought for a moment. "You are who you say you are, right?"

Helena's head snapped back. "Yes, why wouldn't I be?"

"Well, I don't recall Oliver and Amanda having a child." She pressed her lips together thoughtfully. "And you've been away all this time."

"I don't remember living here," Helena admitted. This was a time for honesty, she needed Daisy's help and she suspected if the librarian smelled a lie, she would withdraw all offers of help.

"Then how do you know you are Oliver's daughter?" Daisy tilted her head to one side.

"My mother, Amanda, is in a photograph with Oliver. On the back of the photograph it says Oliver and Amanda Olsen. Although, we grew up with the last name Stanhope." Helena took her phone from her pocket and tapped the screen. "See, this is a copy of it."

"I can vouch for its authenticity," Dario said. "My mom, Valerie, found it up in the hotel attic. There's a stack of old stuff up there from the previous owners."

"Is there?" Daisy's eyes narrowed as she surveyed Dario. "Perhaps I could come by and take a look sometime. I am a volunteer curator for the museum. There might be something there that we could display. That old building and its occupants have some secrets, I'm sure." She smiled, but there was a brittle edge to her words.

"I'll speak to Valerie about it when we're finished up with finding out what we need about Helena's father." Dario put his hand on Helena's shoulder. There was something possessive about the touch and the look in Dario's eye as he stared down Daisy.

"We have a deal." She cracked a smile, but there was something unsaid in her eyes. But Helena had enough mystery on her hands without adding more to the mix.

Daisy turned on her heel and strode back to her desk near the main entrance. After a quick glance at Dario, Helena followed. When they got out of there, she planned to ask him what was up with Daisy.

"Where are you going?" Penny hurried over to them.

"Daisy says there's a retired detective in town who might be able to help us. It sure would be faster to go to the source than to go through all the newspapers." Helena watched Daisy out of the corner of her eye. "Have you found anything?"

"I found Mom and Dad's marriage certificate. They were married here in Wishing Moon Bay." Penny's face was flushed pink as she showed Helena an image of the certificate.

"That was fast." Helena's throat tightened and she swallowed down a lump of emotion. Their mom's familiar signature, the same signature she'd used to sign school permission slips was there in front of her. "Mom."

"We searched around the year of your birth. Added another nine months for the pregnancy. Although Mom could have already been pregnant when they got married... Anyway, we found it." Penny's voice trailed off. "We know for sure who our father is."

Helena held out her arms and the two sisters hugged each other, crying silently in the library in the town they once lived in and called home. They might even have visited here with their mom and dad. Did their father read to them? Did he sit by their bedside and tell them a bedtime story?

"Helena, I have the address." Dario came to them, holding a piece of paper in his hand.

"We should go." Helena wiped her eyes as she let go of Penny. "All of us."

"You don't want Logan and me to stay here and look through the records?" Penny glanced over her shoulder. "Logan is looking for our birth certificates. I want to know if we were born here. If the ones Mom had were fake." She gave a low laugh. "We might even celebrate our birthdays on the wrong day. I might even be the eldest."

"Daisy can't remember us," Helena whispered. "Just like Jeremy."

"But we must have been born before Mom left. Before Dad died. The date on the photograph of Mom and Dad...you would have been five, I would have been three." Penny shook her head. "I don't understand."

"We need to go and speak to this detective. I suspect he might be more useful than these records." Helena ran her hand through her hair, her eyes prickling with unshed tears. "Get Logan. We should go together. This affects the four of us."

"Okay." Penny nodded and backed away. "I'll also need to call Rift and check if he minds taking care of Milo for a couple of hours. I feel as if I've abandoned my son today."

"I'm sure he's having fun with Rift and this is important," Dario said. "This is his history as much as yours."

"You're right. This goes to the very heart of who we are. It's starting to feel as if someone rewrote our past when we left town." She gave a small smile and then went to find Logan.

"I think Penny is right." Dario side-eyed Daisy who was watching them while tapping on a keyboard.

"Which part?" Helena asked quietly.

"That someone rewrote your past." He pressed his lips into a thin disapproving line.

"Is that possible?" Panic welled in her chest and her heart beat so hard it was as if it were trying to break free.

"Sometimes I think anything is possible in this town." He slipped his arm around her shoulders and guided her toward the door. "I need some fresh air."

"And I need some answers."

22

DARIO

"I remember Detective Renshaw. He came to the school and gave a talk on keeping safe. You know, the usual, don't talk to strangers or strange creatures. He seemed like a nice genuine guy." Logan met Dario's surprised look. "You don't remember him?"

"There's a lot about school I don't remember," he admitted. "I'm surprised you remembered that talk, though, since you are a wolf. You always thought you could look after yourself, even before your first shift."

"I remember him saying there are creatures a lot stranger than us out there." He gazed toward the mountains. "But then he might just have come to scare us. With an unsolved murder on his hands and a town filled with supernatural beings, the more people that are vigilant, the better."

"Our father was killed before you came to Wishing Moon Bay, though." Helena had been very quiet since they left the library. Too quiet.

"Yes, if you were five and Penny was three, then the murder happened before either of us arrived in town." Dario got into the back seat of Penny's car. Helena was seated next to him while Logan was in the front passenger seat.

Penny inserted the key in the ignition and started the car. "What about Valerie?"

"Valerie was out of town for a few years before she bought the hotel. She went traveling before she moved back and settled down. I expect the news might have died down a little before she came back. Although, I'm surprised she didn't hear about the case being reopened as a cold case. We'll have to check back with her when we've seen Detective Renshaw."

"*If* he agrees to see us." Penny put the car in drive and headed away from the library, following Logan's directions. "If Detective Renshaw has chosen to live a quiet life away from people, he might not take too kindly to meeting us. Especially since we haven't contacted him before to check if it's okay."

"Or he might be happy to see us. I know everyone else seems to have forgotten we existed but I'm certain Detective Renshaw will remember us. If this case had haunted him, I doubt he's forgotten about the victim's two children." Helena leaned her elbow on the car door and looked out into the gathering darkness.

"Why do you think Daisy and Jeremy don't remember us?" Penny mused. "I can understand Jeremy, I guess. But Daisy. She's a shrewd one. I don't expect a lot gets past her."

"Why don't we leave all speculations until we've talked to Detective Renshaw?" Logan suggested. "We've been going around and around in circles for days with all of this. Detective Renshaw might give us the answers we need about your dad and Barry's connection to all of this."

"That's the weird thing, Daisy didn't know about another unsolved murder in Wishing Moon Bay. So either Barry's father's murderer has been caught and only charged with one murder. Or else the murder took place outside of town. Don't the police here liaise with other police forces?" Penny cast a sideways glance at Logan.

"We've spent our lives avoiding contact with the police," Logan confessed. "We never caused the police to even look at us twice, we had too much respect for Valerie."

"What Logan means is that when there are six young kids together out in town, people look at you with suspicion, so we kept to the beach and the mountains. If there was any trouble to be gotten into, we did it where no one would ever see." Dario chuckled. "It was all innocent fun."

"I am going to need to hear all of these stories one day," Helena told him. "Just so I have a heads-up where our children are concerned." She paused. "If we're lucky enough to have children."

"I am happy to adopt if we are never blessed with our own," Dario admitted. "These last few days I've been thinking more and more about how lucky we were as children to live with Valerie in such a special place. Any one of us could have ended up in a city where no one had a clue what we were."

"And you would like to give another shifter child the same chance." Helena nodded. "I think that's a wonderful idea. Even if we have our own children, I'd be thrilled to adopt a shifter child. Or any child. There are plenty of children out there who need a family of their own."

"Maybe we should think of adopting, too," Penny suggested to Logan.

"The more kids, the better." He flashed Penny a smile.

"We're lucky guys," Dario said. "As shifters, we long to have families, we love any child that's part of our family, which is why we all adore Milo. For Logan and me to have mates who are willing to open their hearts to other children...well, that's just amazing."

"We're lucky women. We have met a couple of keepers.

Which is a good thing, since we have to keep you." She slowed down and stopped outside a dark driveway that led to a house half-hidden by overhanging trees. "This is it?"

"It sure is." Logan looked around. "There's nowhere to leave the car out here. Let's drive to the house and see what happens."

"See what happens?" Helena looked concerned. "Under normal circumstances, I would not have a problem with that. But here in Wishing Moon Bay, it kind of scares me."

"Don't worry, if Detective Renshaw was in the police force, whatever might happen won't be permanent." Dario chuckled as Helena's horror grew. "I'm joking. He's not going to turn us into anything unnatural."

She slapped his arm lightly. "Well, don't joke. Not about something like that."

Penny sighed and drove the car along the darkened driveway, the last remaining sunlight obscured by the overhanging trees. "He's not a vampire, is he?"

"I doubt it, investigating crime would be difficult if you could only go out at night." Logan put his hand on the door, ready to open it as the car came to a halt.

"I was joking," Penny said. "But now you have me worried."

"Sorry, I was never very good at reading people's sense of humor." He popped the door open and got out. No sooner had Dario and Helena gotten out of the car when the front door of the stone-built house opened.

"What do you want?" The silhouette of a man stood in the doorway, his back straight as he called out to them.

"I'm Dario, and this is Logan, we're Valerie's children, from the hotel." That sounded ridiculous since they were no longer children. "We're here with Penny and Helena, Oscar and Amanda Olsen's daughters. We wondered if you could spare us a few minutes of your time. We wanted to talk to you about Oscar's murder. Penny and Helena are trying to find out all they can about their father's murder. I understand..."

"Is this a joke?" came back the reply.

"No. It's not a joke." Helena stepped forward. "We had no idea who our father was until yesterday. Penny found a photograph of our mom and dad together. And I met with a man who told me his father had been murdered by the same man who murdered our father."

"What?" The silhouette sagged forward. "Who told you that?"

"We were hoping you might be able to tell us more." Penny came around the car and went to join her sister. "Please."

"You'd better come in." He beckoned to them and they looked at each other, a silent agreement before they headed toward the house.

"Thank you." Helena was the first to step inside, followed by Penny. Detective Renshaw stood back, looking at them each in turn as he held the door for them. Dario entered last, aware of Detective Renshaw checking outside before he closed the door and locked it behind them.

"I don't know what help I will be," Detective Renshaw confessed. "I never found out who killed your father." He directed them into a living room. "Please, sit down, I'll get some coffee." He stared at Penny and Helena. "Although I might need something a little stronger."

"You look as if you've seen a ghost," Dario noted the man's pale complexion and the way he kept looking at the two women.

"In a way, it feels as if I have. Two ghosts. I never expected you to be here in Wishing Moon Bay." He backed out of the room, but Helena followed.

"Why do you say that?" She stood in the kitchen waiting for his answer as he put a fresh pot of coffee on.

"When your mother left town, she said she would never bring you back here. She didn't want you to know what happened to your father. She didn't want you coming back here and digging up the past." He came back to the living room, his face ashen. "Is she here, too?"

"Mom died a few years back. She never did tell us anything about living here, or our father. Until Penny saw the photo of them together, we didn't know who he was and that we had a connection to the town."

"But the town wants us to know." Penny came to Helena's side. "I was driving past when my car broke down. There was a wrench in my engine that shouldn't have been there. If the wrench hadn't made my engine stall, I would never have found the town or met Logan."

"Logan is your mate. The town does like to connect two people. Maybe it was a coincidence. Maybe not. We'll never know." Detective Renshaw glanced at Helena. "And you followed your sister here?"

"Yes. Because a man came into my life."

"Your mate." He pointed at Dario. "That's some coincidence in itself. Two sisters finding love with two adopted brothers."

"Dario is not the reason I am here." Helena paused. "Well, he sort of is. He did rear up in front of my car and that's when the road to town appeared. But the real reason I was coming here is because a man bumped into me in the street. This is the man who swears the same man murdered my father, and his father. Do you have any idea if that's true?"

"There was no other murder connected with your father's. I'm sorry, I don't know who this man is, but I believe he's lying to you." Detective Renshaw's pity was evident, along with his sincerity.

"Did you have any suspects for my father's murder?" Penny asked. "We might find a link."

"You don't think I have spent my career trying to piece the clues together? Even when the case was officially closed, I worked on it in my own time." His eyes misted with tears. "I knew your parents, they were good people." He chuckled. "His sweets and candies always made people laugh. They were delicious, too. The flavors were so good."

"Why don't we remember?" Helena asked. "And why don't people remember us? We were here at the time of the murders, weren't we? We were living in Wishing Moon Bay. Or did our mom change the dates and years of our births?"

"You were here at the time," Detective Renshaw confirmed.

"Then why?" Penny threaded her fingers through her sister's. They looked young and vulnerable as they stood side by side waiting to hear what the old man had to say.

"Because it was the only way to keep you both safe. Even though your mom was in terrible shock, she knew she had to keep you out of danger. It's what your father would have wanted."

"You think our father would want us to forget him?" Helena shook her head, her brows knitted together. "Why would a father want his daughters to forget he even existed?"

"Because it would be easier..." Detective Renshaw scratched his forehead. "I don't know how to tell you... How to explain to you..."

"Did a vampire do this?" Dario couldn't bear to see his mate in such pain. The truth might hurt but it had to be better than living with the unknown.

"A vampire killed our father?" The blood drained from Helena's face. "Was Dad drained of blood by a vampire?"

"No!" Detective Renshaw held up his hand to calm the situation. "A vampire was not responsible for your father's death. But yes, your mom did ask a vampire to glamor you both."

"Glamor us both?" Penny's eyes widened. "A vampire messed with our heads." Her hands clenched into fists. "Well, he can just *un*mess with them."

"Do you have the name of the vampire who did this?" Logan asked gruffly.

"You need to give this some serious thought before making a decision. Your mom wanted you to forget for a reason." Detective Renshaw's pained expression was a warning but not one Penny and Helena were ready to head.

"Our whole lives have been built on lies. On a cover-up." Helena grasped Penny's hand tightly. "It's time we knew the truth."

"You might not like what you find," Detective Renshaw warned but his shoulders rolled forward, he knew he was beaten.

"I want to know who my dad was. The man that made sweets and candies that made people laugh. I deserve to remember his face. He deserves to be remembered." Helena's breath shuddered through her. "Will you please tell us who took our memories?"

"Your memories were never *taken*. They were simply covered up as if a door was shut on them." Detective Renshaw went to the kitchen and poured five cups of coffee, while they waited in the living room.

When Helena went to follow him, Dario caught hold of her arm and shook his head. "Give him space."

She nodded, her lips pressed together as he turned from him.

I only hope that when Helena and Penny do get their memories back, there won't be a part of them that's missing. Some things might be best left forgotten. His horse hung his head in sorrow.

We need to be strong. We need to be there for Penny and Helena. Together, we can come through this and move on.

They had to. Anything less was unthinkable.

23

HELENA

"Do you know where he's taking us?" Helena asked Dario as Penny followed the headlights of Detective Renshaw's car.

"No." Dario's jaw tensed. "There are a few vampires who live in Wishing Moon Bay, but there's a settlement a couple of miles along the coast where most of the vampires who come here settle."

"It's not just Wishing Moon Bay? I mean there's more than the town here. I know you said the dragons lived across the ocean, but I didn't realize there was more." She swallowed down her nerves. Were they making the right decision? Until Detective Renshaw agreed to take them to see the vampire who had taken their memories, it had seemed like the only decision. She wanted to remember her father. She wanted to recall hugging him and talking to him and playing with him.

Yet there was a sense of dread building inside of her. Detective Renshaw was adamant her mother had made the decision to protect them. Was this the ultimate betrayal? After a lifetime of blaming their mom for not being there for them, for not being the mother she wanted or needed, Helena was about to undo the one thing their mom wanted left alone.

Their mom might not have been there for them when they thought they needed her, but it seems she had been there when they had needed her the most. Helena was beginning to believe that their mom had sacrificed her own happiness, her own future, for her daughters.

"Penny, are we sure?" Helena asked the question burning a hole in her head.

"Sure about going to see a vampire?" Penny glanced at her sister in the rearview mirror.

"About going to see a vampire who can unlock our memories." Helena held Penny's glance before she switched her eyes back to the road ahead and the car they were following.

"We need to know," Penny said firmly. "It's the only way we can ever know we're safe."

"I agree." Logan half turned in his seat. "If you can recall what happened, if you can remember the events around the time of your father's death then you might be able to shed light on what happened. As a child, you might both have been questioned by the police. But you didn't have the knowledge you do now to put things together." He linked his fingers together. "As an adult, you would see how things were linked, a conversation here, a meeting there. You might have seen your father's killer before that day and with your memories restored and the information Detective Renshaw has on the case, it might be possible to bring your father's killer to justice."

"Or the memories might be so painful it would be better if they were left in the past, if they remained forgotten." Dario sighed and reached for Helena's hand. "There is no right or wrong action here. Whichever fork in the road you take leads you down a different path. Your choice is one you have to live with. But Logan and I will live with it, too, and help you in whatever way we can."

"I want to know who I am," Helena finally answered. "Growing up, it was as if there was a part of me missing. Now I know it's true."

"I agree." Penny steered the car off the road and followed the detective down a long driveway with tall trees standing sentry on either side.

"So this is the vampire who took your memories," Logan breathed out the words in a hushed, revered tone.

"He didn't take them, remember." Helena figured it was a good thing to keep reminding themselves that this vampire was not their enemy.

"You're right, he simply buried them deep down, so far down we can't access them," Penny said curtly.

"Because Mom asked him to."

"Or paid him a lot of money." Penny ducked her head and looked out of the front windshield. "Because looking at this house, the vampire who lives here must have a lot of money. And where better to earn it than preying on widows who want to protect their children."

"I think we should keep our thoughts on vampire morals to ourselves," Dario suggested. "If you want this guy to reverse what he did then we're going to need him to take pity on you."

"You want us to play up being sad orphans?" Helena asked.

"I think that's going to get the best reaction from him." Dario opened the car door and got out as Penny pulled up next to Detective Renshaw's car. He was immediately on alert, his nostrils flared.

"Maybe you are the one who needs to relax," she told her mate. "You're all prickly."

"Sorry." Dario rubbed the back of his neck and breathed out a long slow breath. "Vampires give me the shivers."

"Really? I thought nothing frightened you." Logan got out of the car and stood looking up at the large house. It was like a mansion out of gothic horror.

"I didn't say I was afraid," Dario replied defensively. "But if there was anything I was afraid of, it would be a vampire. They're not as easy to fight as another shifter. There's no talisman or ward you can wear to keep them away. The only defense against them is not inviting them into your house. But in this case, it's us making the house call."

"Relax," Detective Renshaw said as he slammed his car door shut and came to join them. "Silas Langdon is a good man."

"Okay, first, he's not a man, he's a vampire," Dario pointed out.

"He's different, yes. But only in the same way that you are different. You might be a shifter, but are you not still a man?" Detective Renshaw's eyes flashed in the moonlight.

"I'm alive, it's different." Dario shook his head. "We're not here to argue about the small stuff. Helena and Penny want answers and you brought us here, so let's have them."

"It might not be that easy." Detective Renshaw didn't elaborate as he walked toward the stone steps leading to an ornate front door. Grasping the large brass door knocker in his fist, he banged on the door.

"Enough to wake the dead," Logan muttered.

"He's awake at this time of night anyway." Detective Renshaw glanced over his shoulder. "Are you sure you want to do this?"

"Absolutely," Helena said with more conviction than she felt.

"Then get ready to bargain," Detective Renshaw warned. "Silas did this for your mother and gave his word that he would never break his promise to her. His word is his bond. Silas does not make promises lightly and he never breaks them."

"Great. So this is pointless." Helena clasped her hands together to stop them from shaking. The urge to turn around and run back to the car and drive far away was almost too much. But she stood her ground along with her sister, Logan, and Dario. This was the right thing to do, she knew it in her gut.

"There has to be something we can give him to make him *un*glamor us." Penny's face looked pale as she stared at the door.

"Maybe he's not at home." Logan sounded hopeful, but then he stiffened. "Someone is coming."

"I always thought if I had shifter senses, my job would have been a whole lot easier," Detective Renshaw said as he stared at the front door.

The door opened a crack and a sliver of light spilled out onto the stone steps. "Can I help you?"

"Colton. It's me, Detective Renshaw."

"Detective, it's been a while. A long while. I take it this is not a social call." The door opened wider, a man in a suit with gray hair slicked back on his head stood in the light from inside the house, his features hidden in shadow. "You are not alone." Suspicion entered his voice, and he closed the door an inch.

"Would you please ask Silas if he'd see us?" Detective Renshaw's voice wavered. "Tell him that the Olsen sisters would like to speak to him."

The old man with gray hair stared at Helena and Penny without a hint of emotion. "My master doesn't like uninvited guests."

"My guess is he'll want to see Penny and Helena. If not,

we'll just leave." Detective Renshaw leaned closer. "I don't think it's your decision to make, do you, old friend?"

"No, it's not. But it's me who will have to put up with his bad mood." With that, the guy closed the door and left them standing outside in the cold.

"Is that it?" Penny asked.

"No, Colton has gone to ask Silas if he wants to see us. To see you." Detective Renshaw turned to face them. "If he says no, we leave. No questions, no arguments."

"Just like that, you expect us to walk away with no answers?" Helena asked. Now that they were standing on the threshold of having their memories restored, the thought of walking away was almost unthinkable.

"Yes. I do. Silas is not a man you mess with."

"Not a man," Logan reminded them.

"Don't start that again," Detective Renshaw rebuked.

"Sorry." Logan paced around in a small circle. "Vampires have always made me nervous."

"Don't vampires and wolves have some kind of history?" Penny asked. "In movies and TV shows, werewolves and vampires are often mortal enemies. Not that I'm calling you a werewolf or anything."

"Vampires and most other creatures, supernatural and otherwise, have a history." Dario rolled his shoulders and stared at the front door as if ready for any sudden movement. "They're dead, after all. While the rest of the world is alive."

"He's coming back." Logan sniffed the air and strode toward Penny, positioning himself by her side, ready to defend his mate.

"My master has agreed to see you." Colton pressed his lips together disapprovingly.

"Thank you." Detective Renshaw entered the house first. Dario followed, with Helena and Penny behind him, while

Logan kept up the rear. She was glad of the protection offered by the two shifters although, from what Helena had gathered from their conversations, if the vampire chose to attack, none of them would escape with their lives.

Or maybe she'd watched too many of those vampire movies for when Colton led them down a long dark hallway and into a room filled with light, the man waiting for them didn't look scary at all.

"Oscar." Silas acknowledged the detective briefly, before casting a curious glance over Dario and Logan. Then his pale eyes rested on Penny and Helena, and there they stayed. "I forget how long it has been since I last saw you."

He smiled, the ghost of a smile on lips the shade of a faded rose. Helena swallowed, he was handsome, much younger than she'd expected. In her mind, she'd forgotten that vampires didn't age. Instead of the old graying man her mind had conjured up, they were faced with a man perhaps in his mid-thirties.

"You remember us?" Penny asked.

"Of course." His pale eyes were mesmerizing as he stepped closer. "I don't ever forget a name or a face." He reached out and stroked her cheek, his fingers icy cold, but there was compassion in his eyes that stole her fear.

Helena stepped back from the vampire. She needed to hold onto her fear, it would keep her safe as she stood in the vampire's lair. "Did you take our memories?"

His lips pressed together into a thin line, but the compassion didn't leave his eyes. "I never stole anything from you or your sister."

"What about from our mother?" Penny stepped forward and gained the vampire's attention, he turned around impossibly fast, his body tilted forward. Logan moved fast, putting himself between the vampire and his mate.

"Let's just calm things down a little, shall we?" Logan put his hand up but didn't touch the vampire's broad chest.

"I am calm." Silas inclined his head slightly. "I am willing to answer your questions and your accusations. But I can assure you I am not a thief. I didn't rob you of your memories and I did not rob you of your father."

"I was thinking more of you robbing our mother of money. She paid you to take our memories, didn't she?" Penny asked harshly.

"She did. I am, after all, a work-for-hire kind of a guy." His eyes narrowed, glowing a little in the dim light. "I am not a charity."

"No, I don't suppose you are." Penny glanced at Helena.

"Silas, will you please tell us what happened?" Helena kept her voice calm and friendly.

"I can tell you about that night. But I am not going to unlock your memories. Your mother made me swear not to. Even if you begged me." He sighed with sorrow and turned away. "And I never break my word."

"Even if it means we might be able to put the pieces together and figure out who really murdered our father?" Penny asked.

"Even if the information locked in our heads might also save us from danger right now?" Helena's question got his attention.

"Danger threatens?" Silas asked.

"Maybe. Before you tell us about the past, maybe I should tell you why we are here." Helena hoped to sway the vampire's decision.

"Go ahead." He swung around and came to stand before her, two feet away from where she stood feet hip-width apart. Dario was by her side, but if the vampire chose to act, chose to rip out her throat and drink her blood, there was little he could do about it.

"I met a man, Barry Matthews. He bumped into me on the street and recognized my mom's earrings." Her fingers lingered on the silver in her ears.

"Someone who knew your mother?" Silas asked. "In the world beyond?"

"In the world outside of Wishing Moon Bay, yes. Until then that's all I knew there was." Helena swallowed down her emotions and composed herself. "He asked me on a date, he was very charming, and I liked him."

"Your point?" Silas asked curtly.

"On the day that Penny was supposed to come and live with me, I got home to find he'd been in my apartment. Uninvited."

"All that proves is he is not a vampire," Silas smirked but his eyes were intently focused on Helena.

"I never made it to Helena's apartment because I found Wishing Moon Bay instead. My car broke down and the road to town simply appeared," Penny picked up the story.

"Ahh, so that's how you got to town."

"Yes, I think I was drawn here because Logan was my mate." She stepped closer to Logan and threaded her fingers through his.

"Fate has its own mysterious ways." Silas stalked away, rubbing his chin thoughtfully. "When your mother asked me to prevent you ever knowing Wishing Moon Bay existed, I knew that I was powerless if fate stepped in."

"I followed Penny here and saw Dario outside of town. I too then found the road through the tunnel." Helena glanced sideways at her mate, but Dario's gaze was fixed firmly on the vampire and the threat he offered.

"So now the two of you are here and you have found that you have history here and want to know what that history is?" Silas asked.

"No, that's not quite the end of the story," Helena said

softly. "I went back to my apartment, we wanted to know why Barry broke in. Specifically, if there was any meaning to him breaking in on the day Penny was supposed to arrive."

"And was there?" The vampire was deathly still.

"He came back. He told me that he was trying to get back to Wishing Moon Bay, that he'd recognized my earrings and knew my mom. He also said that the same person who killed our father killed his father."

Silas skimmed the floor as he moved closer to Helena. "Did he?"

"Yes."

"And you believed him? Did you bring him back with you?" Silas's eyes were mesmerizing, it was as if he had a power over her and she could not lie.

"No."

"Why?"

"Because I don't trust him." The truth was everything. It was like a compulsion, one she was powerless to fight.

"Why?"

"His eyes are cold. There's no warmth when he talks about his father."

"Maybe a vampire was paid to bury his thoughts, too." Silas smiled and the spell he held over Helena broke. "But if that is true, I am not that vampire."

"We need to know what happened to our father so that we can figure this all out. You said our mom asked you to protect us. We need you to keep that promise by giving us the one thing that can help us defend ourselves."

"Your memories." His jaw tightened as he surveyed Helena. "Clever."

"This isn't about being clever or tricking you. This is about protecting ourselves and figuring out what is happening." She leaned toward Dario. "So that we can get on with our lives. Isn't that what our parents would have wanted?"

"It is." He nodded. "What your mother asked me to do was done to protect you, not to hurt you. Most people would have lived a new life outside of this town and never looked any deeper beneath the veil."

"Yet here we are."

"Yet here you are." He inclined his head.

"Will you do it?"

"No."

24

DARIO

"No?" Dario stepped forward, letting go of Helena's hand.

"Your hearing works fine, shifter." The vampire's lip curled up slightly.

"Why not?" Dario's anger surged through him. Faced with this predator, he was ready to fight and his hands curled into fists.

Silas turned his back on the people in the room and walked away. For a moment Dario thought he was going to leave the room, leave them all standing there, but he didn't. Instead, he stopped, his fingers rubbing his temples as he stared at a painting on the wall. "I made a promise."

"Whatever my mother paid you, we'll match it." Penny rushed forward. "If that's what you are worried about."

The vampire's shoulders shook, and Dario shivered at the sound of grating laughter, as if two sheets of metal moved against each other. "You think this is about money?"

"Isn't it?" Penny countered.

"No, it's about giving your word to someone you liked, someone who was your friend." He swung around to face them. "I smothered those memories, I shut them away so you would never have to take them out and look at them. So you would never know the loss and pain of those memories. So you would be safe."

"But we're not safe, are we?" Helena saw a chink in Silas's resolve and went for it. "This man who knows us, knows who we are, is a threat and our memories are the ammunition we need to fight him."

"Bring him here. Let me deal with him." Silas ground his fist into his hand.

"No." Detective Renshaw sprang forward and placed his hand on Silas's arm before pulling it back. "Until we know who he is, bringing him back here is a mistake. If he was thrown out, there would be a reason. If we bring him back here and there's trouble, that blood will be on our hands."

"His blood would be on my hands." Silas held out his hands to Detective Renshaw.

"What pain?" Helena asked abruptly. "You said loss and pain."

Silas switched his cold gaze to her, and Dario fought the urge to drag her from the room. There was something distinctly dangerous about Silas.

"Helena." The danger seemed to dissipate. "Your mother came to me two days after the death of your father. Filled with loss and pain, she set that aside when she asked me to take your memories of your father and place them behind a door. Do you know why?"

"No," Helena admitted.

"Because she wanted to protect *you*. She wanted to protect you from what you saw. Even though that meant robbing her children of their memories of the man she loved. The man you all loved. By asking me to take his memories, it meant she lost him over and over again every day. She could never talk to you about birthdays when your father made special candies for each of you, candies that filled your heads with unicorns and rainbows. Instead, she left a large gaping hole, a wound, if you like, that would never heal."

"Silas is right," Detective Renshaw said quietly. "I was there with her. I know the pain and anguish she experienced. But she ultimately did what she thought was right for you and Penny, knowing full well the consequences." He took a deep breath and looked at the vampire. "And I was in full agreement, even though I was the detective on the case."

"Isn't that like hiding evidence?" Penny asked.

"I suppose it was in a way. But Helena had endured nothing but torment in the hours and days since the murder." He turned soft eyes on Helena, eyes filled with pity.

"We should go." Dario stepped forward and put his hand under Helena's arm.

"No, we came here for our memories and we aren't leaving without them," Helena pulled her arm away from him and he let her go. If he forced her to leave, he would be the enemy and he never wanted to go against his mate's wishes.

But now that we know the full depth of her mom's love, we know those memories are better off buried. His horse longed to throw his mate over his shoulders and gallop off into the night with her.

"Did I see him die?" Helena asked suddenly.

"Yes." The vampire inclined his head, his eyes fixed on Helena's face.

"Oh, no!" Helena covered her face with her hands. "I need to remember so we can figure out who it was."

"You didn't get a clear look at his face," Detective Renshaw answered.

Penny hurried to Helena and wrapped her arms around her shoulders. "Maybe Silas is right. This is too painful."

"What about you?" Helena sobbed. "You deserve to know

who our father was. You deserve to know the good times." She turned to Silas. "Did Penny see, too?"

"No, only Helena." Detective Renshaw glanced at the vampire, who shook his head slightly.

"No, if you don't remember, then I don't want to remember either." Penny shook her head. "That's what hurt Mom for so long, let's not let history repeat itself."

"What if that's what we are doing by not remembering?" Helena placed her hands on Penny's upper arms and stepped away from her. "I want my memories back, all the pain, all the horror. I want to remember. Only by remembering can we use the past to prevent it from repeating."

"Helena, are you sure?" Dario didn't like this one bit.

"I am. I understand Mom had her reasons and it frightened the hell out of me that she wanted me to forget something so terrible that it was worth sacrificing all memories of my father over. But I'm not a child anymore. I can handle it."

All we have to do now is convince the vampire to break his word, Dario's horse said drily.

Everyone has a price. We just have to figure out what it is. Dario's jaw tightened. If only he'd earned more money instead of traveling the world. Then he'd have something to offer a vampire.

"What's it going to cost?" Dario asked bitterly. "What is your price, vampire?"

A smile crept across Silas's face. "I'm not your enemy, son."

"And I'm not your son." But he sure did sound like a petulant child.

Remember, Silas might look ten years younger than us, but he's probably a century or two older. The guy's been around the block a few times.

Maybe too many times, Dario answered.

Are we seriously thinking about taking him on in a fight? His horse didn't sound confident. And he was right, there was no way they could take down this vampire alone.

However, there was something about him that made Dario want to smash his good-looking face in.

You see him as a threat. And he is a threat but not to our relationship with Helena, his horse told him calmly.

What if Silas messed with Helena's head when he unlocks the memories of her father and dumps her memories of us in a locked room instead.

The mating bond would break down any barrier a vampire put up between two mates, his horse said confidently.

"Okay, enough testosterone-filled sparring," Helena put herself between them. "What will it take for you to unlock our memories?"

"I told you, I don't break my promises." Silas's resolute expression said there were some things money couldn't buy. Penny and Helena's memories might be one of those things.

"There has to be something. Perhaps if you repaid what our mom gave you?" Penny suggested.

"And we could pay you instead." Helena dug in her purse for her wallet. "There has to be some deal to be made here."

"You should consider this carefully. Consider your mom's decision." Silas spoke deathly quiet and silence fell over the room.

Helena moved first, she strode up to the vampire and opened her wallet. "I need to know. Penny has a son to protect and the only way we can do that is if we know what happened. Because I'm certain Barry, the guy who broke into my apartment, believes one of us knows something."

"Impossible," Silas replied.

"Why, because you messed with everyone else's head? Is that why people in Wishing Moon Bay also forgot who we were?" Penny asked. "Daisy at the library, Jeremy, who else has no idea that Oliver and Amanda Olsen had two daughters?"

"I'm not that powerful," Silas chuckled. "Daisy is forgetful, and Jeremy was too young."

Helena let out a long sigh. "So it's just us that you glamored?"

"In this case, yes." Silas nodded and thrust his hand into his pocket. "Here, this is the payment your mom gave me." He held out a small golden stone.

"That's it?" Penny picked up the stone. "A wishing stone."

"It was her wish that you forget," Silas replied kindly. "But it seems I didn't make her wish come true."

"What was her wish?" Helena asked softly.

"That her daughters would forget all the bad things that happened that day. That they wouldn't know the sorrow of the loss of a parent. That without the knowledge of what happened or who their father was that they would be happy and not consumed by asking questions and seeking answers."

"Mom was consumed by fear and grief." Penny turned the stone over in her hand.

"She was. But she knew the risks," Silas replied. "I tried to talk her out of it. But when she explained her reasons, they were sound. She was scared that if you came here looking for answers then whoever killed your father would go after the one witness to the crime."

"Helena." For a moment, Penny looked as if she might change her mind.

"I need to know. We need to know." Helena took hold of Penny's hand and they walked forward, standing in front of the vampire.

Logan closed in from the right and Dario moved to stand at Helena's left shoulder. They both knew there was no chance of preventing the vampire from hurting their mates but they both knew they would try. And fight to the death if necessary.

"What's this going to cost?" Helena asked.

"You are asking me to break my word, to go back on a promise I made." He took a moment to look at the four people in front of him. "To break that promise, I ask a promise of each of you."

"What promise?" Dario's suspicions rose.

"I don't know. Yet." Silas tilted his head to one side and studied the horse shifter. "Would you do that? Make a promise, like a blank check, for your mate."

"Yes." Dario answered without hesitation.

Helena swung around to face him. "No, that's not fair."

"None of this is fair," Logan said. "But I'd make that promise, too."

"Ladies? Are you as brave as the men who love you?" The bemused expression on Silas's face confirmed Dario's suspicions.

The vampire is playing with us, his horse agreed.

Or testing us, Dario answered.

"Of course. Whatever it takes," Penny confirmed.

"Helena?" Silas leaned forward, his strange colored eyes piercing in their intensity.

"Yes. With one condition." Helena jutted her chin out.

"Ask."

"Nothing illegal. I want your word that you are not going to ask us to go murder someone for you, or traffic drugs, or whatever bad things vampires get up to."

Silas leaned back, tilted his head to the ceiling, and laughed. It was not a pleasant sound. "I should do this for free. This is the best entertainment I have had for years."

"Promise." Helena jabbed her finger into his chest.

The vampire stilled, all humor gone as he placed his hand over the spot where Helena's finger had prodded him. His entire focus rested on Helena's face, but she didn't blink as she held his cool gaze. "Nothing illegal."

"Then we all promise." She trembled under Silas's gaze, but she stood her ground.

"Then shall we begin?" He placed his hands on either side of Penny's head. She instinctively jerked back but he held her firm. "This is what you want. You have to surrender yourself to me entirely."

Penny rolled her shoulders and relaxed. "Do it."

Silas's eyes were intense as he stared at Penny. "Do you remember me, Penny?"

She nodded. "I do."

"Do you remember what I asked you to do when you were a small child?"

"You asked me to forget my father and to forget I ever lived in Wishing Moon Bay."

"That's right," the vampire purred. "Do you remember what we did with those thoughts?"

"We put them away in a locked room."

"And now it's time to unlock the door and let those memories back in. Can you do that for me?"

"Yes."

"Then do it now." He held her gaze for a long, long time and then he let Penny go. "It's done."

25

HELENA

Helena leaned on Dario as her head swam, filled with memories of her past. Memories that had been locked away for nearly forty years. Her father's smile, his arms holding her tightly and carrying her upstairs to bed. His warm voice as he told her a bedtime story.

Everything she ever dreamed her father would be and more.

Were these memories real? Could she trust them? They seemed too perfect.

Mom. She watched from the table as her mom kneaded bread. She looked so happy and serene, there was no sign of the torment that possessed the mom an older Helena knew.

The sound of the front door opening brought a smile to her mom's face. She left the bread and went to the kitchen door, hugging Helena's father as he entered the room. He bent his head and kissed her lips, the look they exchanged filled with so much love.

"They were happy." She smiled sadly. These were the memories she wanted to cling to, also. She would gladly forget her mom's sorrow and sadness and live with only these memories.

"They were." Penny reached for Helena's hand as the world around her darkened.

Her mind darkened and shadows closed in. A sense of dread consumed her, and she closed her eyes, squeezing them shut, not wanting to look. But this was a memory, and she couldn't shut it out and was powerless to unthink it.

"Daddy." Her father was behind the counter. A man was talking to him. Her dad was scared, she could hear it in his voice.

"I'll just go and see if I have those in the storeroom." Her father walked around the counter, he strode toward Helena, his fingers on his lips, telling her to be quiet, like when they played hide and seek. She had to stay quiet.

Mutely, she allowed her father to put his hands on her shoulders and push her into a small cupboard that smelled of peppermint and sugar. She'd played in here before with Penny, but something told her this was not a game. Terror crept over her as her father walked back into the store, to the man waiting at the counter.

She shouldn't look, she didn't want to look. "Barry!"

"Helena!" Dario's hands on her shoulder shook her out of the memory.

"Barry. It was Barry." She clutched at Dario.

"What was Barry?" Penny asked.

"Barry was the man in the store. Barry was the one who killed Dad!" Her stomach roiled and she put her hand to her mouth as nausea built.

"It can't be Barry," Dario told her gently. "He's not old enough."

"He looked exactly the same," Helena explained.

"Give yourself some time for the memories to settle," Dario stroked her back soothingly. "They are bound to be jumbled up."

"I know what I saw." Tears stung her eyes as she pulled away from Dario. "I need to talk to Detective Renshaw."

She ran out of the room, where Silas had left them after he'd unlocked their memories.

"Helena." Dario was right behind her as she stopped and listened.

"Where are they?" She turned to face Dario, needing him to use his shifter senses to find them.

"Just take a moment to calm down," Dario crooned.

"I know what I saw, Dario." She wiped her hand across her cheek, wiping away her tears. "I saw what happened. I have to tell Detective Renshaw."

"Are you sure it was Barry? It wasn't someone who looked like him?" Dario asked.

"I'm sure. I know him. I went to dinner with him and I danced with him. I know." She inhaled deeply, needing to stay calm. "It all makes sense now. The way he looked at me the first day we met. He expected me to recognize him. When he realized I didn't, he toyed with me, he asked me about my family, the family he destroyed."

"Colton." Dario took hold of her hand and she absorbed the comforting warmth. "Colton."

"I was bringing you some coffee," the elderly man said.

"We need to see the detective, is he still here?" Helena asked.

"He is." Colton glanced at Dario. "Follow your nose and you'll find him."

"Come on." Dario slipped his arm around Helena's shoulders. "This way."

Helena followed, trusting her mate as they headed down a narrow hallway and then took a right turn. The air cooled as if someone had left a door open. Did vampires need heat and warmth or was the house heated for Colton's sake who was definitely human?

"Helena?" Silas appeared in the doorway of a large opulent room filled with pictures and portraits. "I heard you shout."

"I remember the murder. I saw who did it." She gasped, her eyes drawn to a photo on the wall. "That's my mom and dad. And you."

"I knew them well, they were my friends." Silas's sadness was profound. "These are all the people I have known and loved. It's where I come to remember. Not many faces when you consider how long I have lived."

"You truly were their friend." Helena went to the photo and stared at it. This was how she wanted to remember her father. Not the bloody... Her head jerked up. "Detective Renshaw."

"I'm no longer a detective," Oscar reminded her.

"You are to me. You know the case inside and out." She tapped the side of her head. "I need to know if what I am remembering is a mixed-up memory or a true memory."

"I'll do what I can to help you, Helena. But when you were a child, your memories were too hazy. You said that you never saw his face." Detective Renshaw came toward them and stood looking at the photograph of their parents. "They were good people. You were such a happy family. It broke my heart to see your mom after it happened. It has broken my heart ever since."

"Then help me solve the murder." She entwined her fingers with his. "I saw his face when he came into the store. For a split second, I saw him. Then, as I hid, I saw the back of his head, I heard his voice. A voice I know."

"You knew the attacker?" Detective Renshaw asked.

"No. Not then. I didn't know him when I was a child, but I do know him now. The man who killed my father is the same man who broke into my apartment, the man who met me on the street outside of my office building. It might have been a chance encounter, but I believe that's why he tried to get to know me so that he could find out if I had any idea who he was."

"Helena said the man she saw, Barry, looked exactly the same as he does now," Dario added.

"So he knows magic," Silas rubbed his chin thoughtfully. "That makes him more dangerous."

"Will the local police open the case now that they have this new information?" All Helena wanted was to bring her father's murderer to justice and then move on with her life.

"There's no way the police will reopen the case." Detective Renshaw shook his head. "I'm sorry. They need something more. Something concrete. Even for a supernatural police department, this stretches the imagination."

"Not to mention the murderer is outside of Wishing Moon Bay and can't find his way back. That's as good as being in prison for the authorities here. If he's trapped outside of town, he is not their problem." Silas mulled over the information. "Maybe it's time he did come home."

"No!" Detective Renshaw turned to face Silas. "That's not a good idea and you know it. Now that Helena and Penny have their memories back, they are targets. He probably already knows one of them saw him. That information was open knowledge at the time. If he spoke to Helena and ruled her out as the witness, there's a chance he lay in wait at Helena's apartment to..."

"Deal with Penny. He thinks Penny is the one who saw his face." It all made sense now. Barry had gone to Helena's apartment knowing that Penny was coming to town. What his plans were for that day they might never know.

"I didn't see anything, I wasn't even there." Penny and Logan had entered the room, with Colton and his tray of coffee trailing behind them. "Was I?"

"You were with your mom," Detective Renshaw

confirmed. "We have eyewitnesses that put you both inside the grocery store when the murder happened."

"So what do we do now?" Helena asked. "I am not going to live my life looking over my shoulder for Barry. And I don't want to live in fear for Penny and Milo."

"We lure him back here and get him to confess." Dario took Helena's hands. "Or I can go out there and drag him back here by his throat."

"Hell, we could go find him and hogtie him and you can literally drag him back here," Logan ground out.

"If he has magic, he might be extremely dangerous when cornered," Silas warned.

"He's desperate to get back here. He'll take the bait if we go back to my apartment and then lead him here. We can do this," Helena was convinced they could do it without raising Barry's suspicions.

"And I'll be waiting for him when he does get here," Silas replied.

"No, if you get anywhere near him, the authorities will believe that you have tampered with his memories to get him to confess. This needs to be done cleanly and by the book," Detective Renshaw warned.

"Wait." Penny held up her hands. "What will happen to him if he comes back here and gets arrested?"

"He'll spend the rest of his days in prison," Dario replied confidently, then his voice dropped. "If he gets convicted." He glanced at Silas. "If Barry's lawyers find out we have been here, they will accuse you of tampering with Helena's memories."

"And they would be right." Helena nodded. "Tell me, do vampires ever venture outside of Wishing Moon Bay?"

"Only in very exceptional circumstances." A smile spread across his face and his eyes glowed with pleasure. "And this might just be one of those circumstances."

"What are you thinking?" Detective Renshaw asked.

"Why should Barry ever get the pleasure of crossing back into town ever again? Wishing Moon Bay doesn't want him. So why not wipe the memory of the place from his mind, but leave him with the idea that he's searching for something but can't remember what?" Silas rubbed his hands together. "I can ensure he lives in eternal torment for what he did that day."

The vampire's eyes fixed on the photograph of Oscar and Amanda.

"I'm beginning to like you, Silas." Helena put her hand to her head and then closed her eyes, screwing them tightly shut but she couldn't stem the tears as the vision of Barry killing her father flashed into her brain hot and sharp, as if she were watching events unfold in real-time.

"And afterward. When it's done..." Silas took her warm hands in his cold ones. "Will you let me take that piece of your memory and lock it away forever? You deserve to only remember the best of your father."

Helena nodded. "Yes. I'd like that."

For a vampire with such cold hands, Silas had a warm heart.

26

DARIO

"Thank you, Detective Renshaw." Dario extended his hand to the old detective.

"Don't thank me yet. This whole thing could blow up in our faces." The detective unlocked his car and slid into the driver's seat. "But if we get this guy, if it really is the person responsible for the murder of Oscar Olsen, then I'm going to enjoy watching him squirm."

"You're coming, too?" Helena asked.

"Of course. I'm driving. Silas will sleep in the trunk while I drive us to your car." He cracked a grin at their shocked faces. "Never driven with a vampire in the trunk?"

"Can't say that I have," Dario replied.

"We need to get you back to your car. And I'm not willing to wait a couple of days for you to trot on over there. Every day we delay is a day too long. If this Barry guy wants to find his way here, sooner or later he's going to find someone willing to show him the way." Detective Renshaw pushed his key into the ignition. "I don't want him to get the luxury of seeing his hometown again."

"The farther away from Wishing Moon Bay we can keep

Barry, the better. If Silas can make him forget the place exists, that sounds like a win to me." He glanced sideways at Helena. "The only thing that would be better than that would be if we can bring him to justice and make the murder conviction stick."

"I'm going to go home and go over the case files again. I want to see if there's any chance we missed something now that we know exactly what Helena saw." The detective nodded to Dario and Helena. "I'll see you tomorrow. We leave at nine. I'll pick you up at the hotel."

"See you tomorrow." Dario raised his hand as the detective closed his car door and started the engine. "Are you sure you're okay about all of this? We can always change our minds and bring Barry back here to face a court of law."

"Innocent until proven guilty?" Helena wrapped her arms around herself, her face was pale in the moonlight. "But there's no way to prove his guilt. There's no forensic evidence and if I'm the only eyewitness, then it's not going to stick."

"Are you okay about him walking around free?" Dario slipped his arm around his mate's shoulders and guided her toward Penny's car. Penny and Logan were inside with the engine running and the heater on full. They were probably having the same conversation.

"I'd rather he was in jail. There's always going to be a part of me that worries he'll find a way to get his memories back and will one day wind up here." She looked up at the moon hanging over the bay. "But Silas did a great job on me and Penny. We had no memories of the town. And I know we eventually found our way back here, but that was because of you and Logan, not because we got our memories back."

Dario opened the car door for his mate, and she slid inside. "The only thing we can't explain is why Penny recognized some of the buildings when she first arrived in town."

"I have the answer to that." Penny turned in her seat. "I spoke to Colton while you were talking to Silas. He said that Mom came back here with me a couple of years after we left."

"She did?" Helena shook her head. "I wasn't with you?"

"No, it was when you went on a camping trip with the school. You had been having those nightmares and she came to see Silas to ask him if there was a chance that your memories were bleeding through." Penny reached out for Helena's hand. "I don't really remember coming here. I think Mom just told me we were going on a day trip."

"What did Silas tell her about my memories?" Helena asked. "Is that the reason I had nightmares?" She covered her mouth and shook her head. "Or maybe they were a punishment. Maybe I was the monster in the closet."

"Why would you say that?" Penny's fingers tightened around her sister's hand.

"Because I was in the closet when Dad was murdered. If I'd called out, if I'd run for help..."

Penny shook her head. "There was nothing you could do to stop Barry. If you'd called out, he would have hurt you. The man was crazy. Don't ever forget that."

"So why the dreams?" Helena asked. "Why did Mom put up a talisman to ward off the monsters?"

"I don't know. Maybe she was scared in case there was a monster, in case something had followed us out of Wishing Moon Bay." Penny shrugged. "Or maybe they were just normal childhood dreams, but the wards and talismans just made Mom feel closer to this town and her life here."

"I wish I could talk to her. I wish I could tell her I'm sorry for the way I treated her and for not believing in her monsters." Helena wiped her free hand across her face. "It's all such a mess."

"So let's bring the person responsible for that mess to

justice. The only justice he is likely to get." Penny let go of Helena's hand and started the engine.

"There's something I'd like to do first," Helena said. "If nobody else minds. I know you want to get home for Milo, but could we do a small detour on the way?"

"Sure, where are we going?" Penny started the engine as Helena nestled against Dario, welcoming the warmth of his arms around her.

"The beach. I'd like to make a wish." She put her hand in her pocket and drew out the wishing stone.

"In the dark?" Penny glanced in her rearview mirror.

"I'm sure with two shifters we should be able to find the ocean." She smiled up at Dario. "It's something I need to do before we go."

"Then we'll go." He kissed the top of her head and his arms tightened around her.

They sat in silence while Penny drove to the beach. The moon over the bay was like a beacon leading them home. Its bright rays lit up the beach, casting long shadows on the ground.

"It's so cold." Helena stamped her feet and clapped her hands together as she stared at the sky.

"The snow has passed, the skies have cleared." Dario slipped his arm around her shoulders and offered her his warmth. "There'll be frost on the ground in the morning."

"As much as I loved traveling with you across country, I am glad we're making the return journey in a car." She leaned into him and slid her arm around his waist.

"Even with a vampire in the trunk?" Dario chuckled. "I have lived in this town most of my life and seen some weird stuff, but I think this might be one of the strangest things I have ever done."

"So far." Logan patted him on the back. "You have a life

with a mate ahead of you, who knows what strangeness that'll bring."

"What are you implying, Logan?" Penny hurried to join them after locking the car.

"Is Logan afraid of being tied down to a mate?" Dario teased. "Is he scared of belonging to another person and no longer being free to live in his remote cabin and hide away from people?"

"I don't hide," Logan insisted.

"Of course you don't." Dario laughed as he guided Helena toward the steps leading down to the beach.

"Is that what you all think?" Logan asked. "That I hide in the cabin?"

"He's teasing you and you are taking the bait," Penny warned.

Dario chuckled. "Listen to your mate, Logan."

"He's messing with you because you like to think that you aren't frightened of anything," Penny said soothingly as she took Logan's hand.

"But your knees were shaking when we were in the same room as Silas." Dario received a sharp jab in the ribs from Helena's elbow.

"Behave," she whispered.

"Oh, I'm not the one afraid of vampires. When we were kids, you used to hang garlic at the window so they wouldn't come and bite you at night."

"Did you?" Helena asked.

"I might have." He shuddered.

"You're afraid of them?"

"Not afraid. But when I first came here, I met a vampire. I'd snuck out of the hotel one night. It was hard to settle when I first moved here, maybe it's my shifter blood, but the need to be free, to not be hemmed in by any walls just took over me."

"And so you crept out of your room." She squeezed his waist.

"I used to run along the streets, on two feet, I hadn't had my first shift at that time, I was still young. But I used to run until my muscles ached and my lungs burned." She glanced up at the moon. "Sometimes I'd come to the beach and sit and stare at the moon or the stars. I used to wonder if my mom was up there looking down on me."

"Shifter kids aren't a lot different from normal kids, are they?" Helena sounded relieved.

"No, they are just the same, especially until puberty. That's when we change, when our hormones kick in and we gain the ability to shift."

"So you were this lonely child searching for answers, searching for the parents you'd lost?" She leaned on his shoulder as they reached the bottom of the steps, their feet sinking in the soft sand.

"I suppose I was searching for them. I was grateful Valerie gave me a home, but it took me a while to settle down and see it as home. It took even longer to think of Valerie as my mom. But now, that's what she is, the only mom I've ever known." He looked up at the moon.

"And the vampire?"

"Oh, yeah." He'd almost forgotten where his story had begun. "One night I was down here on the beach, sitting down by the tide, the waves gently lapping in. It was summer, twilight came late, and dawn came early."

He could recall the last rays of sun glinting on the ocean, the swell of the tide, the salt in the warm air. He'd been at peace, alone on the beach with only his thoughts. Thoughts that turned over and over the events that had brought him to the very spot he sat on.

Dario rubbed his neck, recalling how his developing shifter senses told him there was someone there, even though he hadn't heard any footsteps. He'd looked up. A pale face, as pale as the moon in the sky, was looking down on him.

He'd jumped and scurried across the sand on his hands and knees as the woman looked down on him. She'd smiled, a kind smile, but haunting. Her loss seemed to match his own as she reached out a hand to him.

"Don't be afraid. I don't want to hurt you." She tilted her head to one side, looking at him with fascination, just as Dario and his brothers looked at bugs going about their day in the dirt.

"I need to get home." He'd stood up, not sure if he should run. His father had always told him not to turn his back and run from a predator unless you knew you could outpace it. Could he outrun this woman?

Was she even a woman?

"I'll walk with you," she offered, her hand still outstretched.

"I'm okay. I know the way and I'm not supposed to talk to strangers." He pushed himself to his feet, his knees trembling. For all the warmth in his body, she made him feel cold. Cold to his bones, cold to his soul.

"There are stranger things than me in this part of the world," she'd purred, her eyes fixed on his.

He'd felt the pull of her, like the pull of a magnet. Her eyes, he couldn't stop looking at her eyes. He'd lifted his hand and reached out for her. Just as their fingertips were about to touch, a voice called out, breaking the spell.

"Move along now, Maughna. He's not for you." Valerie stood on the beach, her feet wide, her hands curled into fists.

"I never knew that story," Logan said.

"It was at that moment that I knew that Valerie would always be there for me, she'd face down demons for me and for those who were my new brothers." Dario shuddered, his eyes glittering with tears. "I've also never forgotten Maughna and what might have happened if I'd taken her hand that night."

"I thought you said vampires don't drink human blood, from humans."

"They don't usually, but I think Maughna saw me and saw something else in me. A lost soul. But Valerie found me that night." He chuckled. "Of course, she could have set the whole thing up, because I never left my room at night for a long, long time."

Logan laughed. "Valerie probably did arrange the whole thing."

"She wouldn't!" Penny exclaimed.

"No, she wouldn't." Dario slid his hand off Helena's shoulders. "So, this is the beach, we've found the ocean and now you have to make a wish."

"I feel bad throwing away the pebble Milo gave me." Helena held it out on the palm of her hand and smoothed her thumb over it.

"That's what a wishing stone is for. Its true value is in the wish it gives you. So throw it out there." Dario swept his hand out in a wide arc.

A little theatrical, his horse commented drily.

I thought so, Dario replied.

"Okay." Helena held the stone in her hand and stared at it for a few moments, then she closed her eyes, as most people did when they finally made their wish. She pressed her lips to the smooth golden stone and then threw it out into the ocean. There was a single plop before the wishing stone was swallowed by the water.

The four people on the shore stood in silence for a long while, each lost in their own thoughts as the waves lapped gently on the shore. Around them, the night air cooled, until their breaths came in clouds of vapor.

"We should go. I've hardly seen Milo all day." Penny

turned her back to the ocean and hurried up the beach toward the car.

"And we need to get a good night's sleep before we leave tomorrow." Dario held his hand out to Helena.

"Yes, since we have no idea what tomorrow will bring." Helena took his hand and smiled at him, her lips red against her pale skin. "But whatever it is, we'll face it together."

"We will."

"And I'll hold your hand when Silas is around, so you don't get scared of the big bad vampire," she told him playfully.

"Now I know why fate brought us together."

"So I can protect you?" She arched an eyebrow.

"No, because fate knows I could only love a woman who makes me laugh." He chuckled as they reached the car and got inside.

I wonder what she wished for, his horse asked.

Maybe she'll tell us when it comes true. Dario stared into the dark, where the endless waves broke on the shore. *Our wish has already come true.*

Now they just needed their happy ever after.

27

HELENA

"Have you gotten over your fear of vampires yet?" Helena asked lightly as they got into her car which remained untouched where they'd left it before their trek across country. As far as they could tell, Barry hadn't been here. Even Dario's shifter senses couldn't pick up a trace of his scent.

"Just because we traveled in the same car as a vampire hidden in the trunk does not mean I like them." He shuddered and then rolled his eyes as she grinned. "You find it amusing."

"Just a little." She turned the key in the ignition and the engine started. Turning the heater up fully, she rubbed her hands together to chase away the cold. "Although, from what you said last night, I think you have every right to be scared. Maughna would be enough to terrify most children."

"Thank you." He inclined his head.

"I shouldn't tease you really. I'm the one who is frightened of monsters in the closet, even though I have never seen one."

"Sometimes, it's what we don't see that frightens us more. With Maughna, it was the thought of what might have happened that scared me more than anything. If Valerie hadn't come along, would she have hurt me, bitten my neck and drunk my blood, turned me into a vampire, or simply taken me home?"

"You're right." She put the car in drive. Detective Renshaw would follow them back to her apartment, from where their plan to capture Barry would unfold. "Maybe that's where my fear of the monster in the closet stems from. Something that frightened me, but I couldn't see."

"Maybe your mom did see it."

"What do you mean?" Helena drove onto the highway, keeping one eye on the detective's car behind them to make sure he followed.

"Your mom lived in Wishing Moon Bay. Perhaps she had a gift for seeing things. Things that even shifters can't see." He shrugged. "It's just a thought."

"And one I'm going to explore once we have dealt with Barry." She stared at the road ahead. What was waiting for them? Whatever it was, they would have to face it alone with only the detective as backup until night fell and Silas rose.

How strange that her life was entwined with a vampire's. His actions all those years ago, to help Helena's mom when she needed it most, had changed Helena's life completely. In some ways, when her father died, she had lost both of her parents. Her mother had faded into a ghost of her former self when they left Wishing Moon Bay and the memories of their lives behind.

Why hadn't her mom asked Silas to hide her own memories? Surely, she would have been happier without the knowledge of what had happened.

"Are you okay?" Dario asked.

"Yes. I was just thinking how sad and lonely my mom must have been. And wondering why she kept her memories of what happened. Wouldn't it have been kinder to shut off the memories of our father's death?"

"I don't think it was about kindness." Dario sighed and stared ahead. "She kept her memories, her pain, and her loss so that she could keep you safe. If she had no knowledge of what happened, then she wouldn't have been prepared if Barry made his move."

"Then why didn't she tell us the truth before she died?"

"By then she would have assumed the threat had passed. She might even have assumed the murderer had died. At the very least he was no threat to you. He'd remained free for so long, why would he suddenly come looking for you?" Dario had a point. Her encounter with Barry had been chance.

Fate.

The same fate that had put her in the path of a certain horse shifter.

"And yet he was out there all this time, just waiting."

"Your mom probably thought he was hiding in Wishing Moon Bay and had never left, that you were safe out here in the other world." Dario sat up straighter as they pulled to a stop outside of her building. "Are you sure you want to do this? We can always try to find him without you."

"No, he wants me, he wants a way back into Wishing Moon Bay." She switched off the engine and half-turned to face him. "And I need to do this. I was there when this whole thing started, and I need to be there at the end."

"I understand." He leaned forward and kissed her cheek. "As long as I'm there by your side. We do this together, or not at all."

"Agreed." She cupped his face in her hands and kissed his lips. "I love you, Dario."

"You do?" He jerked back and she laughed.

"That was not the response I was expecting."

"Oh, I love you, too. I thought you already knew that." He leaned in close, their lips less than an inch apart.

"I still need to hear it." She kissed him, her lips brushing his until a knock at the window made them both jump.

"Hey, I need to find an underground parking lot to stow my car. I can't risk the trunk being opened out here." Detective Renshaw looked around.

"Okay, we can go to my office building and put your car in the underground parking lot there." She turned her attention back to Dario. "I need to visit there anyway. I plan to hand in my notice."

"You do?" His surprise was less than when she told him she loved him.

"I do. I've seen how happy Penny and Milo are in Wishing Moon Bay and I want to be there to watch Milo grow up and maybe give him a cousin to play with. I like the idea of them roaming the mountains together just like you and your brothers did." She nodded. "I know it's the right thing to do."

"I'm certainly not going to argue with you." He kissed her lips then got out of the car. Helena followed, closing her car door and then locking it before she ran across the street to the detective's car.

"Okay, drive along this street. I'll tell you where to turn." Helena directed them to her office building, and they drove into the underground parking lot, where the detective parked the car in a bay with no camera surveillance.

"I'm staying here," Detective Renshaw said. "I can't risk leaving him exposed."

"I'm going into the building. I won't be long, why don't you go fetch some coffee and something to eat?" she said to Dario.

"I thought I was staying by your side." Dario edged closer to her.

"The building is secure. I need to talk to my boss alone."

She placed her hand on his upper arm. "I'll be okay. Honestly, if Barry approaches, I'll scream or something and that'll get the attention of the security guards."

"I don't like it," Dario said but he stepped back. "I'll walk you to the elevator and then go grab some food and coffee." He grabbed his pack from the car and jogged to catch up as she made her way across the parking lot to the elevator.

Helena resisted the urge to look around, she didn't want Dario to know how nervous she was. And how convinced that Barry would more likely make a move while she was alone.

"Keep your cell phone switched on and in your hand," Dario told her. "If you suspect Barry is close then call me and I'll get to you. No matter how much security stands between us."

"You are such a romantic." She kissed his cheek. "I'll be fine."

"I'll be waiting right over there." He pointed to the car. "What floor do you need?" As the elevator doors opened, he leaned in and she pressed the button for the eighth floor. "So I know where to find you."

"I thought your senses would lead you right to me." She kept her eyes focused on his face as the doors slid closed.

"They will," he promised. "Call me. I'll come running."

She nodded as his face disappeared behind the elevator doors. As the elevator rose up through the center of the building, she rehearsed what she planned to say to her boss. She would tell him it was due to family commitments. He'd understand, his daughter had gone through a messy divorce a few years back, and he was well aware of Penny's circumstances.

The doors slid back when she reached the floor of her offices but as she stepped out, it was as if she'd never been here before. It seemed so unfamiliar, despite having worked here for over eight years.

Striding over to the reception desk, she asked Vicky, who was like the central operating system of the office, if Mr. Lyle was free.

"I'll check for you, Helena." Vicky fixed a smile on her face and stared into the distance as she pressed the keyboard in front of her and listened on the headset she always wore, even when she was away from her desk.

Helena strolled away from the desk, turning in a wide circle as she waited to see if Mr. Lyle was available. She could have handed in her notice in writing, but she owed it to Mr. Lyle to talk to him face to face. Although, she had written a formal letter of notice last night after talking with Penny. Their conversation had finally pushed her into making the decision to leave her job and move to Wishing Moon Bay.

They'd talked about their parents as Milo slept quietly. They'd talked and cried over their new memories, of shared thoughts and flashes of insights that taught them about themselves. How Penny had loved playing on the beach, and building sandcastles, while Helena had developed a love of reading at a very young age.

Most of all they remembered the candies and sweet treats their parents made. They recalled the flavors and textures, and the look of pure joy and amazement on people's faces when they popped one of their father's creations into their mouths.

They were part of Wishing Moon Bay, it was their home. It was where they belonged.

"Mr. Lyle will see you now," Vicky told Helena and she broke out of her dream and smoothed down her hair as she headed down the corridor to her boss's office.

The decision to come here now had been spontaneous and she hadn't given much thought to how she looked. Not until she entered Mr. Lyle's office and her boss looked her up and down.

"Sorry, I just got back to town. I came here before going home." She smiled apologetically. Mr. Lyle was a lover of crisp white shirts and ties that were perfectly tied. Women were expected to be equally smart, either in skirts or pants. He had no preference as long as they were neat and tidy.

"What can I do for you? Not an emergency with your sister, I hope?" He indicated the chair in front of his desk, and she sat down, while he slumped down in his own chair. He looked tired, his face pale, not in the same way as a vampire, but from lack of time in the fresh air.

Helena put her hand to her face. Was that how she looked? Or was this what she would evolve into if she didn't make a break and get out of this job?

"My sister is okay, it's not that kind of an emergency. But I have made up my mind to quit my job here. My sister and I are going to travel a little and then find a business we can run together. She needs me. My nephew needs me." She smiled apologetically.

"Are you sure about this? You are good at your job here, Helena. I always thought that you would take on a more senior role in the coming years and maybe even sit in this chair." He patted the arms of his plush leather chair.

"Really?" She leaned forward, a couple of weeks ago she'd have been ecstatic to hear him say that. Helena leaned back and sat up straight. "It's wonderful to hear such praise, but I have made up my mind and I have to stick to it."

"I understand. You want to put your family first." He gave a small smile. "It's funny, but it was precisely because you don't have much in the way of family that I thought you would be the one to rise up through the company."

"It was?" Her fingers curled around the arms of her chair as she tensed.

"Yes, with no husband and no children, you were a prime candidate." His eyes narrowed. "Have you found yourself a husband?"

"No." It was none of his business, but that wasn't the reason she denied his question. Helena wasn't giving her job up because she planned to be a stay-at-home mom. She wasn't being forced into this decision because anyone expected her to. If she chose to stay, she could have handled the job and a family. Dario would have happily stayed at home with their children while she worked...

And that was why she loved him so dearly. Dario, the man who would be by her side no matter what. The man who would always have her back. Her man, her perfect mate.

"Well, I wish you happiness, Helena." Mr. Lyle glanced toward the door, she was being dismissed. He probably had a client waiting, but part of her was a little peeved he hadn't put up too much of a fight to get her to stay.

But Mr. Lyle had seen enough people come and go. He likely could tell she'd made up her mind and there was no shortage of people to take her place.

Helena stood up. "Thanks, Mr. Lyle." She slid her hand into her purse and pulled out the written resignation letter. "I've enjoyed working here."

"If you ever do change your mind, I'll always find a place for you." He smiled warmly. "Be happy."

"You, too." With a lump in her throat, she turned her back on her boss and walked to the elevator, feeling numb. This was the right decision, she was certain, yet it was as if a part of her life was ending.

She pressed the button to call the elevator, not risking a look at Vicky. If she did, she might well cry, and then rumors would fly that she'd been fired or had a mental breakdown.

Pressing the button for the ground floor, she closed her

eyes briefly. When she opened them, an old man was hurrying toward the closing doors.

Helena stepped forward and put her hand out to stop the doors from closing, but the man had a walking stick in his hand and lodged it between the doors. She stepped back as he hurried forward. "What floor?"

"Oh, fourth, please." His voice creaked like an old door.

Helena pressed the button and the elevator doors closed. As they began their descent, she inhaled deeply. A familiar scent tingled in her nose, and her eyes widened as the man turned and grinned at her.

"Surprise." He was old, so much older than the Barry she'd dated, the Barry who had come to her apartment.

"Barry."

"That's not really my name, but it'll do." He tilted his head to one side as she put her hand in her pocket and closed her fingers around her phone. "I don't think we need to make any calls."

He rapped her hand with his walking stick, and she yelped and pulled back her hand. There was no way she was going to let this old man get the better of her. But as she fended off his stick, he pulled a vial out of his pocket, used his teeth to pull the stopper out, and blew the contents in her face.

Her body went limp, but she didn't fall to the floor. It was as if she were drunk, the world around her spinning and her voice slurred.

"All I want is for you to take me to Wishing Moon Bay. I know you have been there. Then I'll let you go." The old man smiled amiably. "If you do as I say, I won't hurt you."

But how could she trust the man who had murdered her father and destroyed her family?

28

DARIO

"She should be back by now." Dario strode toward the elevator doors and stared at them, his hands on his hips as he pushed his senses outward. He tilted his head to the left and right as he tried to locate Helena among all the other people in the building.

Relax, his horse told him. *If you push too hard, you won't find her.*

If I don't push hard, I won't find her. Not when there are so many people in the building.

"I'm taking the elevator up," he called over to Detective Renshaw.

"Okay, I need to wait here." He glanced outside the building. "The sun won't set for another hour. I can't come with you."

"I understand." Anyway, he could travel faster on his own. Even without shifting into his horse.

With one last look around, he pressed the button to call the elevator. The doors opened and he stepped inside, turning to take one last look at the car with the vampire hidden in the trunk. Life sure had taken a turn for the weird.

Our life has always been strange, his horse told him. Compared to normal humans at least. Compared to some supernaturals, our lives are fairly normal. Boring you could say.

I don't say. Dario pressed the button for the eighth floor and looked up as the elevator began to move. That smell.

He inhaled deeply. He could scent their mate, her subtle perfume hung in the air but there was another scent not as familiar, and he'd smelled it before. Recently.

Barry has been here. His horse reared up in Dario's mind, pawing the air, wanting to tear the world apart to find his mate and ensure she was safe.

Dario gripped the handrail running along the side of the elevator, his expression set firm. If Barry had hurt their mate in any way, he was going to find out a shifter didn't need to be a predator to tear someone's throat out.

Calm down, his horse advised. We need to think carefully, we need to use our shifter senses to find her.

Dario closed his eyes and centered his mind as the elevator rose toward the eighth floor. He pushed his senses outward, searching for Helena as if he were searching for a needle in a haystack. He went systematically, floor to floor, pushing further, trying to get a fix on where she was.

Here! His horse stamped his foot, getting Dario's attention as they passed the fourth floor. *She's on this level.* His horse was incredibly confident, and Dario had learned to trust his other side's hunches.

Dario pressed the button for the fourth floor and the elevator slid to a halt. The doors opened but Helena was not in sight. He stepped out of the elevator, ignoring the strange looks cast his way. He didn't fit in here, his clothes were all wrong.

Ignoring the appraising looks thrown at him from several women, he sniffed the air. He might not be able to pinpoint Helena's whereabouts among all the other people here, but he could follow Barry's scent. His cologne hung on the air, leaving a trail.

Down the corridor and to the right, he hurried after his mate, hoping she was okay.

She must be okay, his horse assured him. They passed this way recently and if there was anything too suspicious about Barry and Helena, then the people in these offices would be talking about it. What else do they have to talk about?

His horse was right, and Dario clung to this thought as he rounded another corner. Stairs. Barry had taken Helena into the stairwell. He paused, sniffing once more before going down the stairs, his heart sinking as he got close to the ground floor. Once they were outside in the open air, the trail would get cold fast. Even the slightest breeze would soon cause Barry's scent to dissipate.

I feel her! His horse neighed as he sensed their mate. She was close, they were closing the distance between them. He wasn't going to lose them.

Dario reached the ground floor and burst out into the daylight, which was fading fast. If he could catch up with them soon and subdue Barry, the vampire could do his magic on him and they could all go home.

What a tempting thought, his horse murmured as they looked right then left.

Which way? Dario closed his eyes and focused on his love for Helena as if that would guide him to her side. *Left.*

He set off at a run, sensing her up ahead. They were moving slowly, very slowly, giving Dario time to catch up with them.

There. He spotted Helena on the sidewalk, she was waiting to cross the street, but he couldn't see Barry.

There's an old man with her. His horse sniffed the air. It's Barry.

Barry in his true form. So that's how he got close to

Helena without raising the alarm. He came in the guise of a wolf in sheep's clothing. Dario's hands curled into balls as he slowed his pace and followed behind. He didn't want to cause a scene in the middle of the street if he could help it. They didn't need the police added into the mix, there was no telling what Barry might have up his sleeve.

If Dario attacked an old man, there was a good chance he was the one who would be locked up. Perhaps that was Barry's plan.

Half an hour until it's dark and the vampire can help us, his horse announced.

Let's follow behind. As long as he doesn't hurt Helena, we'll keep our distance.

Why isn't she putting up a fight? His horse studied their mate. She's walking strangely, as if she's drunk.

He must have drugged her. Dario's anger grew as he crossed the street, slowing his pace even more. If Barry looked over his shoulder and saw the shifter then he might hurt Helena.

Where is he taking her, and what does he want? Dario's horse longed to gallop up to them, throw Helena over his back and then gallop off into the sunset.

They turned off the busy street and went down an alleyway. Dario ran on light feet, stopping alongside the alleyway and using his senses to figure out what was happening. Had Barry seen him? Was he lying in wait around the corner?

No, Barry was hurrying down the alleyway with Helena. They slipped around the side of the alleyway and hugged the wall. In the distance, he could see another street. If Barry had a car waiting, then Dario would lose them.

He took a chance, he gambled that no one would see and shifted into his horse.

He ran fast and true, his hooves clattering on the hard ground drew Barry's attention. But he was too slow to turn around and hampered by Helena as she swayed on her feet. He wasn't fast enough to block the horse's attack.

He tore at Barry with his teeth until he let go of Helena. She placed her hands on the wall and stood with her head down as the horse darted around her, putting himself between Barry and his mate.

"I'm not going to hurt her. I just want to find my way back to Wishing Moon Bay. I want to go back home. You can understand that, can't you?" The old man looked pitiful as he stood there in the gathering darkness.

"Is that what you told my father before you killed him?" Helena asked.

"I thought you had no memory of that day!" Barry's shock registered on his face and in the tone of his voice.

"I didn't. But then we went back to Wishing Moon Bay. That's right, we went back there." She took a deep breath as she turned to face Barry. "We found our memories and now I know who killed my father. Perhaps if you hadn't been so vain and had looked your age when we met before, I might not have recognized you. But I saw your face, I heard your voice."

"I lost my temper, I didn't mean to kill your father. I just wanted him to give me one of his candies to unlock my power." He held out his hands. "I have power. I can feel it, I just can't use it."

"You are a wicked man, and you don't deserve power, you don't deserve magic." Helena's temper flared and her back straightened.

Sensing the danger he was in, Barry reached in his pocket, but Helena lunged forward and blew the contents of the small vial into Barry's face. Shock registered there as he called out, "No!" Like a wounded animal he cowered down with his hands over his head. "What have you done?"

"It's time you got a taste of what you have done to others.

You killed my father. My mother was so scared, she had a vampire take our memories and shut them away. Just so we would never go looking for Wishing Moon Bay. So we would never be in danger from you. You see, she believed you were still in town and that we were safer out of it. But she was wrong."

"I left. I was sure they would know it was me. I heard a child had seen my face." He cried and covered his head as if expecting to be beaten.

"I was that child. I saw what you did." Tears streamed down Helena's face and Dario shifted into his human form, holding her close as she faced down the man who had killed her father.

"I just wanted magic," Barry complained. "I wanted to prove my father wrong. He always said I would never amount to anything. He said I was nothing."

"Did you kill him for what he said?" Helena asked. "Is that what you meant when you said the same man killed both our fathers? That man was you."

"He didn't believe in magic. He didn't believe me when I told him. He wanted me to be a bank manager. I wanted to be a warlock and learn to control nature itself." He thrust out his hands as if expecting flames to shoot from his fingers.

"You don't even come from Wishing Moon Bay, do you?" Dario asked.

"I belong there. I saw a car driving down a road I never knew existed and I followed it right through the tunnel and into town. What I saw changed my life forever. I knew that was what I wanted to be. Why should some people be born with gifts and others not?" He held out his hands. "Then I realized I did have the power, I just needed to unlock it. And your father's candies, they were the talk of the town."

"They were make-believe. They had no power to unlock magic inside you." Helena shook her head at the man before her. "You robbed me of my magic. You robbed me of my family. They were the ones who made the magic in my life."

"Helena." Dario put his arm on her shoulders and looked up. "It's time."

He shuddered as Silas appeared out of the darkness, dropping from the sky like a harbinger of doom. With his arms around Helena, Dario tried to turn her away, but she stood firm.

"What is your name?" Silas asked Barry, who stared into his eyes, powerless to fight the pull of inevitability.

"Rufus Mumford."

"Are you the man who killed Oscar Olsen?" Silas's voice was alluring, impossible to block out as he focused on Rufus.

"I wanted magic, he said he couldn't give it to me. I thought if I took his life, I would get his magic." Rufus shook his head. "I just wanted my father to be proud of me."

"He could never be proud of a murderer, could he?"

"No. So I shut him out. I shut him down so he couldn't look at me anymore." Rufus stared at Silas.

"You killed them both."

"I did," Rufus confirmed.

"And you've been trying to get back to Wishing Moon Bay ever since?"

"Yes, it's a magical place. It's where I want to die."

"That's not going to happen."

"Oh, I am going to die. I only have a short time to live. Too many spells and potions, my insides are rotten. Just like the rest of me." He cackled as if he'd told a funny joke.

"You're not going to die in Wishing Moon Bay. From this moment on, you will forget it exists."

"No!" Rufus cried out and grabbed at Silas's lapels. "I will return there. I'm so close."

"No, Rufus. The road is blocked and there is no way for you to return. Even if you saw the road to town, you wouldn't be able to travel it. Each step you take will make you burn as if there is an inferno raging inside you."

Rufus shook his head but no longer protested, as if he'd forgotten what he was protesting about.

"Hear me, Rufus. From this moment on, you will live with your sins and know that you killed. You will feel the guilt you deserve. You will spend your life helping others. That is your sentence for the murders you committed. Do you understand?"

Rufus used Silas to stand on his two feet. "I understand."

Silas let him go and then stood in the shadows as Rufus brushed his coat down and then walked past Helena and Dario as if they weren't even there.

"Will that work?" Helena asked.

"We won't have any trouble from Rufus again. I looked inside of his heart and he's right, he is dying. He's used the spells of others his whole life, drunk potions without caring what was in them all to reach his goal of getting back to Wishing Moon Bay. But the town is lost to him now." He rolled his shoulders back. "And you are free of him, Helena. And now you should be free of what you saw."

She nodded. "I want to remember, but not the...details. Can you do that?"

Silas chuckled. "I have the hands of a brain surgeon. I can cut out just the right parts. And it won't hurt a bit."

29

HELENA

"What did I miss?" Detective Renshaw ran into the alleyway and slid to a halt as Rufus walked past him. His eyes widened and he stared at the man before looking up at Silas for confirmation.

Silas inclined his head slightly in acknowledgment. "That is Rufus Mumford."

"Rufus," Detective Renshaw ground out.

"Oscar, why don't you follow Rufus home? I'd like to know where he lives so we can find him again if we need to. I'll catch you up."

Helena put her hand to her temple. "Is that it? Is it done?"

"It is." Silas brushed the tips of his cold fingers over her temples. "Don't try to force your way in there. Normally I would take away any knowledge of the event that's locked away. With you, I have left as much intact as I can." He smiled sadly and curled a tendril of her hair around his finger. "You look so much like your mom."

Helena reached up and held his hand, it was so cold, but she didn't share Dario's fear of vampires. Even though she probably should. "Thank you. For everything. I know when my mom came to you, she was hurt, and you did what you thought was right."

His strange eyes narrowed as he stared into her face. "It was right, Helena. You and Penny grew up in safety. You grew up without the nightmares that would have haunted you every night. A child should never see their parent murdered before their eyes."

"In a way, my mom sacrificed her own sanity for mine, didn't she?" A tear trickled down her cheek and he brushed it away.

"She loved you both so very much. You were a happy family, never forget that."

"It makes what came after much harder." She inhaled deeply and straightened her shoulders.

"You have her strength." He stepped away from her. "I look forward to seeing you in Wishing Moon Bay. You and Penny. I'd very much like to get to know Milo. You are staying, aren't you?"

"We are, we talked it over last night, we are thinking of opening a candy store, just like the one Mom and Dad owned." Her nose wrinkled. "Or do you think that's a terrible idea?"

Silas shook his head. "No, I think that is the best idea. It will help you heal." He glanced toward Dario who had stood back from them. "It's good to meet you, Dario. I have been watching you and your brothers grow into men."

"Really?" Dario asked.

"When a dragon lives so close, it would be foolish not to." He smiled a secret smile and then walked away, fading into the shadows as if he'd never been there.

"Maybe I should have asked him since he's so interested in us and he loved your parents if he would cancel his fee." Dario slipped his arms around her shoulders.

"It would have been rude to ask since he's done so much for us. And a promise is a promise."

"That's what worries me." Dario guided them back toward the road.

She rested her head on his shoulder, she was so tired, even though it was barely six o'clock. "You are so warm."

"You're shivering." His arm tightened around her. "How do you feel, after...you know?"

"I feel okay. It's strange, like when you walk into a room and can't remember what you were looking for. It's there but I can't reach it." She pushed her awareness into another part of her brain, the part that loved the touch of her mate. Silas's advice not to push against the barrier keeping her memory sealed echoed through her head.

"It's best out of reach, don't you think?" Dario asked as they reached the road. "Which way? I'm lost in this town of yours."

"Not as lost as I am in yours."

"Wishing Moon Bay is not my town, Helena. It's our town. You belong there just as much as I do."

"I suppose I do." She held out her cold hands, the chilly night air creeping into her bones. "But there's no magic in me. Or Penny. I don't think our parents had any magic at all."

"Not everyone in Wishing Moon Bay does. But your parents belonged there." He squeezed her and chuckled. "And from what people say, I think your parents did have magic. They made people happy, they made people laugh. And that's the greatest magic of all."

"I suppose you're right." She lifted her hand and hailed a cab. "Let's get back to my apartment." She looked around. "Do you think Silas and Detective Renshaw will go straight home?"

"I expect so." Dario looked up at the sky. "If they travel at night, Silas won't have to sleep in the trunk."

"True." She slid into the back seat of the cab and leaned back. It was over. Barry, or Rufus, was no longer a threat. She was free to live her life with Dario.

As the taxi took them back to her apartment, she watched the old familiar places pass by. After living in the same town for years, she no longer felt connected to it. It was as if getting her memories back had severed her ties with the world outside Wishing Moon Bay.

"Come on, sleepy." Dario shook her gently awake.

"Oh, I didn't realize I'd dozed off." She scrambled out of the cab and leaned against him as she paid the driver. "Come on, let's grab the stuff from my car and get inside. I am freezing."

Dario helped her to the car and grabbed their luggage from the trunk. Carrying their bags in one hand, he wrapped his right arm around her and helped her into the building. Her legs were leaden as she walked to the elevator. All she wanted to do was lie down and sleep.

The last couple of days had zapped her energy, her legs ached from the long ride across country and she felt emotionally drained from the new memories she was processing. It all caught up with her as she stumbled into her familiar apartment.

"Okay, I've got you." Dario dropped the bags on the floor and scooped her up in his arms.

"I feel like such a fool," she told him as she buried her head in his neck.

"There is nothing foolish about admitting you are done in. It's like that door in your head, if you fight it, it's just going to hurt more. You're safe here, I'll make you something to eat and get you some tea while you rest." He kissed the top of her head as he settled her down on the bed.

"Thank you." She kicked off her shoes and took off her coat before pulling the covers over her. "My mom used to take care of me when I was sick." She smiled. "I used to like being ill because she would sit by the side of my bed and watch over me. She always looked so peaceful. So serene."

"She loved you. You know that." The bed dipped as Dario sat on the mattress.

"I do. I always did." She brushed a tear from her cheek. "I wonder if somewhere in my subconscious I recalled what she was like before we left Wishing Moon Bay, before Dad... I wonder if somewhere deep down I knew she'd changed and just wanted her back as she was before."

"Honey, let it go." He leaned forward and cupped her chin in his hand. "I spent so much time going around and around in circles in my head over what-ifs. Don't torture yourself over it. What happened, happened. Your mom did her best and so did you. It's the past, let it go."

He leaned forward and kissed her lips. Helena slipped her hands around his neck and pulled him down onto the bed beside her.

"I can let the past go, but I can't let you go. Not ever."

Dario lifted his legs off the floor and kicked off his shoes before sliding beneath the covers. "I'm here for you for eternity. You won my heart and soul."

"Unless a certain vampire wants them as his own." She pushed his jacket off his shoulders.

"Not even a vampire could steal them away from you." He sat up and peeled his sweater and shirt off, casting them aside.

"All of a sudden I am too hot." She placed her hand on the mattress and levered herself to a sitting position.

"I can help you with that." He tugged at the hem of her thick sweater and pulled it over her head. Then he nimbly unbuttoned her shirt and pushed it off her shoulders. Bowing his head, he pressed his lips to the swell of her breasts. She shivered with desire, curling her fingers in his hair as he unclasped her bra.

With a sigh, she closed her eyes as he claimed her nipple with his mouth. Rolling his tongue around and around, he teased her, chasing away the remnants of cold in her bones. He was warm, he was life. He was hers.

Reaching for his belt buckle, she undid it and pushed his jeans down over his hips. He kicked them off and angled his body so he could undo her pants.

Naked beneath him, she stroked his back, her lips leaving a trail of featherlight kisses along his shoulder as he entered her. He thrust forward, slowly, so slowly, until he had completely penetrated her. Her fingers dug into his flesh as she urged him on. Urged him to make new memories with her, to create a future with her.

She wanted his children more than anything. Squeezing her eyes tightly shut, she recalled the moment she made her wish on the beach. As she kissed the golden stone, she wished with all her heart that she would raise a family with Dario, the man who owned her heart.

Dario pulled out of her and then lunged forward, impaling her on his hard length. Resting his weight on his right elbow, he cupped her left breast in his hand, his thumb brushing the taut bud while he claimed her lips with his.

Her mate consumed her with his touch. Each new sensation was sweeter than the last as he pushed her to new heights.

With a groan, he came, his seed pulsing into her. Helena arched her back as her climax hit her and they raced together like two wild horses across a mountain plain.

"I'll go make something to eat." His lips brushed hers and he went to get out of bed, but she pulled him back toward her.

"Not yet, I like you being next to me." She snuggled closer.

"I'm scared if I close my eyes, when I open them again this will all have been a dream and I'll be in my lonely apartment with no mate."

"I'm not a dream. I'm very real." He stroked her upper arm with the tips of his fingers. "Our love is very real." He lowered his head and kissed the top of her left breast. "You can feel me in your heart. Just like I can feel you."

"You say the sweetest things." She stroked his cheek as he raised his head and looked into her eyes. "I love you."

"I love you, Helena." He smiled down at her, his eyes roaming her face as if he were trying to memorize every line, every curve.

"Let's eat and sleep, and then tomorrow I'll pack up some of my stuff and we can go home."

"That sounds like a plan." He slid out of bed and grabbed his clothes. She watched him while he dressed, her eyes growing heavy.

She placed her hand over her heart. Dario was right, he was in there. He was real. And he was all hers.

30

DARIO

"Wait, before you unpack, there's something we want you to see." Penny clapped her hands excitedly as Logan came out of the hotel with Milo in his arms.

"We don't even get a cup of coffee?" Helena groaned as they were ushered into Penny's car.

"You have to see the surprise first," Milo told her as he grabbed her hand and pulled her toward Penny's car.

"This had better be good. We've spent the morning packing up my apartment and loading the car and then I've driven all the way here." Helena grinned as Milo shook his head at her. "Okay, we give in."

"It's great," her nephew assured her.

"Come on, Dario." Logan beckoned to his brother.

Logan isn't one for getting excited about many things. So if he's excited, it must be good, his horse told him.

You might be right. Dario stretched his arms above his head. But the thought of getting back into a car isn't a good one. Not when I was looking forward to something to eat from Ivan's kitchen.

Some things are more important than your stomach, his horse reminded him.

Don't I know it. His eyes lingered on the excited face of his mate, who had caught Milo's infectious enthusiasm and was climbing into the back seat of the car next to the child.

"So, what's the big surprise?" Dario asked Milo as he climbed into the back of the car.

"It's a secret surprise," Milo told him seriously. "You have to wait until we get there."

"And where is there?" Dario asked.

"Don't try to trick my son into telling you where we're going," Penny warned.

"I wasn't," Dario replied innocently.

"You were never good at keeping secrets." Logan chuckled as his mate started the car and drove away from the hotel.

"That's because not all secrets are good secrets," Dario replied. "Just like not all surprises are good surprises."

"This is a good one," Milo said firmly.

"And I believe you." Helena put her arm around the boy. "How do you like it here, Milo?"

"In Wishing Moon Bay?" His eyes lit up, reminding Dario of his brothers when they were that age. Particularly the twins. The two bear shifters, Aiden and Caleb, had come from a cramped apartment in the city. Valerie was told that the person caring for them was not a family member but knew they were bear shifters and planned to sell them to a collector.

Dario's horse shuddered. Who would do such a thing? They were just children.

People can be cruel when there is money involved and I suspect the twins would have fetched a high price. At least they were spared that.

As far as they were aware, no one knew who their parents were or how they ended up in the apartment. When they were taken away, there were no arrests, the apartment had been empty, aside from the twins, and despite a police stakeout, no one returned to the scene. The police suspected someone tipped off the person holding them captive.

"That's terrible. I had no idea." Penny glanced at Milo in the rearview mirror.

"So, I like surprises," Helena said. "And I think I'm going to like this one."

"Life certainly has had plenty of surprises in the last few days." Logan placed his hand briefly on Penny's thigh. "Most of them good."

Penny covered her mouth briefly with her hand and nodded. "Most of them good."

"Are you all right, Mom?" Milo leaned forward, his expression full of concern.

"I'm fine. I'm just really happy we're all here together." She turned onto a street with small stores on either side of the road. This was the main shopping area in the town. Grocery stores stood next to stores selling potions and spells. Some clothing stores catered for modern dress, like jeans and work boots, while others sold long flowing robes and cloaks. There was no discrimination between the magical world and the mundane world.

I have an idea of where we are going, his horse said.

I think I have some idea, too. A thrill of excitement mingled with apprehension. Would this crack open the door behind which Silas had hidden Helena's memory of her father's murder?

"This is it." Penny parked the car on the street outside a store with two large display windows that were currently empty.

"It's the candy store. I remember it." Helena got out of the car and stared at the building. "Has it been empty all this time?"

"Silas bought the building after...it happened. No one else wanted it, and he hated to see it fall into disrepair, so he bought it. He's kept it in good condition, heated in the winter, and air conditioned in the summer." Logan put his hands on his hips and looked up at the store. "I also wonder if he put a glamor on the whole town because I don't recall ever taking any notice of this place."

"Me neither," Dario agreed. "And I must have walked along this street a thousand times or more over the years."

"Thank you for bringing me here. I should thank Silas, too." Helena choked back tears. "It brings back so many memories."

"Shall we go inside?" Penny took Helena's hand. "If you want to."

"Are we allowed?" Helena asked.

Penny dangled the key in front of her. "Silas dropped this off at the hotel last night. He said he never knew what to do with the building until now."

Helena's brow furrowed. "I don't understand."

"If we want it, Silas will gift us the building. He said it belongs to us more than him." Penny smiled weakly, unsure of Helena's reaction. "He said you mentioned opening a candy store just like Mom and Dad. And he thought it would honor their memory if we reopened this candy store. I think he said the witches who used to help with the sweets and candies would be willing to help us."

"I don't know." Helena put her hands to her face. "I'm not sure."

"Shall we take a look inside and then decide?" Dario took her hand and Helena nodded.

"I suppose a look won't hurt." She smiled weakly.

I hope she's right and a look doesn't hurt, his horse said.

We'll be there for her. If there's any sign this is undoing what Silas did then we'll get her out of there. Dario followed Penny and

Helena to the front of the store while Logan came behind holding Milo's hand.

"I love it!" Milo skipped a step. "And I'd really love to own a candy store." He licked his lips in anticipation.

"What do you think?" Penny stepped into the store and looked around, her face bright with excitement. "Do you remember any of it?"

"Yes. I remember Dad standing behind the counter, with all the sweet treats behind him. The special ones, at least, the everyday candy was on this counter." Helena went to the old-fashioned wooden counter and ran her fingers along it. "It's been dusted recently."

"Silas did say he'd kept the place in good repair. He's done a good job." Penny held out her hand to Milo. "What do you think?"

"I love it." He held out his arms and she lifted him up.

"Do you know anything about making candy?" Dario didn't want to put a damper on things, but he was a realist.

"We can learn." Helena ducked behind the counter. "All the equipment is still here. One of our marketing ploys can be old-fashioned candy. We could also make some to sell in the outside world, minus the magic."

"Your aunt is planning to build a candy empire." Penny kissed Milo's cheek.

"We should take a vote," Logan suggested. "We should all agree. This is going to need all of us working together to build it into something we can all be proud of."

"I don't know." Dario held out his hands. "I don't have the first clue about any of this."

"I thought you would be ideal for the job." Helena took his hand. "You have been all over the world. You've tasted local flavors in so many countries. We could have a line of candy and sweet treats inspired by your travels."

"Say yes, Uncle Dario." Milo slithered out of his mom's arms and ran to him.

"I think I'm outnumbered." Dario laughed as Milo jumped up and down, filled with pure happiness. "Are you already on a sugar rush?"

"Oh, Milo is full of jumping beans. He doesn't need candy to make him jump around with happiness." Penny laughed and grabbed her son's hand. "Shall we go and look in the storeroom?"

"Yes!" Milo tugged at his mom's hand. "We might find some candy that has been hidden away for years and years."

"If we do, you promise me you won't eat it. I don't want you turned into a frog."

"Are you sure you're okay with this?" Dario asked Helena as they stayed behind alone in the store where her father met his tragic end.

"I am. I don't remember...you know. I know my father died here, but that's all." Tears misted her eyes. "I want to do this. I think it'll make me feel closer to my mom and dad."

"Then let's do it." He cupped her cheek in his hand. "I love you and all I want is for you to be happy."

"I think I'll be happy here. With you. With Penny." She nodded. "This feels right. Out of all the things I've ever done in my life, this feels like the right move."

"I always wondered what I'd do with my life." He kissed her softly. "I never saw myself as a store owner."

"I never saw myself as the mate of a horse shifter. So that makes us even." She laughed and tugged at his hand. "I can just see you behind the counter."

"I don't think I want to be in the store, I'd rather be in the back making candy." He followed her around the back of the counter.

"No, you can stand here, and our children will come in

and you can pick some of the sweetest candy for them to eat." She stared ahead as if seeing the ghosts of the past.

"Are you sure?"

"I am. We've come home, Penny and me. It's taken a long time and the road has been rocky, but we're here and this is exactly where we're supposed to be." She kissed him, her hands cupping his face as her lips moved against his.

Dario closed his arms around her and held her tight. She was right, this was exactly where they were supposed to be. Together, ready to face whatever life held for them and to make a future together.

EPILOGUE

"And we're officially open." Helena turned the sign on the door to open.

A small cheer and the sound of clapping came from the group of people outside, which was larger than they'd expected since they hadn't made a big announcement.

"Come in." Helena opened the door. Milo was waiting impatiently, holding Rift's hand. Aiden followed close behind with Valerie. Caleb and Ivan were back at the hotel. They would pop in later and say hi. They'd all been so supportive and helpful while they got the candy store ready to open.

"Am I the first customer?" Milo asked hopefully.

"You are." Helena held out her hand to him. "What can we get for you?"

"I'd really like to try the candy that makes you croak like a frog." Milo tugged her hand, and they went to the counter.

"Hey, Milo. What do you think?" Penny came around the counter and held out her arms for her son.

"I love it." He smiled broadly. "You put a banner up."

"We did. And we placed a photo of Grandma and Grandpa on the back shelf. So they can watch over us."

Penny lifted Milo up and caught Helena's eye as she turned around.

Helena smiled sadly, her eyes lingering on the photograph. One day she hoped to be able to look at her mom and dad without experiencing pain and sadness. But she wasn't there yet.

"I'll go see if anyone needs my help. Come and croak at me later, Milo." She let go of her nephew's hand and headed to the back of the store, where Dario was talking to various people about their merchandise.

Her hand lingered on the cupboard where she'd hidden as a child. That was the last thing she remembered about that day until the police found her. Was she the monster for not coming out and helping her father? Or were there other monsters in her life?

She looked over her shoulder at the photo of her mom and dad smiling down on them. Had her mom protected her from something else?

She might never know.

"Helena." Detective Renshaw came into the store, his eyes scanning the shelves. "This is incredible. You've all worked so hard."

"We want the store to be a success. Not just because otherwise we're going to need other jobs." She smiled, her mood lifting. "But because we want to pay homage to our parents. And bring a smile to people's faces."

Over by the counter Milo let out a loud croak.

"I think you've done that." Detective Renshaw chuckled.

"Is there anything I can get for you?" Helena asked as Dario came to join them.

"No, I have to watch my diet." He rubbed his stomach.

"It's good to see you." Dario shook his hand.

"And you, Dario."

"Could we speak to you outside?" Dario glanced around the store. "It won't take a moment."

"Is everything all right?" Detective Renshaw asked.

"Yes." Helena placed her hand on her stomach. "It's very all right."

"You're pregnant!" The detective grinned and then hugged them both. "I'm so happy for you both."

"We wanted to tell you, since you were so kind with everything that happened." Helena swallowed hard. "You worked so hard to bring justice for my family."

"Our family." Dario placed his hand on her shoulder.

"Our family." Helena sighed. "It's a good family."

"And growing bigger." Detective Renshaw glanced up at the store. "It looks just the same."

"We hope when people come inside, it feels as if they are stepping back in time." Dario put his hands on his hips. "It's not how I envisaged spending my life. But being here, being part of the town, has reined in my wanderlust."

"A family does that." The detective spun around, and Dario stiffened.

"What's wrong?" Helena reached for her husband's hand. They had married within the first week of their relationship. It had been a joint wedding with Penny and Logan.

Valerie and Logan had hastily transformed the hotel into a wedding venue, while Ivan prepared a small intimate dinner for the guests. They'd kept it mostly to family and a few close friends. Silas had arrived at the hotel in the evening with gifts and stayed for a while, dancing with the brides and then with Valerie.

It wasn't a lavish wedding, but it was the best day of Helena's life. When she said her vows and Dario slipped a ring on her finger, it was as if she'd left her old life behind and stepped into a new one. A happy one. A life filled with love and the promise of a new tomorrow.

"There's someone coming."

Helena's hands balled into fists as she stood side by side with her mate. No one was going to ruin this.

"Aiden." Dario turned as his brother left the store and came outside.

"There's someone coming." Aiden's eyes were unfocused as he stared across the street.

"Who is coming?" Helena asked, wishing she had shifter senses.

"A fae," Detective Renshaw replied.

"My mate," Aiden added.

THANKS FOR READING!

I hope you enjoyed my book!

The next book in this series is 'Her Fae-vorite Bear', which you can find on my website: harmonyraines.com/all-books/bond-of-brothers-series

If you'd like to keep up with my new releases, and any offers, you can follow me on Facebook at:

facebook.com/harmonyrainesauthor

Or you can head over to my website and sign up to my newsletter for notifications about releases and exclusive deals.

Feel free to message me on Facebook, or send an email to harmony@harmonyraines.com.

Harmony.

HER FAE-VORITE BEAR

THE BOND OF BROTHERS - BOOK THREE

Get it here:
US: amazon.com/dp/B08YPB48MM
UK: amazon.co.uk/dp/B08YPB48MM

FLORA

"Calm down, I don't want to cause trouble." Flora stopped around ten feet away from the small group of people staring at her. With a slight tilt of her head, she surveyed the broad-chested, dark-haired man, his eyes a little out of focus, but fixed on her. "Or maybe you would like me to hurt you." She smiled disarmingly.

"What do you want?" Oscar Renshaw, an older man in his mid-sixties stepped forward, his chin jutted out in defiance.

"You." She put her hands on her curvy hips and lowered her gaze, challenging him.

"Why?" Another man stepped forward. She lifted her chin and sniffed the air.

"Don't be alarmed, horse shifter. I only need to speak to the detective."

"I'm not a detective anymore," Oscar replied.

"That's immaterial. You were a detective. And I need knowledge of a case you worked some years ago."

"And you expect me to help you?" Oscar had enough run-ins with the fae to be wary, but she needed him to trust her.

"I do." She bowed her head and relaxed her stance. "I'm

sorry. Maybe if we start again and I introduce myself." Flora stepped forward.

"I know who you are, Flora Delavere, Daughter of Evander, High Lord of the Starlight Realm," Oscar replied.

"Ah, that explains the slightly hostile behavior." She looked at each of them in turn. "I'm only here for information and then I'll be gone."

"Dario, why don't you and Helena go back to the store? I'll handle this." Oscar nodded at the horse shifter and the woman by his side.

"And the other one?" Flora pointed to the man who was still staring at her. A bear shifter. A true warrior among his kind. Her eyes lingered on him longer than they should but there was something about him that she found...attractive. Great. As if her life wasn't messed up enough.

"He's your mate, Flora." Oscar took pleasure in those words.

"Oh, no. I am not in the market for a mate." She waved her hands at the shifter. "You're probably a really nice guy and everything but a shifter is not the man for me. Thank you."

"You know you have no choice in this." Oscar's eyes twinkled. "And neither does your father."

Her jaw tightened. Oscar was wrong, her father had a couple of choices. But that trouble could wait for another day. "My father has other things on his mind right now. So, why don't we get to the reason I am here. The rest can wait."

"Can it?" Oscar asked.

"Are you going to be unreasonable?" She arched a perfectly curved eyebrow.

"Would it matter if I was?" Oscar stared at her. He didn't like her. Most people in Wishing Moon Bay didn't. They judged her before getting to know her. The fae were not the friendliest of people outside of their realm. And in response, people were not friendly toward fae.

"Oscar. May I call you Oscar?" She respected the detective. His reputation for bringing criminals to justice was well known even in the realm of the fae.

Oscar bowed his head. "You may, *Flora*."

"I need some information on a case you worked on some years ago." Would he help a fae? They were not renowned for helping the authorities, preferring to deal with their people in their own way, even if the crime was committed outside of the fae realms.

"As you mentioned." He stepped closer, his voice low. The bear shifter stepped closer, too, his eyes never leaving her face. "I am going to need a little more information."

"It's..." She glanced at the candy store. There was a child outside croaking like a frog and a sudden need to *not* talk about this in front of him overwhelmed her. Great. Not only was she attracted to a shifter, she was now experiencing maternal feelings. She didn't have time for distractions. "Could we talk elsewhere?"

"Tell me what information you seek." Oscar closed the space between them.

"Children. Missing children." Her lip trembled and she lowered her eyes. "*Please*, I need your help."

Oscar's eyes widened and he gave a curt nod. "We can go to my house. My memory isn't as good as it once was. If it's about what I think it is, then I need to access my files." Oscar glanced at the bear shifter. "Why don't you give Flora a ride? I'll meet you there."

"I could ride with you," Flora called out, but the detective walked away without turning around. "Bear shifter."

"Fae." His eyes came back into focus, he'd lost the dreamy look. Instead, he was filled with suspicion. "Why are you looking for missing children?"

"Where is your car?" Flora looked around. This was none of his business. She'd only come into town to find Oscar and ask him for help. She wasn't here to make small talk with a shifter. Even one as growly as the man who was supposed to be her mate.

Although, if he knew what he was getting mixed up in, he'd have turned around and run back into the candy store. His life would be a whole lot easier if he forgot all about her.

"This way." He strode down the street and even with her long legs, she struggled to keep pace with him. Great, another male who intended to show her he was stronger than her, had power over her. Well, he had another thing coming.

They walked in silence until they reached a truck that had seen better days, like most of the vehicles in Wishing Moon Bay. People here didn't travel too far, they were happy to stay in town. If they drove anywhere, it was to the mountains or the beach, places where they would leave their cars and then stop and walk.

Only those folks who left the town more often bought newer cars. They traveled more miles...

"Are you getting in?" the bear shifter asked.

"Yes." She reached for the passenger door handle and pulled it. The door swung open, no creaks, no groans. When he started the engine it purred like a kitten. The truck might be old, but it was well cared for.

This shifter deserved better than her.

"Tell me why you are looking for missing children?"

"What am I supposed to call you, *mate*?" She was a master at not answering the questions of others. *Non*-answers caused much less trouble.

"My name is Aiden. Why the children?" Aiden waited for her to answer, the key poised over the ignition.

"A fae child has gone missing. I've been sent to help bring her back." It was a half-truth, but it was not a lie.

"And why does this relate to a case Oscar worked on?" Aiden pushed for answers.

"I received information from a trusted source." She glanced sideways at him. "Does it pain you that your mate is fae?"

He sighed. "No."

"That face says differently, as does your tone."

"I know what fae think of shifters."

"I know what shifters think of fae."

A small smile crept over his face. "Why don't we just pretend we are two people who have just met and leave our prejudices out of it?"

"A shifter with a brain. How marvelous." She looked down at her hands clasped in her lap.

"I'm being serious, Flora." He didn't rise to her jibe, instead, he turned his heartwarming, soft brown eyes on her.

She swallowed hard and inclined her head. "That would be...refreshing."

"Okay. So, tell me more." He pushed the key into the ignition and started the engine.

Flora let out the breath she'd been holding. "A friend of mine. Delphine. She lives in the world beyond."

"*The world beyond*. That's what your people call the world outside of Wishing Moon Bay?"

Flora nodded. "Yes, that's the name we give for the non-magical world."

"And your friend lives there?" He stared at her for a moment. "And she is fae?"

"Yes." She understood his surprise. But he didn't know the circumstances and Flora wasn't ready to explain them, not to him. Not yet.

"And it's this friend whose child was taken?"

"Yes."

"Did they get a look at who took the child?" Aiden drove out of town toward where the retired detective lived.

"No. They have no idea as to the identity of the kidnapper. However, a friend of the family concerned mentioned another case, one Oscar has knowledge of." She shouldn't be telling this shifter, but if he truly were her mate, she could trust him with her life. "When my friend investigated further, they found there was a spate of these kidnappings over a period of time. Children considered supernatural are taken. Shifters mainly. This is the first time a fae child has been stolen."

"Ah, so that's why you are interested, not because you want to bring down the people involved but because someone dared to take one of your special fae children." Aiden's jaw tensed.

"That's not true," she said firmly. "We are only interested now because we have knowledge of it."

"Because it involved a fae child. It doesn't bother you that this has been going on for decades?"

"Decades. I never said decades." He knew more than he was saying. She wasn't the only one with secrets. "You know of these cases?" Flora asked. Perhaps this was the reason she had been drawn to Aiden. He might be the key to the whole thing. She had come to meet Oscar, but that was just fate leading her to where she needed to be.

"I am one of those cases. My brother and I were taken as children. We were found in a cramped apartment. Apparently, we were going to be sold. Because we were shifters." He stared ahead, not looking at her as they arrived at Oscar's house.

"And this all happened outside of Wishing Moon Bay?"

"Yes, we were born in your world beyond." He glanced

sideways at her. "We were lucky, sometime after we were rescued, we were adopted by Valerie. She runs the hotel..."

"I know of Valerie Kelts." She rested her chin on her hand and stared out of the window. "Will you come with me? Will you help me find the missing child?"

"What do you think?" Aiden ground out.

"I think you are angry that I am your mate." Her heart ached like a wound that wouldn't heal.

"I'm not angry." He relaxed his shoulders. "I'm just..."

"Disappointed?"

"No. Concerned."

"Concerned." She gave a short laugh.

"Yes. That you won't take this seriously. I know how fae feel about shifters."

"Then you will have to change my mind." She blinked rapidly and swallowed down her emotions as she'd been taught to do since a small child. "But our mating is secondary to the need to find the child."

"Agreed." He parked the truck and got out. "We'll find the child. Then we'll figure us out."

"*Us*." She joined him and they walked to the house together. Oscar had already arrived and was waiting for them at the front door.

"Yes. Us. You and me." He glanced sideways at her. "You find that amusing."

"A little." She stopped walking and stuffed her hand in her pockets. "The fae are very...individual. I suppose in some ways selfish."

"Really?" He arched an eyebrow.

"Oh, we do sarcasm, do we?"

"We do, although it's more of my brother's thing."

"Is he older or younger?" Flora tilted her head to one side.

"We're twins."

"Twins. Identical?" This had her interest.

"Yes. Although, I'm the better-looking one."

She nodded solemnly. "And I will agree with you because you are my mate, and we should agree on all things."

Aiden laughed. "A fae with a sense of humor. This is going to be interesting."

"You have no idea, Aiden. No idea at all."

As they reached Oscar, he opened the door and went inside. Flora followed behind Aiden, pausing to glance over her shoulder. The skin on the back of her neck prickled as if she were being hunted.

She'd hoped to get out of town before her father realized she was gone. Evander, High Lord of the Starlight Realm, would not condone her risking her life to help Delphine.

Not when she should be at home planning her wedding.

AIDEN

"Right. Aiden, why don't you go into the kitchen and make coffee while I go and dig out the files I need." Oscar removed his jacket and hung it up in the hallway before rubbing his hands together and heading into the first room on the right.

"And what shall I do?" Flora asked.

"Stay right there. Don't touch anything and don't talk." Oscar stared at her for a long moment. Flora opened her mouth to speak but then closed it again. Oscar's eyes twinkled and he cracked a smile. "I was just testing you."

She frowned. Flora didn't seem to get people at all. "Testing me for what?"

"To see how serious you were about all of this. Fae are not known for holding their tongues or doing as a mere mortal tells them." His smile faded. "But you were willing to."

Flora stepped forward, an air of menace surrounding her. "I assure you, this is deadly serious."

"Then you'd better come this way. We have a lot of files to go through." He inclined his head toward the door. "Aiden, there is some cake in the cupboard. Perhaps you can root it out and bring it in when the coffee is ready."

"Sure." He turned on his heel and went to the kitchen to make the coffee.

We have a mate, Aiden's bear sounded as stunned as he was.

We do.

A fae.

A fae. Aiden grabbed the empty coffee pot and made fresh coffee before checking through the cupboards for the cake.

Taking a tray from the counter, he placed the coffee cups and cake on it, then added plates. Feeling like a server at the hotel, he carried the tray into the room where his mate and Oscar were talking quietly.

"Ah, just what we need." Oscar set down a handful of files on a desk and Aiden put the tray down next to it.

"What is all of this?" Aiden asked.

"This?" Oscar waved his hand at the files. "This is what I do in retirement. They are copies of all the cold cases that have never been solved. Cases that the authorities in Wishing Moon Bay will never reopen."

"And you work on them?" Aiden asked.

"Some. And some of them are for reference. Like the case of Penny and Helena's dad's murder. They came to me for answers and I gave them. If they had gone to the authorities, they would either have been ignored or it would have taken months for someone to get back to them." He shrugged. "That's just the way things are."

"Have you found the files you need? The ones concerning missing children?" Aiden handed the coffee cups out.

Is that all we're going to be? The coffee boy. His bear shook his head, a simmering anger building inside him. Not because they were serving coffee. His anger went much deeper than that. Aiden and Caleb were lucky, they'd been found before they were sold. Other shifter children were not as fortunate.

No, it's not all we'll be. Aiden soothed his bear. *We will have our part to play. There's a reason we are here. That reason is wrapped up in why fate decided to make Flora our mate.*

So we can catch whoever is taking children? So we can end the suffering.

His bear had always harbored deep anger toward whoever stole Aiden and Caleb from their parents. If they were older, if they had undergone their first shift, he would have defended them. If he'd been there, the twins would have grown up with their biological parents.

Not that his childhood in Wishing Moon Bay hadn't been incredible. He'd loved every moment of it and was forever grateful to Valerie for adopting them.

Yet there was a hole inside him, a dark abyss which he could never get rid of. He yearned to know who his parents were. Were they still alive? Were they hurt or injured when the twins were taken? Or had they done the unthinkable and willingly given up their children?

When Aiden and Caleb traveled outside of Wishing Moon Bay, they would look at the people they passed on the street and try to tell if they were their parents. Was the woman standing at the street crossing their mother? Or the cab driver their father?

Not knowing kept that abyss open.

"We have found some of the files. I'm trying to think if there are any more." He helped himself to a piece of cake and took a bite. "Help yourself. It's a good cake."

"Thank you." Flora licked her lips and took a piece, placing it on a plate. "It smells sweet."

"Honey cake." Oscar glanced at Aiden. "I can't tempt you?"

"Here, eat." Flora picked up another piece and handed it to Aiden. "You will need your strength for what lies ahead."

Oscar met Aiden's eyes and winked. "I think she might be right. In more ways than one."

Flora ignored Oscar's comment and wandered around the room while savoring her honey cake. "This is good."

"I'll give you the recipe. You can make some for Aiden when you get back."

She pressed her lips together. "Fae don't bake, and I certainly don't intend to become a housewife."

"The files." Aiden didn't want to think about his future with Flora.

We have always longed for our mate. We might even be blessed with children, his bear replied.

Okay, it's not that I don't want to think of our future. It's more like the future we envisioned, with a house in the mountains and a brood of children playing in the trees, is not the future we will have with Flora.

Fae were secretive, they lived in another world. Literally. And...they were not the nicest of people.

I get the feeling Flora isn't like a normal fae. His bear turned and walked away.

"Okay. So these are files concerning missing children from five years ago. These are from a couple of years before that. And these..." Oscar picked up a slim file. "These are from twenty years ago."

"Aiden said he and his brothers were taken from their parents and held in an apartment. Is there any chance their cases could be linked to this new one?" Flora dusted the crumbs off her fingers. "Are all of these cases linked?"

"No." Oscar paused. "As far as I know. They were too random. Different places, different times. Some were from families who lived outside of town but came back here in the hope the lost children had found their way here. Some were from families who were out of town for vacations. Many of the cases involve older children who might simply have run away from home. Teenagers who didn't get along with their parents, that sort of thing."

"There were no threads to connect them?" Flora could certainly understand a child wanting to be free of their parents' control.

"Not really. Some were shifters, some were not. An occasional witch or warlock. But never a fae." Oscar fixed his gaze on Flora. "But then your people usually tend to deal with these things themselves."

"They do. Usually." Flora didn't meet Oscar's gaze and he let it go.

"These are the open cases. While I worked for the authorities, we did find some of the children who went missing." He placed his hand on a file. "Usually a location spell worked, and the child and parents were reunited."

"My friends tried a location spell," Flora replied. "It didn't work."

"Which puts the case on this pile." Oscar picked up a couple of files. "These are cases that share some similarities with yours. Mainly shifter children who disappeared and were never found."

"Never? No clues at all?" Flora's faced paled.

"No. One was a child who was orphaned while the family lived out of town for a few years. The father got a good job in the north and the family moved away. After the parents died in a car crash, the child was placed in foster care. That's where she disappeared from."

"Did the local police help in the search?" Flora asked.

"Yes, they used their forensic teams while we tried all the usual things. Location spells for example. It was as if the children just disappeared."

"Or were cloaked." Flora perched on the edge of the desk. "Have you tried a location spell recently?"

"What difference would that make?" Aiden asked.

Oscar's plate clattered on the desk as he grabbed a file and flicked it open. "The cloaking might have been temporary. As the child grew up into adulthood...with the first shift..."

"Spells also break down over time." Flora put her hands on her face. "A spell to make yourself look young and beautiful doesn't last unless you keep feeding it. It takes power to keep it going."

"So, there's a chance that some of these missing children are no longer cloaked. And if we cast the location spell again, we might track down the child who was taken and that might lead us to those who kidnapped her," Aiden mused.

"You aren't just a pretty face." Flora patted his cheek. "I'm so relieved."

Heat flared where her fingers touched his skin and her breasts heaved, she'd felt it, too. Despite her outward defensiveness pushing him away, she felt the mating bond, she felt the connection between them.

But she's fighting it. This is too important to her, his bear said. She needs to focus on finding the fae child.

"The problem is, we don't have anything to use for the location spell. These files are just copies of the originals. I don't have anything that belongs to any of the children." Oscar flopped down in his chair, looking defeated.

"Do you know the whereabouts of the foster parents? Do you think they might have kept anything belonging to the child?" Flora's intensity set her eyes aflame. They glowed but not in the same way as Ivan, who was a dragon shifter. Flora's were violet.

"Possibly. They were cut up about it. They'd fallen in love with the child and talked about adopting her. They live in a town called Bear Creek. They are bear shifters, like Aiden. That is where your search should start."

"Bear Creek. Delphine lives near there. You're right, it is a good place to start." Flora nodded. "I'll need to collect a few things I need for the location spell." She turned her attention to Aiden. "Then we leave."

"I'll go and grab a few things. Where do you want to meet?"

"I'll meet you on the other side of the tunnel." Flora placed a hand on the files. "Can you get me a copy of everything in the files and email it to me?" She grabbed a pen from the desk and scribbled down her number. "This is my cell phone number."

"Okay, I'll scan everything and send it to you. I'll text you the address of the family in Bear Creek." Oscar moved swiftly, gathering up all the files. "Safe journey."

Flora nodded and then turned and left the room.

"Be careful," Oscar murmured as the front door closed. "I know she's your mate but the fae are a strange race."

"I know." He ran his hand over his head, taking a moment to let the events of the last hour sink in. He had a mate.

"And this business..." Oscar waved his hands over the files. "It's messy and dirty. You might uncover things you would rather not know."

"Or I might uncover things I need to know. I am one of these children, Oscar."

Oscar nodded. "When you arrived in town, Valerie spoke to me about your case. I did some digging." He went to a filing cabinet and opened it. Shuffling through the numerous files, he pulled one out. "Here."

"This is about me and Caleb?" His hand shook as he reached for the file.

"It is. What little there is of it. There were no leads. The police involved found no clue as to what happened to you and your brother or where you came from." He shook his head. "I was a young man. I had no authority. I did what I could, but we didn't have the resources or the knowledge we have today."

"Do you think our cases were related to the others?" Aiden asked.

"There's no way to tell. If they were then this has been going on for a long time. Which means we are dealing with a ring of offenders. Or one incredibly old individual."

Aiden nodded. "Can I have this?" He curled his fingers around the file.

"Yes. There's little in there. But I don't want to share it with Flora. This is your story, this is your life. If you choose to share it with her, that's up to you." Oscar patted Aiden on the shoulder. "I know the fae are a strange race. They have a reputation for being cold-hearted. But I sense something else in Flora. Something a man like you could unlock."

"Are you an old romantic, Oscar?" Aiden asked.

"I might be." He grinned. "Take care. If anything happens to you, Valerie will be knocking on my door and I'm too old to fight her."

"She's still recovering from her knee operation. I don't think she's too tough at present." Aiden tucked the file under his arm and headed for the door.

"Don't ever underestimate Valerie. And don't ever underestimate a mother whose child is in danger." He leveled his gaze at Aiden.

"What does that mean?" His eyes widened. "You don't mean... Does this child belong to Flora? Is she the mother?"

"Oh, goodness no. If this were Flora's child who was missing, her father would tear the world apart to find it."

Aiden let out a sigh of relief. Not because he wouldn't have loved a child fathered by another man, but because he would hate for Flora to live through the ordeal of losing a child.

"Thanks, Oscar."

"You're welcome, Aiden. And good luck."

"Because we're going to need it, right?" He opened the driver's door and climbed into his truck.

"More than you could ever guess." Oscar waved his hand as Aiden pulled the door shut and drove away. He hadn't left Wishing Moon Bay for years, now he was going to trek across the outside world with his mate by his side.

Life sure did take the strangest of turns.

Printed in Great Britain
by Amazon

61760819R00170